"Climb in the back."

Nelson took hold of the edge of the wagon and then paused. "You do realize that this is kidnapping?"

Sylvia shut out the twinge of guilt she felt. Tommy was all that mattered. "Can't be helped."

"I could shout. Call out for he'

"Everyone is at the town ' one around to hear you."

"You've planned elf into the wagon be ey would hear a gun

"I don't thin hat chance, now, do you, Doc? off the land most my life. I don't miss wha or."

"I see your point."

"Now, lay down on your back."

"I hardly think that is neces—"

She threw a tarp over him. "I'm in charge here, in case you ain't noticed. Now, no more shenanigans. I never heard someone talk so much during a kidnapping."

"So this is a common occurrence?"

"Ya gotta come with me, Doc," she said softly, mostly to herself. "I can't give you no choice in the matter."

Her heart hurt, tight with remorse. It wasn't right, her using him this way—especially after he'd done her a good turn a few days back at the mercantile—but it couldn't be helped. Tommy came first, despite how guilty she felt about forcing the doc.

She snapped the reins. "Get up, Berta!"

Author Note

My life before writing full-time entailed years as a professional nurse. I drew on that background in writing about Dr Graham and his medical practice in 1880. Medicine in the United States at that time was in its infancy. In Boston, where Dr Graham attended school, medical education consisted of going to lectures by part-time instructors and taking an exam at the end. All that was required to start that school was payment for the individual lectures and a high school diploma. Things have certainly changed!

I was fortunate to have in my life a 'city' grandmother and a 'country' grandmother. Sylvia Marks is the embodiment of my country grandmother in her can-do attitude, her generosity, love of family and common sense. I remember going with my grandmother as she delivered fresh eggs from her chickens to all her neighbours along the long country road where she lived, visiting with each for a moment to catch up on their lives and their families—no phones! She truly cared about and enjoyed people.

Sylvia Marks has had to work hard, homesteading a patch of Kansas dirt with her son, using nothing but common sense and optimism. When she encounters Dr Graham sparks fly. I hope you enjoy this story, in which opposites attract.

THE PRAIRIE DOCTOR'S BRIDE

Kathryn Albright

Published in Great Britain 2017
by Mills & Boon, an imprint of HarperCollins*Publishers*
1 London Bridge Street, London, SE1 9GF

© 2017 Kathryn Leigh Albright

ISBN: 978-0-263-93262-1

Our policy is to use papers that are natural, renewable and
recyclable products and made from wood grown in sustainable
forests. The logging and manufacturing processes conform to the
legal environmental regulations of the country of origin.

Printed and bound in Spain
by CPI, Barcelona

Kathryn Albright writes American-set historical romance for Mills & Boon. From her first breath she has had a passion for stories that celebrate the goodness in people. She combines her love of history and her love of stories to write novels of inspiration, endurance and hope. Visit her at kathrynalbright.com and on Facebook.

Visit the Author Profile page at millsandboon.co.uk.

Dedicated to my Grandma Gladys,
a heroine herself in all her optimism,
common sense, generosity and love of family.
And to my father, a man who inherited
the best of her traits.

Chapter One

Western Kansas 1879

Sylvia Marks stared at the gold-and-green sign swinging over the Oak Grove mercantile, then dropped her gaze to the corner of the large display window. The crack was still there—a casualty from her last visit before Christmas. Mr. or Mrs. Gallagher, the owners of the store, had stuffed old copies of the *Oak Grove Gazette* into the opening to keep out the cold. They wouldn't be excited to see her back again—or Tommy.

The main street of town was deserted this early, even the livery stable doors were shut tight. She hoped the store would be empty of customers. It was why she had come as soon as the sun rose enough for her to see her way across the river. Most folks were still in bed—at least she hoped they were. It wasn't herself she worried about. She had long ago grown tough enough to endure their stares and whispers. It was Tommy she worried for.

She glanced down at her son. She'd wrapped him up as best she could, but at seven years old, he was growing out of near everything he owned. Spring had better hustle along a little faster so that she could see to shearing Jeremy and Petunia. Besides selling the sheep's wool, she would be able to knit Tommy a larger sweater and make them both new socks and stockings. As it was, snow melted from her worn boots and the wet seeped inside, working its way down through the frayed wool strands and settling against her skin. Guess it was one more thing to make her tough.

She took a deep breath—best to get this done. She took hold of her son's hand and strode through the doors of the Oak Grove mercantile. She knew exactly what she had to get: two yards of cheesecloth for rendering her cheese, along with two cases of jars with lids so that she could bottle her honey come late spring. That, and some flour and oats.

"Be right with you!" a man called out from the back room.

Her gaze caught on a bowl filled with silk ribbons of every color at the close end of the counter. It looked like the storekeeper had been cutting them into lengths. Large scissors lay beside the bowl. She couldn't keep herself from touching the length of dark blue silk that shimmered pretty as the night sky. Wouldn't that feel nice in her hair? She'd always been a fool for pretty things, but in her life pretty always had to walk a step behind practical. A bit of twine worked just as well or better for tying back her hair.

Mable Gallagher stepped through the curtained doorway.

Sylvia grabbed her hand back from the ribbons immediately, feeling guilty even though she'd done nothing wrong.

Mrs. Gallagher's brows drew together in a frown. "What do you want, Miss Marks?"

She didn't sound happy about being pulled from whatever she was doing in the back, or perhaps it was more a matter of Sylvia's way of doing business that the woman didn't care for. Out of necessity, Sylvia bartered more than she bought outright. She had precious little coin for any extras…like the ribbon.

"Just got a few necessities I'm aimin' to buy. Won't take but a minute."

"See that you hang on to that youngster of yours. I won't have a repeat of last time."

Sylvia tightened her grip on her son's hand. What had happened was an accident. Tommy had not meant to knock over the tower of canned goods. Mrs. Gallagher should have known better than to stack them so close to the window. Any fool could figure the outcome of that. Children liked to climb things, and Tommy more than most. She leaned down. "Don't you pay her no mind," she said softly in her son's ear. "What's done is done and a lesson learned. Just stay close."

She straightened. "I got my wagon out front. I need a sack of flour and another of oats."

"That all?"

"No. I need two yards of cheesecloth and two cases of canning jars and lids. I got three crocks of sorghum molasses and a dozen eggs to barter." She set her basket of eggs on the counter.

"Are these fresh?"

"Wouldn't bring them if they weren't fresh."

Mable Gallagher picked the stub of a pencil from over her ear and started tallying up in her ledger.

Sylvia was halfway through haggling out a satisfactory exchange rate when Mrs. Gallagher stiffened.

The pungent smell of the stockyards snuck into the room. The hair on the back of Sylvia's neck stood on end. Only one person could make both Mrs. Gallagher and herself uncomfortable—Tommy's uncle. She tightened her grip on her son's hand and turned to face him.

Carl wore the same brown britches and coarse cotton shirt that he always wore and each time she saw him they were dirtier and smellier than the time before. Looked like his long hair was getting streaks of gray in it. He was young for that to happen and she wondered if Thomas, had he lived, would have grayed early too.

"Well, well. Who we got here?" He swaggered up to her and stopped too close for comfort, staring down his long nose at her. By the way he acted, she could tell that he'd been into a bottle of spirits already. Being that it was so early could only mean he'd been up half the night drinking.

She stood as tall and stiff as she could, and still only came up to his chin. "Morning, Carl."

"Ain't you a purty sight this early come to town."

His gaze roamed over her, making her queasy in her gut. He must have seen her wagon out on the street. Of all the people in town, he was the last one she wanted to see.

"Who you got hiding there in your skirts? That my kin? Well, step out here, boy, and let me have a look at you."

"We don't want trouble, Carl," she said, moving to shield Tommy with her body.

"Why, I don't never cause trouble." The insolent sneer on his face deepened. "Come out here so you can say a proper hello to your uncle." Moving faster than she'd thought possible, he snaked his hand around her and grabbed her son by the arm.

A cry of pain erupted from Tommy as fear leaped into his brown eyes.

Carl stuck his hands under each of Tommy's armpits and whisked him up into the air, letting his legs dangle. Then he shook him. "You sure he's a Caulder? He don't hardly weigh three stone."

"He weighs just what he should. Now, put him down. You had your fun."

"He needs to grow a little backbone. Gotta be tough in this world. Ain't that right, boy? Your ma had to learn that." Carl shook him again. Harder this time.

Mable Gallagher pushed aside the curtained doorway to the back storage area and called out. "Henry! Get out here!"

Sylvia trembled with anger. "Put him down!" She inched closer to the large scissors lying at the end of the counter. She had never hurt Carl before, but she would to protect her son.

Carl tossed Tommy aside as if he was no more than a sack of potatoes and slammed his hand down on top of hers, pinning her fingers to the wood. "Now, what are you doing, woman? That ain't very hospitable of you."

Henry Gallagher strode into the room. He wasn't as tall as Carl, but what he lacked in height, he made up for in muscle. He was a stocky bull of a man.

Carl relaxed the pressure on her hand, giving it a last squeeze before pulling completely away from her.

Immediately, she crouched before her son. "Are you all right?"

Tears brimmed in his big chocolate-brown eyes. He nodded—the motion barely detectable.

"You gotta quit mollycoddling the boy," Carl said. "He's a Caulder. Should act like one. Not some namby-pamby."

She stood up, her gaze colliding with Henry Gallagher's. His wife was no longer in the room. He looked from her to Carl and pressed his lips together. His censure was no help. It wasn't her fault that Carl had shown up and was the one causing the fuss. Yet it seemed her link to that name made everyone judge her accordingly.

She stiffened her spine. The sooner she and Tommy could leave, the better. "I need two yards of cheesecloth and two cases of canning jars. I already negotiated for them with your wife."

With a glance at Carl, Henry walked over to the corner stock of canning and pickling supplies. "These will have to do. It's the only size I have left over from last summer. There'll be a new shipment in June."

"They'll do fine," she said crisply. She just

wanted to get out of town as quickly as possible, before Carl got any more mean ideas.

Mr. Gallagher got the cheesecloth and picked up a case of the jars and carried them out to her wagon.

As soon as the man disappeared through the doorway, Carl sauntered over to the counter. "These yours?" He held up her basket of eggs, the handle balanced on one stubby finger as he swung the basket to and fro.

Her chest tightened. "Carl, why are you being like this? You'd best put that down."

Carl shrugged. "You ain't been by to see me in a long time. I near forgot how you looked. Just catchin' up is all."

The arc of the basket's swing got wider and wilder. One egg flew out and splattered on the floor.

Anger exploded inside. Her chest tightened. Such waste! "What do you think you are doing?" She rushed forward, reaching to steady the basket.

He held it just beyond her reach. His mouth curved into a taunting jeer. Another egg flew out and met the same end on the mercantile's plank floor. "What'll ya give to get them back?"

Her heart pounded. "Now, you listen here. Those eggs belong to the Gallaghers now. There's no sense in what you are doing."

He grabbed her wrist, his fingernails digging

into her skin, as he held up her arm just high enough to put her off balance. "Don't you point your finger at me, missy. You always did think you were better than me and we both know it ain't so."

His words hurt—cut—as much as those grimy nails of his. She hadn't made the best choices in life, but she couldn't think about that now. Not with Tommy looking on. It was better to let the anger take over than to let what he said get to her inside.

Heat built up and rolled through her. Her jaw tightened. "You let me go."

He huffed out a breath. "Or what? What you gonna do? You ain't no bigger than a mite."

"Mama?" Worry filled Tommy's high-pitched voice.

She hated that he was a witness to Carl's bullying, but there was nothing she could do about it. She twisted her arm, glaring back up at Carl. "Let go of me."

"I'm just having a little fun. You know what that is? Fun?"

"This ain't it. Not by a long shot." She stomped down with the heel of her old boot on his foot. Hard.

Surprised, he loosened his grip for a moment, only to grab hold again. His jaw tightened. "Why, you little—"

"What's going on here?"

A man stood in the doorway, his silhouette outlined by the early-morning sunlight on his back. He was tall as an oak tree with a deep voice to match. Sylvia couldn't recall ever seeing him in town before.

Carl's grip loosened. She wrenched from his grasp.

Carl sneered and let go of the basket.

Before she could think to react, the tall man scooped it up, saving the eggs just inches from the hard floor. His actions were so quick and precise that Sylvia stood there in shocked silence, her mouth gaping open, as he handed the basket back to her.

"It appears none are injured," he said in that deep voice.

She closed her mouth.

His gaze, green as the pines in the Shenandoah, skimmed over her, before he turned back to Carl. "How's that rope burn?"

Carl scowled. "Healed up."

"Glad to hear it." The man didn't budge. He seemed to be just fine with waiting for Carl to make the next move.

Carl scowled again. He tugged his wide-brimmed hat down over his ears. "Guess the fun's over. Gotta get back to the stockyards anyways."

It was all Sylvia could do to hold in her relief as he stomped away. The apple didn't fall far from the tree, and in the case of the Caulders, she'd learned it was half-rotten before it hit the ground. Only Thomas had been different, taking after his ma's side of the family instead of his pa's. She'd been wary of Carl for some time, but when he didn't come around for a while, she thought things were better. For years, he'd had a woman friend over near Fort Wallace who kept him busy. If that wasn't the case anymore, guess she would have to watch out for him from now on whenever she and Tommy came to town.

"What can I do for you, Doc?" Henry asked from behind the counter.

Doc? Sylvia turned back and stared as the tall man walked over to the counter. So, this was the doctor that Mayor Melbourne had talked into staying in Oak Grove. She'd heard tell of him a year or so ago but never had a reason to meet the man face-to-face.

She took in the way he was dressed—his white shirt was a bit rumpled, but clean. He wore one of those shoestring neckties she'd heard tell of and it wasn't even Sunday! His dark burgundy vest had fancy stitching along the edges, like something she'd seen when she lived back East. He had dark brown scruff along his jaw and chin and upper lip. Seemed he wasn't sure whether he was growing a beard and a mustache or not. His wavy hair was so thick it sprung like a soft cushion from his head. That, she could tell because he didn't wear a hat or overcoat.

Didn't he have the sense to know he'd catch his death of a cold in this wayward weather? Spring in Kansas was nothing to sneeze at, half the time cold, wet and windy and the other time sunny, hot and still windy. But today was a sunny one, so guess he had a right to enjoy the feel of it on his head after the fright of a winter they'd had.

"I passed the supply wagon late yesterday on my way back from Putnam's ranch. Thought I'd check to see if my order of medicine and books came in."

"I haven't had a chance to look through the packages," Henry said. "If you'll wait, I'll open them up."

Funny how accommodating Mr. Gallagher was with other people. Guess some folks just counted more than others. Tommy inched up beside her and slipped his hand into hers. A peace stole over her as she felt the warmth of his skin against hers. Maybe she didn't count to these townsfolk, but she sure as shootin' counted to Tommy. And for her, that meant everything.

She walked up to the counter and set her basket down. "I have your eggs here. Let's settle up. I gotta start back." She caught a whiff of some fancy lotion or soap the doc had used on himself. Mmm, but he smelled good.

"Soon as I take care of the doctor," Mr. Gallagher said.

She frowned. She'd been in town long enough and would have been long gone by now had it not been for Carl. "I got me a young 'un to watch out for. 'Sides that, Miss Petunia is in a family way and shouldn't be left on her own too long."

The doctor cocked his head. "Miss Petunia? I haven't come across her in my outlying visits."

He'd mistaken the name of her sheep for a woman! A chuckle nearly escaped before she clamped her lips tightly shut. She didn't intend to correct him, seeing as how she probably wouldn't run into him again.

Slowly, he took in the length of her down to her worn boots, before coming back to her face. With his chin, he pointed at her wrist— the one that Carl had gripped so hard. Only now that Carl was gone did she feel the sting. She hunched her shoulders to coax the end of her sleeve down over the reddened and scratched skin.

"Might want to put salve on that. I've got some back at my office."

She moved away from him, covering her wrist with her other hand. Whether he did or not, she wasn't going anywhere with him—no matter that he'd saved her basket of eggs. "I can take care of it myself."

"I'm sure you can, Mrs....?" He let the word

hang there. When she didn't supply a name, he continued. "I'm Nelson Graham, the doctor here in town. The salve I have is made in Kansas City by a reputable apothecary."

Maybe he was only trying to be helpful. Carl had put her on edge—made her realize all over again how foolish she'd been in her youth to get involved with the Caulder family. She'd learned her lesson, but there was no turning back, no undoing what had come about. She'd keep to herself and take care of herself and that was the end of it. "I thank you for catchin' these eggs before that scallywag dropped them all on the floor. I needed them to finish this here piece."

His brow furrowed. "Transaction?"

She frowned right back. Didn't he know English? "That's what I said."

She waited while Mr. Gallagher transferred the eggs into a pail, all the while knowing the doctor watched her. It made her uncomfortable…more than it would had he been someone else from town. She knew where she stood with them. This Doc Graham looked down at her like she was a puzzle and he wanted to figure her out. Well, she liked her privacy and he'd just have to be satisfied with some disappointment.

"I find it odd that I've been in town for some time and never knew there was a midwife nearby."

She stiffened. He just couldn't keep his nose

out of her business! "If you call helping my sheep in her time of confinement midwifing, then I guess that's what I am." She didn't wait to see what his reaction would be but pointed out a twenty-five-pound sack of flour and another of oats that she needed. "That too, Mr. Gallagher."

Henry hoisted a sack under each arm and carried them out to the wagon, and she followed with the second case of jars.

Her conscience pricked her. Maybe she had been a bit testy with the doc. After all, he had been a big help with Carl.

"Go on and get in the wagon," she told Tommy. She waited while Tommy clambered up onto the wagon seat. She always had the impulse to help him, after all, he was only seven years old, but she resisted the urge. Her son liked to climb. Seeing that he was settled, she turned back toward the doctor.

He stood in the doorway, looking comfortable and relaxed and infuriatingly confident, with a half smile on his face. She'd like to ask him what was so amusing but didn't figure she'd care for his answer. "Nice to make your acquaintance, Doc Graham."

"Same here. Except I still don't know your name."

She had plumb forgot about that. Still, she hesitated, hating to reveal yet again to another person her marital state. He'd learn of it eventually. Carl had made sure of that years ago and the Gallaghers liked to gossip—at least Mable did. "It's Marks. Miss Sylvia Marks."

She hurried outside, deposited the box she held in the back of the wagon and climbed up next to her son. She didn't care to gauge the doc's reaction on learning who she was. She unwrapped the reins from the brake lever and called out softly to her mule. "Giddup."

She couldn't leave town fast enough. Nothin' but trouble in town. Nothin' but trouble.

After watching the wagon pull away, Nelson Graham turned back to the counter. He considered it his duty as the town doctor to know who lived in the area. Miss Marks was as backwoods as he'd ever seen and an interesting mix of spunk and pride. Not bad-looking either, and despite her small frame, not easily overlooked. He would have remembered her, had he met her before.

"Interesting woman," he said when Henry returned from the storage room. He carried the two heavy medical books that Nelson had ordered a month ago.

Henry snorted. "Always seems to bring trouble with her when she comes into town."

"As I saw it, she didn't have much choice."

"I don't involve myself in the squabbles between folks. If I take sides, my sales go down."

Nelson had been told nearly the same thing in medical school. *"Don't involve yourself in the politics or prejudices of your patients. Your job is to heal. You won't always agree with your patient, but you've given an oath as a doctor to care for everyone."* Trouble with that was, in Nelson's mind, he was a man first before he was a doctor.

The fact remained that Carl Caulder was twice as big as Miss Marks and a bully. Nelson couldn't abide bullies. "I thought I met everyone in these parts when I first arrived."

"Miss Marks stays to herself. And if you happen by and surprise her, you might get a load of buckshot in you."

Nelson stifled a smile at the image of the small-framed woman with a big rifle in her hands. "Doesn't encourage me to visit her anytime soon. Where's the boy's father?"

"I heard he took off a few months before the boy was born and never came back. Carl says he died, but knowing Carl, that's not necessarily true."

Nelson absorbed that bit of information, feeling more and more like he was prying instead of gathering facts that might help him provide better medical care for the pair. He withdrew a few bills from his inside vest pocket. "Well, what do I owe you here?" Once he'd paid, he picked up his books and headed for the door.

Henry followed him outside to the boardwalk. "This came for you too." He handed him a letter.

Nelson glanced at the return address. Boston. His parents. A weight dropped in his stomach. What could they possibly want?

He tucked the letter inside his vest pocket. "Thanks, Henry."

"The train is due in tomorrow from Bridgeport. More women wanting to marry are arriving. Are you going to the station to look them over?"

"I didn't fare so well the first time." By the time he'd made up his mind which bride he wanted from the first train, he was too late. Mary McCary would have been a suitable fit. She knew how to cook and she had displayed a caring attitude toward the injured cook out at Putnam's ranch. It was too bad that spending all that time with Steve Putnam had turned her head toward the rancher. They seemed satisfied with each other. More than satisfied. He was happy for them. It was just that he was left high and dry.

He nodded a goodbye to Henry and started for his house.

Although he had sworn off matrimony after his short-lived engagement, he figured in a small town it was the only course to take. People here tended to trust a married family man more than they would a bachelor and he also needed the help in his medical practice.

What he really wanted was a nurse—not necessarily a wife. Yet he couldn't very well advertise for one. Any woman would cringe at the thought of traveling so far from her home for a mere nursing position. And no marriageable woman of good character would agree to spend constant time at his side without a ring on her finger. Tongues would wag in this little town where there were so few women. Even if he did find one to employ as his nurse without making her a missus, it wouldn't be two months before another man would woo, marry and whisk her away.

His only other option was to hire a widow twice his age. He'd been on the lookout for just such a woman. Unfortunately, in the two years he'd lived here, even the older women quickly became brides again or left Oak Grove.

No. His only choice was marriage—preferably to a woman who could look after herself and not throw a fit if he missed supper now and then. Doctoring was more than a job to him, more than a profession. It had become his passion, a calling as much as any parson's call to the cloth was a calling, and it took as many or more hours in a day. He needed a wife who would understand and be of help to him. Someone practical.

He stepped up on the porch and entered his

office. Passing through the front room that served as his parlor and waiting room, he strode back to his office and set the journals and the letter on his desk. He wanted to delve right into the journals, but the letter was another matter. Word from home was seldom happy. He wished he could leave it for another day.

The address was written in his mother's script. Nothing unusual about that. His father had never written to him. He heard from his mother only when there was something important to pass on—once a year at the most. He broke the fancy seal and unfolded the letter, then paced the length of the small room while he read.

And came to a standstill.

His parents were coming to visit.

Stunned, he reread the letter. Not once before had they visited him. Once they had stuck him in boarding school, it was he who did the traveling to see them, not the other way around. Not even when he graduated from medical school did they make the effort. This was unprecedented. They would arrive in two weeks. He turned the letter over once more, inanely hoping he'd find more written somewhere else on the page. He wished he could read between the lines.

What was really going on?

Chapter Two

"But it hurts!" Wiley Austin mumbled to his older brother, Kade. His eyes started to tear again as Nelson probed the boy's thumb with the end of a needle. The large splinter had embedded itself under several layers of skin.

"Toughen up," Kade said as he looked on. "Quit your slobberin'."

"I ain't slobberin'."

"Are too."

"Ain't neither!" Wiley wiped the snot from his nose with the back of his hand.

"You're doing fine," Nelson murmured, concentrating on the splinter.

"Ouch!" Wiley jerked away.

Nelson straightened and stretched his back. "Shake it out and we'll try again in a minute." The grandfather clock in the hotel lobby chimed three times, reminding him that the train carrying the brides would be arriving at any moment. After a busy morning in the office, he'd finally made up his mind to be there…until Wiley's splinter happened. "Ready to tackle this again?"

The boy wiped his nose again and stepped closer, holding out his hand. It shook slightly.

"I'm almost there." Nelson pressed against the far edge of the splinter with his thumb, picked up his tweezers and eased the splinter out. He held it up. "That's a big one. You were brave. Not every six-year-old could handle such a big operation."

Wiley let out a huge sigh of relief.

Nelson dabbed at the drop of blood with his handkerchief and then slathered a small bit of unguent on the nearly invisible exit hole.

The train whistle blew once more and with it came the last chug and wheeze as the wheels slowed to a stop. Shouts sounded from the street as men headed toward the station.

"Thank you, Dr. Graham," Sadie Austin said as she descended the steps from the second floor. "I just had to get the last of the rooms ready for the women and Wiley wouldn't stand still for me to help him."

"Not a problem, Mrs. Austin. Glad to help out."

"Ma! Can me and Wiley go meet the train?"

Mrs. Austin hesitated a moment and then

nodded. "We'll go together. I can't have you two anywhere near the tracks or the train's wheels. Your father would have a fit. Now, you take hold of your brother's hand, Kade."

"Aw!" Wiley whined.

"I mean it!" she said.

Nelson settled his Stetson on his head. For a woman who had never had children of her own, Mrs. Austin was doing a fine job of mothering the two boys. "Going there myself, ma'am. I'll walk with you."

She grabbed her shawl from the table in the entryway as they headed out the front door of the hotel. "I'm glad to see you still here in Oak Grove."

"Still here," he said. People here had worried he would pull stakes and head back East when things didn't work out with the first set of brides that rolled into town nearly a year ago. What they didn't know was that the words he'd had with his father before leaving home for good had left a gaping chasm in their relationship— one not easily bridged. The only way he would consider going back to Boston would be if he received a heartfelt "I'm sorry" from his father. Unless their visit had something to do with that argument, he didn't expect an apology to happen anytime soon.

"I like the town and the people. And with the

new brides there will be more people to doctor in a few years."

With Kade and Wiley jumping and yelling between him and Mrs. Austin, Nelson strode down the main street of town to the train station. A number of cowboys had come from outlying ranches for the excitement and they spilled out of the Whistle Stop Saloon ahead of him, lining up, shoulder to shoulder and bowleg to bowleg. As the women descended from the train, their long dresses pressed against their legs from the strong wind. Nelson tugged his hat farther down on his head, so as not to lose it to the blustery spring day.

"Gentlemen! Back up! Give the women some breathing room," the mayor said in his booming voice from where he stood on the train steps. He had already been inside the train to welcome them in his official capacity. "The train must keep to its schedule, so you men help unload the trunks and get their belongings up to the hotel. The ladies will appreciate that more than having you jabber at them as their things ride on to Denver. We'll have a welcome party tomorrow, once they've had a chance to rest and freshen up."

Nelson pulled Kade and Wiley back to keep them out from underfoot as a few men surged forward and responded to the mayor's instructions. Then the line of remaining cowboys

parted and the mayor strode through the opening with the women—five of them—following.

Nelson quickly removed his hat, as did every
other man there at the station, and watched the
parade of women walk past, their long dresses
swishing in time with the twitch of their bustles
and the bob of their heads. It was quite a sight
for Oak Grove.

Leading the group was a dark-haired, rather
stern-faced woman in a black skirt with thin
white stripes and a black shirtwaist. She took
long, no-nonsense strides that could match any
man's. When she came near, he realized with
something of shock that she was as tall as he
was, which meant she had to be nearly six feet
without the heels on those shoes of hers.

The next two women walked arm in arm
and were close enough in appearance that he
wondered if they were sisters with their nonde-
script brown hair confined in buns, brown felt
hats with flowers and dark brown wool coats
that covered them from head to toe. One looked
about the town and men with open curiosity in
her intelligent expression as she walked, while
the other had a severe case of nerves and kept
covering her lower face and giggling into her
gloved hands.

The next two women walked single file, surrounded by the last of the cowboys from the saloon, who hid them so much that he couldn't get

much of a look at them. One looked to be quite attractive with pretty chestnut-colored hair, dark eyes and a wine-red hat that matched her cloak. The other appeared to be a blonde with wide cornflower blue eyes. She was a bit older by the small lines near her eyes. She might do—someone with experience in life could be an asset.

Mrs. Austin, with her young charges in hand, took off with the entourage toward the hotel. It would fall to her to help the young ladies get settled into their rooms. Left to himself, Nelson considered the notes he'd made earlier that day and withdrew the paper from his vest pocket. It was a "wish list" of sorts. Likely, no woman would meet all his expectations, but perhaps it would help him stay on course as he considered each of them.

Amiable.

Biddable.

Able to take constructive criticism.

Skilled in domestic chores: cooking, laundry, cleaning, sewing and gardening.

Willing to work by his side as his nurse.

Quiet. He didn't want a woman who disrupted his research or his daily habits.

Willing to put another's needs ahead of her own.

He'd added the last as a cautionary point, remembering his fiancée. He'd thought they were compatible in all things, but then suddenly she had broken off the engagement, unable to accept the numerous times he'd been called away to help someone who was ailing.

He wouldn't let that happen again. What he needed was a practical woman as his wife. She didn't need to be a raging beauty, but like any man, he wouldn't mind if she was pleasant to look upon.

He tucked the paper back into his pocket and headed to his office. Now all he had to do was interview the ladies, one at a time, and see which one came closest to fulfilling his wish list.

Who knew? With his parents arriving in two weeks, perhaps they would find themselves attending his wedding.

He stopped before his two-story home that doubled as his office and surveyed it critically. Prior to residing in Oak Grove, he'd worked as the physician for the railroad company. The job entailed constant travel—something he'd had enough of after two years. This was his first office, the first place he'd ever been able to "hang his own shingle" and be in business for himself. He hoped his parents would be impressed with it when they arrived. It wasn't up to Boston standards, but it was a start for him.

A wedding might be just what was needed to bring them all closer together. A wedding, after all, meant children would come next. The idea fascinated him. He was an only child, and

a large family would be wonderful. But would
his parents welcome grandchildren when they
hadn't ever made him feel welcomed? Likely,
all his dreams were just that—dreams and nothing more.

Chapter Three

Sylvia threw the last of the wet clothes into her basket and traipsed back to the house from the creek. The day was uncommonly warm this early in spring, and she figured she'd better not misuse it. With her washing done, and soon to be spread on the line, she and Tommy might have time to hunt for mushrooms. Her mouth watered at the thought of them fried up in butter and piled high on a chunk of hearty bread.

"Tommy! Fetch a pail from the lean-to and let's take a walk down the road," she called out.

"Not till you find me!"

That boy! He was full of vinegar! She couldn't blame him, not one bit. The warm sun shining down beckoned her to put work aside and have a day of fun. "Can you give me a hint?"

"Nope!"

He must be behind the shed. She set her basket down and ducked under the clothesline. She couldn't believe the shed still stood after the winter they'd had, but Thomas had been good with his hands and smart when it came to making things.

"I'm coming!"

"Won't get me!" her son cried out.

The happy sound filled her heart with gladness. She peeked behind the shed, ready to catch him if he raced by.

"You ain't even warm yet!"

"Then where are you?" She tiptoed over to the stand of brush that edged the expanse of prairie and buffalo wallows beyond. The line of brush hid their place from prying eyes and made their small cabin feel cozy and protected. "I give up."

A giggle escaped Tommy. "Right here!"

She spun around. Her son's voice had come from above her. A flash of blue caught her eyes and she finally spied him. He'd managed to climb atop the shed and now lay sprawled across the slanted roof on his belly.

"How'd you climb way up there? Come on down now."

He grinned. "All right, Ma."

He stood and took a step, the old wood and tarp cracking and then giving beneath his foot. He flailed his arms out and his eyes widened.

"Tommy!" She moved closer. "Careful!"

But the fear in his big brown eyes clutched at her heart. "Ma… *Ma!*" Suddenly, he pitched forward, scraping against the edge of the roof and crying out in pain as he fell.

"No! Tommy!" she screamed and scrambled toward him.

He landed hard on a patch of weeds and lay still.

She knelt at his side, afraid at first to touch him. Hoping…hoping…that he would open his eyes or squirm or even jump up and laugh at her for being worried.

He didn't.

"You all right?" she asked gently, her chest tight with worry. Of course, he wasn't all right. He wasn't moving. He wasn't even hearing her. "Tommy! Wake up! I'm here! I'm here…" She barely got the words out before her sobs choked them off. Her gut coiled into a hard lump. She reached for him. He was her baby—the only thing she cared for in this life. Oh, why…*why*… had he been born with the overpowering urge to climb things?

Maybe he'd just had the wind knocked out of him. Maybe she just needed to give him a moment.

Trembling, she took hold of his small hand. His face was deathly pale.

"Tommy, please wake up…"

His chest moved and then he gasped, pulling in air in a short burst, and then in a longer, slower drag as his lungs started working again.

"Oh, my stars! Tommy, are you all right?"

He rolled farther onto his back and took another breath. A deep one this time. "I don't feel right."

"You fell from the shed, baby. Where does it hurt?"

"Everywheres."

"I don't doubt that. Can you move?"

At that, he clenched his hands into fists, then tried to use his arms to sit up. Immediately, he fell back to the ground, breathing hard. "My head. My leg."

"Let me look at you." Gently, she turned his head to the side and smoothed her fingers through his hair. She felt something sticky and wet. There—a lump the size of a black walnut swelled up. He winced.

She turned to his legs. The one closest to her moved just fine. When she tested his far leg—his left leg—Tommy yelled.

"All right, all right…" she said. She had barely moved the leg and he'd had pain. What was she to do?

"Ma…I hurt all over."

She swallowed. She couldn't leave him out in the weather like this. The ground hadn't given up the cold of winter yet.

"I gotta git you warm, son. I'm gonna get

the quilt from the house to cover you. Then I'll figure this out. You just rest. I'll be right back." She squeezed his hand firmly and then scrambled to her feet.

She raced to the house. Yanking the quilt from her son's straw pallet, she rushed back out to him. He was deathly pale. His eyes were half-closed.

"This ain't going to feel good, son," she said as she snugged the quilt over him and tucked it around his little body, especially tight around his legs. "But you be brave. I'll get you fixed up."

Sneaking her arm under his knees and her other behind his back, she lifted him up and carried him to the house. If it was possible, his face paled even more when she laid him on his pallet by the hearth. Beads of sweat glistened on his upper lip and forehead.

"All done moving." She used her apron to wipe his forehead, then raked his long shock of dark blond hair away from his face. "You were as brave as brave could be."

"I don't feel so good." His usually boisterous voice was thin and weak.

She took his hand. It was cold and moist. Fear as she'd never known it before gripped her. "You hang on. I'll get you—" His brown eyes drifted closed and his hand fell limply from hers. "Tommy!"

His chest rose and fell with each shallow breath.

Grabbing the fire iron, she stirred up the ashes in the hearth and then tossed on a cow chip.

She had best look at that leg. Carefully, she unwrapped the quilt from Tommy, then took a knife from the cupboard drawer and cut away his trousers.

And sat back, staring at the ugly wound on his leg. Her gut tightened. It looked bad. Real bad. A flap of skin had been scraped back in a wide swath along the side near the ankle. The skin was swollen and purple. Could she fix it?

Then another thought took hold. Had he broken his ankle too? It had all happened so fast. Maybe she couldn't fix either of his ailments.

She took a closer look at his head, wincing at the size of the lump that had formed. He'd bled through the coarse cotton covering of the pallet, but she'd heard that head wounds always bled a lot. The flow of blood seemed to be slowing, congealing now. She couldn't do anything for a head injury. It would have to heal itself. She felt so helpless.

She got to her feet, grabbed the soap and the bowl and the pitcher from the table, and came back to him. "I sure hope you don't wake up and feel this, son, 'cause it will break my heart if I'm a-hurtin' you."

With that, she set to work rinsing out the dirt and splinters of the old roof and cleaning out the wound. Then she slathered a layer of honey over it and wrapped it in a clean cloth.

She wished that someone at the DuBois farm was home. Adele would know what to do, but just yesterday the family had stopped by to tell her they were on their way to Salina to purchase a new ox.

Sylvia pulled Tommy's pallet closer to the fire. Not knowing what else to do, she sat down in her rocking chair and watched him for signs of rousing.

She took comfort in the fact that he was breathing. The steady rise and fall of his chest was sweeter to her than a meadowlark's song. Surely he'd wake up soon. Surely the Lord wouldn't take Tommy from her too.

But the next hour brought no change. Her confidence in Tommy's recovery slowly eroded. It seemed that a child should bounce back quick and this wasn't quick. She gave him a little jiggle, pushing on his shoulder. Then put a cold cloth to his face. He didn't stir.

Pale sunlight streamed through a small window and slanted across the dirt floor. It would be dark in another hour.

She wasn't used to sitting. Wasn't used to letting life happen to her. She preferred to go out and meet it. For seven years, she'd worked hard to make a life for the two of them. She wasn't about to see that stop, not if there was an ounce of strength left in her body.

Chapter Four

The sun cast a pink glow over the entire town when Nelson left his office and walked toward the Oak Grove Town Hall. Since the evenings still carried the chill of winter, the shindig was taking place inside the building that Jackson Miller had just completed. From the street, he could hear the muffled sounds of conversation and laughter through the tall windows.

He stepped up onto the boardwalk and through the front doors. The new construction held the strong scent of fresh-cut lumber and varnish. He scanned the packed room, grateful to be a head taller than most of the people inside. The bachelors that had donated to the bride fund through the Betterment Committee milled about along with several other families from outside town. Guess they were anxious to gather and socialize. Another few weeks and they would be up to their necks in planting their fields or caring for the newly born calves. Getting away from their farms and ranches to have a moment of fun would not be possible until summer arrived.

A heavy hand clasped his shoulder. "I wondered if you would throw in with the rest of us, Doc."

Graham turned. "Hello, Jess. Giving it another try?"

A wide grin covered the younger man's face as he grasped Nelson's hand in a strong shake. "Practice makes perfect, right, Doc? May the best man win." Jess moved closer to the front of the room.

As he looked over the brides, Nelson reminded himself that he really needed a nurse. That was primary. Of course, he couldn't very well blurt out his intentions here. The men of Oak Grove would likely show him the door. They wanted wives, helpmeets in life, and they wouldn't take kindly to his motives.

His own parents' marriage wasn't the best standard to judge what a good marriage looked like, but it was all he had to go by. And what with his failed courtship, it seemed to him that sticking to a nonemotional, practical union made the most sense. It was safer.

Mayor Melbourne climbed the two steps to

the small stage and stood there, gripping the lapels of his silk vest and surveying the group. He waved his hands for everyone to quiet down. Then he motioned to the new brides to come to the front of the room. He introduced each of the five and said a small bit about them.

The two older women stood next to each other, looking poised and lovely, while the three younger ones clustered together in a clutch like barnyard chickens. He grimaced. Perhaps that was a bit critical. Being observant was a good attribute to have in medicine, but not in social gatherings. It reminded him of something his father would say.

The mayor cleared his throat, drawing everyone's attention. "I'll have the bachelors that donated to the Betterment Committee, and only those, line up now and introduce yourselves *briefly* to the ladies," he announced.

Nelson counted twenty men who lined up. He stepped toward the back. As the men made their way across the stage, some were quiet and sincere, some cracked a joke to cover up their nervousness and some were eager to the point of embarrassing. It came to him that he was none of these. He simply wanted to assess each woman as unemotionally as possible. That way he could be sure his decision would be based on facts and not feelings.

His turn finally arrived, and he made his way

down the row of five women, making mental notes as he went from one to the next.

Miss Vandersohn: Chestnut hair, dark green eyes. Petite like a china doll and well dressed. Beautiful.

Miss Pratt: The tallest. Older, black-haired and stern of face. Instead of curtsying as did the others, she gave a sharp nod of her head.

Miss O'Rourke: Older, blonde with cornflower blue eyes, with lines at the corner of her eyes. Pleasant-looking. He wondered what had happened that some young man hadn't already snatched her up.

Miss Simcock: Youngest in appearance and a dishwater blonde. She blushed to the roots of her hair when he asked her a simple question and then barely got an answer out due to giggling nervously.

Miss Weber: Younger, chestnut hair, gray eyes, wine-red hat and cloak. Shy. By the shiny indentation on each side of her nose, she appeared to wear glasses, although she wasn't wearing them now.

The moment the introductions were complete, the mayor motioned for the music to start. The bachelors surged back toward the five brides, in their excitement trying to muscle him to the side of the room. He didn't budge.

He stood there a few minutes more, observing the hoopla. None of the women would be able to focus on him with all the other men in the room. He would rather visit them at another time when he wouldn't be interrupted.

"That exam table working out for you, Doc?" Jackson Miller said as he approached.

Nelson shook his hand. "Fine. Not a splinter gained among any of my patients so far. Fine work."

"Glad to hear it."

They stood there a moment, arms crossed over their chests, watching the melee in communal silence.

"I wonder what surprises will appear among these women," Miller mused out loud. "I don't think any will match the amount that my Maggie made."

Nelson chuckled. "Probably not. I can't see any of these landing in jail."

Miller's wife had arrived on the first bride train, along with her sister, Mary. At the time, Nelson had had issues with the tonic Maggie tried to pass off as a remedy for just about every conceivable ailment. A family recipe, she'd said. Since then, the reticence she once carried toward him had begun to ease. A good thing because Miller's Cabinetry Shop stood near his office and they crossed paths often.

"I don't see you rushing in with the rest," Miller said. "No one strikes your fancy?"

Nelson surveyed the women once more. "Five does."

Miller's eyes twinkled with amusement. "Five? As in number five? Better not let the lady hear you call her that."

"Miss Weber. I think she'll do just fine."

"Do?"

Nelson nodded but didn't elaborate on his thoughts. She was young and strong. She was also quiet. He liked that. If she took instruction well, he could train her precisely how he wanted things done.

The clear bell tones of a woman laughing sounded. Number One drew his gaze. She was a stunning woman. There was a reason he didn't want a beautiful woman, but at that moment it escaped him.

Beside him, Jackson took a long swallow of beer.

"On second thought," Nelson said, "I think I'll start with Miss Vandersohn and go through them one at a time."

Jackson spit out his mouthful of brew. "You're serious!"

"Yep. That's how I'll do it. Steady and methodical."

A slow grin grew on Jackson's face. "I'd try to warn you off such a crazy plan where women are concerned, but I don't think it would do any

good. Take it from me. You don't stand a chance
if the right one comes along."

"We'll see who is right when the time comes."

"Sure, Doc," Jackson said, shaking his head
as he walked away.

A sense of purpose filled Nelson. By the end
of the month, per their contract, the women
would have to marry. He had four weeks to get
this part of his life in order. He would call on
Miss Vandersohn first thing in the morning and
start things moving forward. A stroll perhaps to
show her the sights of the town.

His decision made, he spun on his heels and
headed out the door, leaving the gaiety and the
noise behind him.

Chapter Five

Sylvia was no good at waiting. When she drove her wagon into town just after dusk, she had expected Doc Graham to be home. She hadn't a clue how she was going to convince him to travel all the way to her place. She had nothing to pay him with for his services. All she knew was that she was scared for Tommy and with each minute her desperation was growing bigger and bigger. It might end up choking her if the doc didn't show up soon.

She paced the length of his walkway a few times, her arms crossed over her chest. Then she sat down on his steps. For all of one minute. Then she was up pacing again.

On her way to town, she'd come face-to-face with the fact that a man who wore a silk vest, a man who had an office, was not likely to come over to her side of the river to see her son. He'd expect payment, which she didn't have. He'd probably expect her to bring her boy to him—and she wasn't going to move Tommy. She might hurt him worse.

At least she was sure this was the doc's house. A brass sign on the porch said Doctor's Office plain as could be. She'd checked three other houses, peeking in the darkened windows, before she was sure she had the right house. There was some big hullabaloo happening down in the new building next to the bank. Maybe that was where everyone was. Maybe she should check down there.

She hated to walk right in on the entire town. Her whole life she'd made it a point to avoid as much of the people here as she could.

But what if he never came back tonight? What if he was out on a call? Maybe somebody was having a baby. Or somebody was sick. The thoughts plagued her.

Maybe she should have asked Carl for help… She recoiled at that when she remembered how he had treated Tommy at the mercantile. No… Carl would have made things worse. She'd done the only thing she could and that was to leave Tommy by himself. Doing that weighed on her something fierce. He was too hurt to wander off. The way he had whimpered once, like a kicked puppy, just crumpled her insides. He needed the doc. She couldn't go back without him.

A shout came from somewhere on the main street. Then a door squeaked open and shut on one of the buildings—maybe the hotel. A dog barked.

Someone was coming.

She tiptoed up the porch steps and pulled into the shadows.

It was a man. His long strides gave that away. The silver clasp at his neck gleamed in the small amount of light left. The doc had worn the same tie in the mercantile.

Her heart pounded. She swallowed, nervous. What could she possibly offer him by way of bartering? What would he accept?

Now he was on the steps. He stood taller than she remembered. She hesitated. Maybe this was a fool idea. There was no way she could force him to go with her if he had a mind not to.

As he crossed in front of her, she caught a whiff of that fancy-smelling lotion he used. He reached for the door handle...

She gathered her courage. Tommy was worth it. Tommy was worth everything. "How much do you charge for a doctor visit?"

He froze at the sound of her voice.

"Would you take a chicken in payment?"

"I hate chicken," he said evenly in his deep voice.

Her gut tightened. What to do? What to do? Then he started to twist around.

"Stay as you are!" She panicked, fumbled with her satchel and withdrew her pistol. She shoved it against his lower back. "I got me a gun here, don't you know."

It was her nerves talking. She was making a muddle of everything.

"I dislike being accosted at gunpoint."

She would have laughed at the absurd statement had her skin not been crawling in her nervousness. Instead, she scowled. "Most people do, but you're mighty calm for bein' in such a condition."

"Believe me. I am not calm at all. I simply can't see any value in making the situation worse."

"Well...that's a good thing. Now. Enough talk. You got to come with me."

"What is this about? I assume someone is hurt or sick."

How much could she tell him without him saying no to crossing the river? If he wouldn't take a chicken, she had nothing to give him. She had nothing to spare.

"Are you alone?"

He was asking too many questions and this was taking too long.

"I said quiet! Just move on down to the wagon there."

He started to turn.

She didn't want him facing her! She stepped farther into the shadows.

"If you need my medical skills, then I must insist that either you or I bring my medical bag."

She scowled again. "Fine. Get it. But don't try anything."

She followed him to a room in the back of the house, where he picked up a brown leather bag the size of a bread box from his desk.

"I'll need my—" He reached for a drawer.

"Oh, no, you don't!" She cocked her gun. He could store anything in there—a gun or a knife. "You git a move on."

The rustle of heavy material sounded as he grabbed his coat off the back of his chair and shrugged into it, then picked up his bag again. She stepped aside to let him pass and followed him outside.

Light from the moon cast the town in shadows of gray and black and blue as he strode to her wagon. She didn't want him sitting next to her. He might get the upper hand and wrestle her gun away from her. Then where would she be? Where would Tommy be?

"Climb in the back."

He took hold of the edge of the wagon and then paused. "You do realize that this is kidnapping?"

She shut out the twinge of guilt she felt. Tommy was all that mattered. "Can't be helped."

"I could shout. Call out for help."

"Everyone is at the town hall. There's no one around to hear you."

"You've planned this well." He swung into the wagon bed. "If I forced your hand, they would hear a gunshot…"

"I don't think you want to take that chance, now do you, Doc? I been living off the land most my life. I don't miss what I aim for."

"I see your point."

"Now, lay down on your back."

"I hardly think that is necess—"

She threw a tarp over him. "I'm in charge here, in case you ain't noticed. Now, no more shenanigans. I never heard someone talk so much during a kidnapping."

"So, this is a common occurrence?"

"Ya gotta come with me, Doc," she said softly, mostly to herself. "I can't give you no choice in the matter." Her heart hurt, tight with remorse. It wasn't right—her using him this way especially after he'd done her a good turn a few days back at the mercantile, but it couldn't be helped. Tommy came first, despite how guilty she felt about forcing the doc. She snapped the reins. "Get up! Berta!"

Chapter Six

This was a first for Nelson. Kidnapped by a bit of a woman no bigger than a broomstick. At first, he'd thought to wrestle the gun away from her, but then realizing the depth of her desperation, he'd decided, for the time being, to let her have her way and let things play out. If she kept waving that gun around, someone—likely he— was bound to get hurt. Besides, she hadn't demanded money, so this wasn't a robbery. The only thing she seemed to want was him. The idea of it tickled him a small degree. Kidnapped! He'd never been wanted so badly in his life. He only hoped he wasn't going from a bad situation to worse. One tiny woman wouldn't be a problem, but if she transported him to a den of outlaws, that would be another thing entirely.

In the dark, he hadn't gotten a good look at

her, but something about her was familiar—her voice, the way she pronounced certain words. He couldn't place it, but he'd heard her speak somewhere before.

The wagon rumbled along and he felt every small rut and bump on his backside. He shivered against the chill in the air, smelling snow. Suddenly, his weight shifted as blood rushed to his head. The wagon traveled down a steep slope, then hooves clopped on wooden boards. The wagon leveled out and stopped.

There was the rustle of cloth and a few feminine grunts, then he felt a strange rocking sensation. At first, he was confused, but then the sound of water trickling over rocks came to him and he realized the wagon was floating. The only river nearby was south of town—the Smoky Hill River. And the only ferry crossing was southeast, about a mile from the train tracks. At least he had his bearings now.

When the wagon started moving over solid ground again, he knew they had reached the opposite bank. He popped his head out from under the tarp. Clouds obscured the moon. With so little light, how could the woman see the trail? All he could make out was the manly shape of her hat against the darkness. A snowflake landed on his eyelash. He swiped it away, feeling more confident that he could find his way back to town if need be. A light layer of spring snow would make it easy for him to follow tracks.

"Ma'am?"

"No talking," she said curtly.

"But don't you think this has gone far enough? Why do you feel the need to drag me out—"

"Shut your mouth, Doc."

"If I can be of service, I am certainly willing."

"I got no call to believe a word out of your mouth or any man's. You'd only force me to turn around and take you back and I can't do that. There's only one thing I want from you and you ain't leavin' until it gets done."

"Then you intend to release me after I do whatever it is you want?"

"Figure I've said enough. So have you," she said stubbornly.

Another snowflake landed and then melted on his lip. He'd offered to help, but it seemed she wanted nothing of it. Fine by him. Let her handle things on her own. She was obviously strong. She'd managed to maneuver the pull-line across the river. He hunkered back down under the tarp. Cantankerous, stubborn woman!

After what seemed hours but was more likely fifteen or twenty minutes, the wagon stopped. He heard the squeak and jostle as his captor jumped from the small, rickety wagon.

"Doc? You awake?" She flung the tarp off,

shaking out the light layer of snow on top, which ended up flying into his face.

If he had slept—which he hadn't—he'd be awake now. He sat up.

The dark blanketed the woman's face as surely as the tarp had blanketed him. "You can get out."

For a moment, he thought about the gun in his medical bag. He'd thought about the derringer several times on the ride and whether to grab it or not. He kept the gun as protection against snakes and to warn off cougars. He'd never pointed it at a man, much less a woman. He knew instinctively that this entire affair was not about anyone getting hurt. The woman was desperate. That thought stayed his hand and kept the derringer stored away. He needed to find out what was going on.

"I said, get out," she repeated.

Nelson climbed from the wagon, medical bag in hand. The snowfall was heavier. He doubted that it would stick—just a fitful spring snow destined to melt away once the sun came up. He hoped it stayed just long enough for him to find his way back to town.

"In the house. Be quick about it."

He could barely make out the silhouette of a low-slung building a short distance away. Candlelight flickered in the window. He made his way there over lumpy ground, found the door and stepped inside.

A banked fire in the hearth emitted enough of a glow to cast the one room in a low reddish-gold light. A table stood in the center of the room. A tall cupboard stood against the far wall that was made of stacked bricks of sod. "Why did you—"

Then he heard a moan. The sound came from the floor. He walked around the table. A small boy lay on a straw pallet, his eyes open and feverish. Immediately, Nelson strode over to him.

He set aside his medical bag and dropped to his knees. "What happened?" Dried blood congealed on the boy's matted hair and smeared the thin muslin cover behind his head.

"He's awake! Oh, Lord be praised! Tommy! I'm here, son. Mama's here. You just lie still now. I fetched the doctor."

Nelson glanced up and for the first time recognized the woman he'd met in the mercantile two days earlier. She wore the same hat she'd worn then, a man's old felt cowboy hat that had lost its shape from years of use. It had fallen back between her shoulder blades, held there by its chin ties. Her brown hair, loosely braided, fell over her shoulder to her belt buckle. She had tears in her large brown eyes.

"So…it's you."

She met his gaze with a stubborn one of her

own. Then she swallowed before resolutely lifting her chin. "You'll fix him."

Nelson raised his brow. He wasn't used to being ordered about. He was the one who usually did the ordering. "What happened?"

"He fell from the shed this afternoon. Hit his head good and hard. He wouldn't wake up."

"It's a good thing he's awake now." Nelson took a moment to look down the boy's body. The left leg had been tended to. It was now wrapped in a thick piece of wool material. "Looks like he did more than hit his head."

She hovered over him, unmindful of the fact she still had that pistol in her hand. She waved it about. "Hurt his leg too. Happened when he went through the old roof. Foot got caught up and he lost his balance. Might be broken." She pointed with the gun to his left foot.

"Put that gun down before you shoot somebody, woman! As upset as you are, that thing will go off before you know it."

She pulled back.

"I don't do well at gunpoint." He held out his hand. "Give it to me."

She frowned at him. "How do I know you won't shoot me once I let go?"

He huffed. "Because if I wanted to shoot you, I would have done so already with the pistol in my medical bag."

Her eyes widened. "Oh." Slowly, she put the gun down on the table.

He turned back to the boy and crouched down again. He directed his words to her. "It sounds like a nasty fall. Where were you when this happened?"

She stiffened. "I was tending to chores." Then her face crumpled. "You'll fix him, won't you?"

She truly was beside herself and not thinking straight. He guessed a lecture on keeping an eye on her son was unnecessary at this point, although he'd surely like to give her one. What kind of mother consented to letting her youngster climb something so high? "What were you doing up on top of the lean-to, young man?"

"He's always climbing something, Doc," Miss Marks answered for her son. "Never had a fear of heights like most people. It ain't natural, but there you have it."

He stared her down. "Does he know how to speak?"

She looked confused. "Why, yes."

"Good. Then he can answer for himself."

She clamped her mouth shut and glared at him.

"Bring that candle over," he ordered. "Or, better yet, if you have a lamp…"

He continued examining the boy while the woman bustled about the room. He was barely aware that she'd lit a lamp and carried it close, holding it steadily to help him see her son better. Tommy followed his instructions—holding his head still and following the lamp with his eyes, his pupils constricting and then opening again with the distance of the light. That was a good sign.

"How old are you?"

The boy stared silently at him with a wary expression.

"He's seven."

He set his jaw. The woman was impossible to work with. "Then he's old enough to answer my questions. I will have you step away, ma'am, if you don't hold your tongue. I need to hear him talk, to make sure he is not slurring his words. It helps to determine the extent of his injury."

He turned back to Tommy. "Now, young man, how old are you?"

The boy looked from him to his mother.

"Answer me."

Tommy swallowed. His lips parted. "Seven." The word was barely a whisper, croaked out between dry lips.

"Tell me where you hurt."

Systematically, he examined the boy, questioning, peering and probing until he was satisfied that he understood the boy's injuries. When he unwrapped the makeshift dressing from the injured leg, Tommy gave a swift gasp.

He'd been so quiet, and now to hear him, Nelson realized the boy had been hiding much of his pain. Nelson gentled his touch. "It is the air hitting the wound that hurts." He leaned closer, surprised at the cleanliness he encountered. The raw wound had been scrubbed. "Did you clean this up?"

"Are you asking me? Or Tommy?" the woman asked.

He gritted his teeth. "You, of course."

"I did the best I could. There was lots of dirt from the shed's roof."

He grunted. Surprised she'd done such a thorough job of taking care of the wound. As much as she was worried about her son being in pain, she hadn't skimped on scrubbing it. He peeled back a small section of the skin flap. The wound was nearly to the bone.

Tommy cried out. Large tears filled his eyes. His breathing grew erratic.

The lamplight wavered. His mother, still holding the lamp close, knelt beside him. Tears filled her eyes too as she grasped her son's hand with her free one.

Nelson replaced the flap of skin, approximating the edges as best he could. It would need stitching, but there was one more thing he had to do before he was completely satisfied with his exam. "I'm sorry to have to hurt you. I'll go as quick as I can to lessen the pain. Ready?"

The boy set his jaw once more and then nodded bravely.

Nelson ran his fingers down the two long bones from the shin to the wound. Then, grasping above the wound with one hand, he took hold of Tommy's foot with the other and moved it through all the proper positions.

"Very good." He pulled his medical bag closer and rummaged through it for his needle and supply of catgut. "It needs to be stitched. Brace yourself, Tommy."

"No."

He let out another sigh. "Miss Marks."

"So you do remember my name. Don't matter. You're not poking holes in my son."

"It's the only way to keep the skin together so that it will heal."

She shook her head. "He's hurting enough. Wrap it back up and let it heal on its own."

He wasn't used to having his directions contradicted. "I don't think you understand how deep his wound is. If the tissue doesn't bind correctly, your son could lose much of his ability to walk."

She'd been so set to argue that it took a minute for his words to sink in. Then her shoulder slumped and her brown eyes clouded. "You're sayin' he…he might not walk again?"

"That's right."

She swallowed.

"I've seen this type of injury before when I worked for the railroad. I know what to do. You will have to trust me."

The war going on inside her was evident on her face. She wanted to protect her son from further hurt—that was what her gut told her. And she didn't know whether he was skilled or not. Her bottom lip trembled. "You'll make it so he walks again?"

"I'll do my best."

Tears brimmed in her eyes.

"Ma?"

She met her son's gaze. "We got to trust the doc, Tommy. You hold on to my hand tight. I'm right here." She looked up at Nelson and nodded, her expression resolute.

Nelson finished his preparations.

"Hold him," he said to Miss Marks.

She set her jaw and then lay across her son, gripping his leg to hold him still.

He made the first stitch.

Tommy tensed and yelled out.

Nelson had done this procedure on grown men. Never on a young boy with his mother looking on. If he messed up, there was the chance he might sentence the boy to being a cripple the rest of his life. That thought made him extremely careful.

When he was done, he glanced up to see how Tommy had weathered the treatment and found

Miss Marks watching him intently. Her face was pale, but no less determined than it had been earlier. "Get me another bandage."

She scrambled to her feet.

"You did well," he told the boy. "I'm all finished except for wrapping it up."

Tommy didn't answer, but he relaxed his jaw. Sweat beaded his upper lip.

"How are you feeling?" Nelson asked.

Tommy let out a shaky breath but still didn't answer.

Of course, the boy still hurt. "You did well," Nelson said again. "I've had grown men who didn't handle stitches as bravely as you."

Miss Marks returned with what appeared to be clean rags and a small jar of honey.

He took the rags and wrapped the ankle. "You can get him a blanket now. Keep him here by the fire for the next few days. He needs lots of rest. Nothing appears to be broken. It's probably a bad sprain. I'll know more in a few days, once the swelling has gone down and the wound has a chance to bind together."

"Then…he'll be all right?"

He nodded. "Young boys are resilient about such things."

A ragged breath shuddered out of her. She sank to her knees beside her son. "Ya hear that? You're going to be all right, Tommy." A tear trickled down her cheek.

"What are you cryin' for, Ma?"

She cupped the boy's jaw with her palm. "I'm happy. That's all. You heard what the doctor said. You rest now."

Nelson squirmed. Such an outpouring of love was something he'd never experienced with his own mother. He turned away, clearing his throat.

At the sound, Miss Marks rose to her feet. "You look piqued, Doc. I'll get you some water."

He hadn't realized he was thirsty until she said something. "Thank you."

She also filled a glass for her son and handed it to Tommy first. Then she set a full glass on the table for Nelson.

"Now you know why I had to make you come."

"At gunpoint," he said, glancing pointedly at the gun still lying on the table.

"You wouldn't have come otherwise."

"You didn't give me a choice."

"I had to know Tommy would be all right. I couldn't get him to wake up."

Something stirred inside Nelson. "You should have sent someone. It was dangerous for you to leave your son alone."

Her expression crumpled. "Like you, I didn't have a choice either."

He looked away—anywhere but at her. Female sentiment shook him up more than he cared. Female hysteria unhinged him. Give him a man to doctor any day. A man who would keep his feelings in check.

He looked about the cabin. Two chairs, a table, a fireplace. A curtained-off doorway, likely one that led to a small bedroom for her. She had so few things. There was nothing he could see that was not essential—no pictures on the walls. How long had she lived here on her own with her son? He wanted to ask but held the question back. It was best that he not get involved with that part of her life. He should keep a professional distance, keep things objective.

As he pondered this, Miss Marks moved back to her son. She crouched down and lovingly swept the shock of dark blond hair from his forehead. The ministration, and the look that passed from her to her son, spoke volumes. As did the calm adoration in her son's eyes for her. This woman might not have pictures on her walls or fancy clothes, but she had what was most important in life. It was something he had never had.

He measured the darkness visible at the edges of the oilcloth covering the window. Dawn wouldn't arrive for several hours. The woman looked exhausted. He should offer to sit up with the boy and let her rest. He wouldn't be fresh to call on Miss Vandersohn in the morning, but that seemed inconsequential now. That decision seemed like a year ago—the bright celebration at the town hall last evening a far cry from this dark, dank soddy.

She placed another chip of dried dung on the small fire, then stirred the ashes with a poker. A small, steady flame sputtered up and took hold. "I'll take you back as soon as it's light, Doc."

"Then you'd better get some rest. I'll sit up with your son."

Tommy was already falling asleep. She stood and, with her fist to the small of her back, arched her body in a quick stretch. The firelight flared, the light revealing dark smudges beneath her eyes. "I'll be taking care of my own."

"After all this, you still don't trust me? Not even a little?"

She raised her chin.

He let out a tired sigh and sat down on a chair, his back to the wall. "All right. Then we'll both stay up with him."

She plopped down in the only other chair available and stared at the fire in the hearth.

It came as a bit of a surprise that he was warm—warmer than he would be at his fancy two-story house in town, where the wind whistled and made the boards creak. Here, there were no cracks or knotholes for the breeze to pass through. Whoever had built this home had done a decent job with the materials at hand.

Before long, her breathing became deep and even. Her eyes drifted close as she slid slowly and surely to rest her head in the crook of her arm on the table.

He moved the gun out from under her elbow and took a moment to consider her. She must be somewhere around twenty-five by her unlined face and the lack of gray in her dark brown hair. Her skin was smooth and pale. He liked the slight upturn of her nose at the end. Considering the flash in her eyes when he mentioned the catgut, the shape of her nose went along well with her stubbornness. Unguarded like this, with her frown replaced by a peaceful expression, she was…attractive. Immediately, he looked away. She was just a young and determined mother. That was all. And, annoying as it had been to be kidnapped, he admired her spunk and her devotion to her son. To notice anything more about her was…unsettling. He pushed the thought away and settled back in his chair to keep watch the rest of the night.

Chapter Seven

She woke with a start to the daylight streaming through the windowpanes and her cheek mashed against the table. Her entire body ached from sitting in the chair through the night.

Across from her, Doc Graham slept with his head cushioned by his arm. The other arm was stretched most of the way across the table. His dark hair, longer on top than on the sides, flopped over his face with just enough wave in it to make him appear boyish in his sleep. A coarse, dark stubble had grown on his jaw overnight.

She shook the remaining cobwebs from her mind, stood, stretched briefly and then crouched down to check on Tommy. His breathing was even and deep. He slept. Peacefully. She peeled back the cover over his feet to check his ban-

dage. It still looked fresh. Why hadn't the doc
wanted to use her honey? Didn't he know it was
good for cuts and such? And Tommy's cut was
the biggest she'd ever seen. She'd make sure to
add some when she changed the bandage later,
after she returned from taking the doctor home.
She put Tommy's cover back on and stood.

The doc had done his part. Tommy was healing. The least she could do was offer him breakfast before taking him back to town. She sure
didn't have any money to pay him for his doctorin'. Didn't even have any eggs to send with
him! She filled the tin pot with water from the
pitcher and threw in two handfuls of chicory.
Then she hung the pot on the hook and swung
it over the hearth. She set another chip on the
fire and stirred up the ashes.

Quiet as a mouse, she slipped outside to see
to her needs and those of her animals. An inch
of new snow had fallen during the night and
the air was crisp with the tang of winter's end.
In the shed, she gave Berta a measure of oats,
checked on her sheep and milked her goat. Then
she walked to the chicken coop and gathered the
eggs. Seven eggs—that was plenty for the three
of them and the number was a good sign. She
carried the pail and basket back to the house.

When she walked through the door, the doc
was crouched over Tommy.

"Is he all right?" she asked quickly.

"He might have some dizziness for a few days."

She knelt before the hearth. "I'll have breakfast for you directly." She pushed the iron skillet closer to the hearth. "Then I'll take you back to town."

She heard the door close behind her. Had he left? Was he walking back to town? She jumped to her feet and rushed to the window. He stood in the middle of the yard and stretched. My, but he was a tall man! Much bigger than Thomas had been.

She took in the yard, trying to see it through his eyes. It was always a bit muddy and dreary this time of year. Only the hardiest of weeds had gotten a start in the dirt. At least last night's snow covered most of it and made the yard look clean. She let out a sigh. It wasn't much to look at. Not when compared to the fine houses in town. Each new house that was built in Oak Grove looked bigger and finer than the last.

Well, it was all she could do to keep the place running as it was. There was no time for prettying up things. But it was her place. Hers and Tommy's and built by his father. And that meant something. She wasn't going to apologize for it.

He headed for the rain barrel on the far side of the cabin, moving with a measured steadiness that had a way of calming a person. He leaned over and splashed water on his face. His gasp and quick shudder at the coldness amused her.

The man probably had someone warm his water at home—straight from a pot on a fancy stove. Well, he would just have to forego that kind of coddling here.

She couldn't seem to hold back from stealing one more glance. If coddling made a man weak, like Carl had said, the doc didn't look weak in the least. His shoulders were broad as a barn door and his linen shirt stretched over them in a manner that made butterflies suddenly swarm in her tummy. He looked full of health...full of vigor. Her cheeks warmed at the thought. It had been a long time since she'd noticed a man's qualities.

When he stepped inside the privy, she pulled away from the window, not wanting to puzzle out why she had stood there watching him for a spell when she had so much to do. Not wanting to decipher that at all. She moved back to awaken Tommy and help him with his morning needs.

The doc strode through the door and stopped when he saw the spread on the table. Coffee, fried eggs, toast and jam. She fixed a plate for him and set it across the table. Then she fixed another plate for Tommy and gave it to him there on his pallet. Last, she fixed one for herself.

He waited for her to sit down, like a gentleman. She said grace, adding at the end how grateful she was for Tommy feeling better and for the doctor's skill. Then the man waited for her to take a bite of food.

"It'll get cold fast, Doc. Eat up." She was awkward with his ways. The last person who sat at the table with her, besides her son, was Tommy's father and he'd not been one to wait on her to start eating first.

"This is every bit as good as the breakfast I get at the restaurant in town," he said, after a few bites.

"Can't mess up eggs and toast, Doc," she said, amused.

He gave a derisive snort.

"You mean you can't cook a simple thing like this?" The thought struck her as comical. "Didn't you learn growin' up?"

He shrugged. "I've always had someone cook for me. I take my meals at the restaurant, often with Mayor Melbourne. Sometimes the sheriff joins us. It gives me a chance to catch up on what is happening in town. Things like kidnappings and such." He added the last smoothly.

She pulled a sharp breath. She hadn't thought through what would happen next after forcing him here. If he went to the sheriff…

She put down her fork, no longer hungry. All she'd done to get him here…was wrong. She was ashamed she couldn't pay the doc like most folks and instead had to go and do such a terrible thing. It couldn't be helped, she told herself for the tenth time since Tommy had hurt himself yesterday. She'd do it again if she had to. But Tommy was innocent in all of it and she didn't want him sharing in the burden of the guilt she now carried.

She stole a glance at her son. He was done eating and had lain back down. His eyes were closed, but his breathing wasn't the deep, even breathing of someone who was asleep. Most likely he was listening to all that was being said. She didn't want Tommy hearing what she'd done.

Doc Graham leaned back in his chair and studied her.

Her gut knotted. It was like he knew the predicament he'd put her in by his words. Guess she'd better say something despite Tommy. The doc deserved that after all he'd done. She couldn't look him in the eye, so she stared at her plate. "I'm sorry for the way things happened last night. I — I guess I panicked some. I was afraid if you knew I couldn't pay you, that you wouldn't help Tommy. I just didn't know any other way to make you come here."

"All you had to do was ask."

His soft words struck right to her core. She drew in a sharp breath, feeling even more remorseful.

"I take my oath seriously, payment or no payment, although a hearty breakfast eases the lack of coin immensely. While I was learning medical skills, you were obviously learning to cook."

He liked her cooking? The tightness inside her eased. Slowly, she raised her gaze. He was sopping up the yolk with his toast and appeared to be enjoying the meal immensely.

"Seems a man who can't cook should hire one," she said cautiously. "That'd be the smart thing. Then maybe he wouldn't be out in the evening and getting himself caught up like a rabbit in a snare. Ain't nothing good that happens after the sun goes down."

Did his eyes just twinkle?

"Odd you should mention that. Those were my exact thoughts. The celebration going on at the new town hall was to welcome a handful of women from back East. They came to marry. I hope to take one of them as my wife, thereby solving my problem of lack of a cook."

"Can't believe a woman would come so far just to marry a man. What if she ends up with a lout?" Carl came to mind. Anyone who ended up with him was in for a rough time of it.

Then she realized that she'd as much as called the doc a lout. "Not that you are a lout, Doc."

He flashed a grin. "I've been informed that I would be impossible to live with. That I am married to my work."

Her astonishment must have showed on her face. His eyes twinkled—again! "You mean a woman said that straight to your face? In my mind, a man who takes his work seriously is a good thing."

"She said it right after I'd missed our third social engagement at the opera house in Boston. A patient was in need of my medical skills. Josephine called off the courtship that night. Looking back, it was smart—a practical response. At that time, I didn't have time for a wife or a family. And she was correct. I did put my career ahead of everything else."

She thought about Tommy. "Well! There are some who would appreciate that quality in a man. I surely would."

He didn't say anything for a moment but studied her silently.

Her cheeks heated. Guess the conversation was getting a mite personal. She finished her toast in one dry mouthful.

"Doc, you could easily get tricked and end up married to a woman who can't cook but one thing. Or you could end up with a nag. A woman wanting to marry might not show you that part of herself until after the vows are said."

"True. It is a risk—for me as well as the woman."

"It's a scary thing to contemplate," she said, shaking her head. "I can't figure why anyone would do it." She and Thomas had known each other since they were babies. Their families had grown up in the woods there in Virginia.

She couldn't remember a time when she hadn't known him. Meeting a stranger and deciding to spend the rest of your life with them seemed like a crazy thing to do.

"I've come to the conclusion that there are many valid reasons. A person must realize their circumstances need changing and then they do something about it. Not all women are that brave."

She hadn't thought of it like that—being brave. "You got a gal in mind?"

He shook his head. "Not yet. I want to speak with each one individually. I have certain qualities I'm looking for to narrow my choice down to the best woman."

She'd never heard of such a thing. "I guess you've figured a way to find a flower among the weeds, then. Could be smart," she said slowly.

He raised a dark brow. "I'm so glad you approve."

He was teasing her, she realized, her heart skipping a beat. Like they were friends. Imagine that! A man like him—smart, intelligent and handsome.

In the next breath, she reined in her delight. *Don't be silly*, she told herself. *You're a grown woman with a seven-year-old son. No doctor is going to want to be friends with you. He's just being kind.*

She stood abruptly. "It's time I got you back."

She checked on her son once more and then grabbed her coat. When the doc stood and reached out to help her with her sleeve, she pulled back from him with a sharp tug. "I can handle it myself." She plopped her old hat on her head for emphasis.

He looked to be about to say something but then turned to her son. "In the future, please refrain from climbing on the shed and scaring your mother. You may like to think you are a cat with nine lives to spare, but you are a boy with only one life. You need to take care of it."

Sylvia looked from her son to the big man. He took a lot on himself to school her young 'un. Schoolin' Tommy was her place. But what he said had truth in it.

"I'll get my mule," she said.

She hitched Berta to the wagon and fifteen minutes later they arrived at the river. They journeyed along a short piece, among the fledgling cottonwood trees that grew only along the southern bank. Buds had formed. Wouldn't be long before leaves unfurled.

Nothing like her insides that were curled up tight.

Now that the deed was done, she couldn't let loose of fretting about it. Would he tell the sheriff what she'd done? Would the entire town know that he'd spent the whole night at her place?

"Why was Carl Caulder bothering you at the mercantile?"

She tightened her grip on the reins and kept her gaze on the road. "We go way back. He's Tommy's uncle and thinks that gives him the right to boss me and Tommy around."

His brows drew together. "I wouldn't call what he was doing bossing. More like bullying."

"I know. He's hard to take," she whispered. "Especially when he's feeling all high-and-mighty and had a couple drinks. His brother wasn't anything like him. Thomas was a good man."

They came to the ferry crossing. Thankfully, the flat raft remained on this side of the river. She started to lead Berta down the bank and onto the wooden planks when she felt the doc's hand on her arm.

"I'll find my own way back from here."

She held the reins taut while he climbed from the wagon and grabbed his doctorin' bag. He returned to her side of the wagon and looked up at her, squinting against the sunlight. "I'll check on Tommy in a day or two."

"No need. I can care for my son now."

He frowned. "I should be aware of how he heals."

"It ain't… It ain't that I don't appreciate the thought."

"Then what is the problem?"

The reason stared him in the face! Didn't he have any sensibilities? She let a twig drift past as she contemplated how to answer him. Seemed all she could do was be blunt.

"I can't pay you."

"I thought you understood. That isn't a problem."

"It is for me," she hurried to say. "It may be late in comin', but I pay my debts."

It pained her to have to ask, but she had to know where things stood between them. "You going to tell about this? The sheriff—or anyone else?"

He pressed his lips together. "I won't say anything to Sheriff Baniff. And I can't see why it is anybody else's business."

It was as if the notion of being improper was not something he ever dealt with. Here she'd been dealing with it practically every minute of her entire life. She swallowed again. "I—I mean about stayin' the night."

"Oh. No one will hear a word of it from me."

She breathed a sigh of relief.

"Believe me. It's an easy decision. Should I say anything, questions will arise not only about your virtue, but also about my inability to thwart my kidnapping. People would know that you, a small mite of a woman, bested me. I can't afford that. *My* reputation might never recover."

He was teasing her in that way of his. Nothing seemed to ruffle him. In every moment, he was confident and strong. She wished she could soak up some of that. It would be nice to feel that sure of herself again. Guess when Thomas left her, any sureness she possessed had evaporated.

She smiled slightly at his quip. "Thank you kindly for your help."

He stepped onto the ferry and slipped the tether line off the stump. Taking hold of the heavy rope that was suspended across the river to the opposite bank, he put his back into it and pulled hard. The flat raft eased out into the current and carried him across the water.

Once ashore on the north bank, Nelson followed the wagon trail toward Oak Grove.

The early-morning sun warmed his back and quickly melted the thin crust of snow into a slushy mess. After he brushed past, the weeds and grass lining the trail sprang back to attention with only a few casualties bent and crushed under his boots. He was vaguely aware of this while he walked and mulled over the strange encounter with Miss Marks.

He could have wrestled the gun away from her at any time. Why didn't he? What had held him back every time that he'd thought to try it? Was it the desperation of the act? Tommy was worth everything to her. She would go to any lengths to make sure he was well and safe.

He couldn't imagine his own parents breaking the law in order to take care of him. They had packed him off to boarding school when he was Tommy's age— with a formal, undemonstrative goodbye. Miss Marks would never have let her son go away at all.

It had to be impossibly hard for her to survive on that piece of land. Almost any other woman in her situation would have moved into town long ago. What was it that kept her there? That plot of land or her unmarried status?

She was an interesting woman—very different than any he'd ever met before. She was self-sufficient, stubborn and emotional all wrapped up under that ugly, floppy hat. And oddly enough, charming in an unsophisticated way. She had her pride. And she had certainly been worried about him being there all night even though it was her fault he was there in the first place. Guess she hadn't thought that all the way through until morning came—another indication of how desperate she'd been about her son's condition.

He stopped walking as a new thought occurred. Maybe it wasn't her own reputation that she had been worried about. Maybe it was ruining *his* reputation that concerned her.

He started walking again.

Now, there was an interesting concept.

Just over the rise, a jumble of wooden buildings came into view, the white church steeple at the far end of town was the tallest and easiest to spot. The town hadn't looked like much two years ago when he had first come to Oak Grove, but it was growing. Each season brought new people to settle the town and, with them, new improvements and new problems.

The odor from the holding yards swirled around him. He barely noticed it now. The local ranchers had already brought their herds for transport on the train. Being the first of the season gave them a better price per head from those who would soon arrive up the Chisholm Trail. Josiah, the mayor, had been careful when laying out the town by building it west of the holding yards. The stench of cattle meant the town would thrive, but at least the wind blew most of the odor eastward and away from town.

Oak Grove wasn't Eden, but it was far from Boston, and that had been his main thought to settling here. Denver would probably have been smarter for his career. In Denver, he would have had more patients with the increase in population and they would have paid for his services with coin. There would have been other physicians to consult with and to discuss things. Here his patients paid with chickens and canned goods and he was the only doctor within two hundred miles, but here he was needed. That was more important to him than a fancier house and the things he could get in Denver.

The thought brought him back to Miss Marks and Tommy. What kind of ointment had that woman rubbed all over the boy's ankle? It had been nearly clear. Some home remedy, he imagined, and suited more for the pantry than the boy's leg. With the tissue scraped off nearly to the bone, Tommy would have been crippled for the rest of his life if she hadn't forced Nelson to come and see her son. He had a feeling it was the boy's unconscious state that had frightened her more…as it should have. The healing of head injuries was up to time and the grace of God. Doctors had little they could do.

He would have to make another visit out to her cabin to check her son's mental faculties and make sure there were no residual symptoms from that nasty bump to his head. He wanted to make sure the boy's leg healed properly too. He wasn't about to leave that up to Miss Marks and her backwoods medicine. He would go in three days. That would give the edges of the wound time to bind together and Tommy a chance to get over his dizziness.

For now, he was ready to get acquainted with the new women in town before they were all scooped up by other suitors. Perhaps one of them might accompany him out to Miss Marks's place later in the week. It would give him the oppor-

tunity to see how the woman reacted to someone who was ailing.

He frowned as he considered the ruse. Would
any of the women jump at such an offer when
they were being wooed with fine dining and pic-
nics by half the men in town? All he really had
to offer was a comfortable house that doubled
as an office. No…he'd leave Miss Marks out of
his search for a bride.

He crossed the railroad tracks by the small
station and headed up Main Street, bypassing
the restaurant. He wasn't hungry. Miss Marks
had seen to that need quite adequately. He would
wash up, change his shirt and then call at the
hotel on Miss Vandersohn.

Chapter Eight

Nelson never got a chance to call on any of the women who had come to be brides. From the moment he stepped through his door and for the next two days after his kidnapping, he saw a constant stream of people who needed his care.

Now, finally, he'd found the time to take a stroll with Miss Vandersohn. She walked beside him, twirling her white ruffled parasol, which rested on her shoulder. The apparatus framed her face becomingly, but with the way she held it, did little to shelter her from the bright rays of the sun.

"So, Dr. Graham," she said, "I would love to hear of Boston and what it is like there. What was your favorite thing to do?"

"I had my nose in a medical book most of the time," he said, taking her arm to assist her across the street. "But in my rare moments of free time, I enjoyed sailing."

"You had a boat?"

"No. But an acquaintance of mine—"

A sharp yell came from the vicinity of the livery.

A moment later Teddy White rushed from the building, scanned the road and headed straight toward him. "Doc! Wally Brown is hurt!"

Nelson took two steps toward Teddy and then remembered Miss Vandersohn at his side. "I need to check on him."

"Then by all means…go."

Together, they hurried into the livery. A quick examination revealed that Wally had a broken arm.

"We need to get you to my office so that I can set it. Can you walk if we help you?" he asked the older man.

"Dang mule," grumbled Wally, glaring at a mud-colored mule nearby.

Nelson helped him to stand, and with Teddy's help, they made their way to his office. Nelson didn't like the way the color drained from Wally's face, but once the wiry man was resting on his exam table, he seemed to get some of it back. Miss Vandersohn kept an eye on Mr. Brown while he gathered his supplies and then mixed up the plaster compound for a cast.

He glanced about the room. Teddy had disappeared after bringing him the pitcher of water he'd asked for. Wally had no family that Nelson knew of. It was fortunate that Miss Vandersohn was willing to stay and help. He made sure the major bones in Wally's arm were aligned and then instructed her, "Hold his arm, just so."

For the next fifteen minutes, he concentrated on wrapping strips of cloth that had been soaked in the plaster solution around Wally's arm. He was so engrossed in his task that he barely heard the knock at his office door.

He glanced across the exam table. Mara Vandersohn still held Wally's arm as she had been instructed, but her face had paled considerably. Wally was the patient, although at this point, that was becoming more difficult to ascertain. How long she could continue was becoming the issue as she swayed alarmingly to one side. In a moment, he'd have two patients, and if whoever was on the other side of that door had anything to say about it, likely a third.

"Doc! Doc! You in there?" The door burst open and Brett Blackwell rushed across the small parlor and into his exam room.

"What is it, Blackwell?" he asked…although he had a foreboding he knew what it was. Brett's wife, Fiona, was seven months along with his first child.

"I think it might be time."

It was too early for the baby to come. He'd

warned Fiona about trying to do too much, but
having had two lively children from her first
marriage, her body knew just what to do and
was anxious to get started.

"I can't stop in the middle of this. I'll be there
as soon as I am able."

Noticing Wally for the first time and then
Miss Vandersohn, Brett moved farther into the
room. He whipped his hat off and crushed it in
his hands.

Nelson dipped a length of cloth in the bucket
of plaster of Paris solution. Then he patted the
wet cloth around Wally's arm. Nelson had to get
the cast finished and the entire arm elevated.
Time was of the essence.

"Well...what should I do about Fiona?"

Nelson needed to remember that Brett was
a first-time father and all this was new to him.
Fiona was probably handling things better than
her new husband. "Make her lie down. Give her
some water to drink. And keep those young boys
out of her room."

He dipped another length of cloth in the plaster solution. Nelson could feel Brett's heavy
breathing on his own wet hands. "What are you
waiting for? I'll come as soon as I can."

"How soon will that be?"

"Soon as I am done here."

Brett spun around and walked out the door.
This day was shaping up to be like any other

day. He had too many people in need of his services and not enough of himself to go around. And besides that, he was hungry. He had missed lunch.

"Dr. Graham…" Miss Vandersohn said tentatively. "I'm not feeling well."

He glanced up at his assistant. Perspiration had popped out on her forehead. That, along with her chalky appearance, which easily matched the color of the cast he was making, made him drop the strip of cloth he held over the bucket edge and rush around the table to her. He was just in time to take hold of Wally's arm, but not quick enough to catch Miss Vandersohn from slumping to the floor.

She went down gracefully, in a soft, rather slow crumpling, her petticoats and gingham skirt billowing out around her. He could only hope they afforded a bit of cushion as she sank to the floor and toppled over, for he certainly could not let go of Wally.

"Drat," he said under his breath. He lowered Wally's casted arm carefully to the table. "Don't move." He grabbed a nearby wet rag and wiped what plaster of Paris he could from his hands, then crouched down to check on the woman on the floor.

"Miss Vandersohn?" Gently, he jiggled her shoulder. "Mara?"

"She all right, Doc?" Wally asked, sitting up slightly to see.

"She's coming around." The return of color to her cheeks was a good sign. Her eyelids fluttered open. "Lie still, Miss Vandersohn. You're fine. You just fainted."

A soft moan escaped her thin lips. Actually, it sounded more like a gasp.

Not what he expected.

"Uh—Doc?" Wally tilted his head toward the open doorway.

Miss Marks stepped into the room.

He realized, with sudden clarity, that she was the one who had emitted the gasp.

She set a package she held on a nearby chair, grabbed his coat from the wall peg by the door and folded it into a bundle as she strode quickly to Miss Vandersohn. Crouching down, she stuffed it under the woman's head.

Miss Vandersohn stared first at him and then at Miss Marks.

"You had a spell," Miss Marks said softly. "Lie there for a bit until you get your thoughts all going in the same direction. No need to rush. When you are ready, the doc and I will help you get up."

The woman nodded, her eyes still wide and vacant.

Nelson frowned. He wasn't used to anyone usurping his position in his own office. "I have to finish with Mr. Brown. She will weather it if we get her up now."

"You sure, Doc? I think she will just pass out again."

There was half a chance Miss Marks was right. He was willing to risk it. He had Wally and then Mrs. Blackwell to see to. And the longer Miss Marks argued, the better the odds were that Miss Vandersohn would recover and do fine.

"I had spells such as this when I was carrying Tommy. Getting up too fast was the worst, 'cause I'd pass right out again. You go ahead with whatever you are doing there. I'll help her up when she is ready."

Relieved with the offer of help, he turned back to Wally. He dipped another length of cloth into the plaster solution and applied the strip to the man's arm, working in silence for a few minutes. He glanced up once when Miss Marks helped Miss Vandersohn to her feet and then over to a nearby chair. No issues there, so he returned to finishing the cast.

"Dr. Graham? I believe I will take my leave."

Miss Vandersohn was at the door. She held herself stiff, with her chin up even though she didn't look completely recovered.

"Very well, Miss Vandersohn. I'm sorry our walk was cut short. I will call on you later."

There was a pause.

"That isn't necessary. A bit of rest is all that

I need. Perhaps I will see you at services on Sunday."

He glanced up. *Sunday?* That indicated a step backward in his timetable. He'd thought they were getting along well during their walk.

At the moment, however, they were both in agreement. He had work to do and she should go back to her hotel room. "Yes. Fine," he murmured, concentrating on wrapping the wet cloth loosely between Wally's thumb and first finger to allow for movement and possible swelling of his arm.

Silence enveloped him after she left. He preferred silence. Preferred concentrating on one thing at a time.

Done.

"You must lie here for several hours," he instructed Wally. "At least until suppertime. It will take that long for the cast to dry and set." He poured water from his pitcher into the bowl and washed off the remaining plaster from his hands.

"I could use some vittles."

At the mention of food, Nelson's stomach rumbled.

"Ha," Wally said, hearing the sound. "Guess you could use something to eat too."

"I need to check on Mrs. Blackwell first." He would have to leave his bucket and plaster mess until later. And Miss Vandersohn's parasol leaned against the wall. She must have been in more distress than he realized.

Then he remembered Miss Marks. She'd disappeared too. Why had she stopped by? Perhaps something had gone wrong with her son. He should have inquired.

"Did you see what happened to Miss Marks?"

"She left with that other lady."

Nelson walked to the window. The slant of shadows on his sundial indicated it was past noon by two hours. Although it didn't sit well with him, he would have to leave Wally and go check on Brett's wife. Hopefully, Brett had done as he ordered and made the woman lie down.

Miss Marks suddenly appeared in the shadow of Miller's Cabinetry Shop. She strode briskly down the road toward his office. Nelson walked to the front door and waited for her to climb the steps. High color filled her cheeks and her brown eyes shone bright and clear. Her face glowed in a pretty, wholesome way. He hadn't noticed that before, probably because she wore that ridiculous hat. She had it on now with her hair pulled back into one long loose braid. Flyaway strands of straight, dark hair framed her face.

She stopped on the porch and peeled a few flyaway strands of hair from her face. "That woman ain't got much of a stomach, Doc."

He felt responsible for Miss Vandersohn's distress. "What happened?"

"She made it all the way to the hotel and then puked right in that fancy brass umbrella stand inside the door."

"You saw her all the way back?" It wasn't far, but still it was his place to accompany Miss Vandersohn back. He was the one who had asked the woman out.

"Well, I couldn't very well let her go on her own now, could I? Not with the way she was weaving. She was all shades of green. Crossing Main Street, she might have got run over by a horse!"

She certainly had a colorful way of talking, peculiar and different from other women he had known. "What is it you've come for? Is it your boy?"

"No," she said. "Tommy's doin' fine. Healin' up good."

"I intend to stop by and remove the sutures."

Her chin jutted up. "Did that this morning."

He was shocked. Nearly speechless. Her audacity knew no bounds! "You took his stitches out?"

She passed by him and walked into his parlor as if performing surgery was something she did every day. "Yes. They were itching and he was scratchin'. Figured it was time."

He followed her. How dare she usurp his place as Tommy's physician! She was the one who had forced him out that night in the first place. "You had no right to do that. Did you make sure to get every single one?"

"'Course I did!" She let out a huff, frowning up at him.

"And there was no pus? No festering?"

"No! Like I said, Tommy's healin' up fine."

Her answer did not mollify him in the least. She had gone too far. "You have a lot of nerve taking that on yourself."

She swallowed and glanced toward Wally, then leaned toward him, lowering her voice. "It's like I said, Doc. I don't have the means to pay you for comin' way out there to see to something that I can do myself."

She certainly could be frustrating. Money was not the issue here. "I distinctly remember telling you that I didn't expect further recompense. Pride is a—"

Her chin jutted up again, and stubbornness sparked in her eyes, effectively halting his lecture. "I brought something for your help. I thought you might take partial payment. Guess I was a bit frazzled that night with him being injured and not thinking straight." She turned and picked up the burlap sack from his chair and held it out.

He blew out a breath, and with it, some of his anger abated. Pride went both ways. His, for his profession. And hers, for her ability to care for her own. What was important was that they both wanted what was best for Tommy. That her son was healing was the main thing.

He focused on the sack. It wasn't moving. A good thing. With his city upbringing, he knew nothing about livestock. Whenever a grateful patient would pay him with an animal, he'd immediately take it to the butcher's or to the restaurant.

He loosened the cinched end and peeked inside. A jar and a loaf of brown bread—still warm from baking—nestled in the bottom of the sack. The aroma wafted up and made his stomach grumble. Reaching inside, he pulled out the jar. Once in the light, he realized it was filled with a thick golden liquid and a few light-colored particles floating within it.

"I plum forgot that I had a few more jars of honey stored up in the root cellar. This is from the best hive in the territory."

He supposed it would be good to have around. Once he married, his wife might have a use for it. "Thank you, Miss Marks."

"I figure a little sweetening might help your disposition."

He met her gaze. She was serious? "My attitude is just fine."

She cocked her head. "Well, it sure wasn't for that young lady that skedaddled out of here. She was fit to be tied."

The difference between the two women was

a mile in each direction. One was a princess and the other— He studied Miss Marks and her beat-up hat. Just how would one describe her?

"Doc!" A shadow blotted out the sunlight that had streamed through the open door. Brett stood there again, a frantic look in his eyes.

"I'm on my way," Nelson said. He set the jar of honey on his side table. "Duty calls, Miss Marks. Thank you for the honey and the bread." He picked up his medical bag.

Her eyes clouded over. "What about this man lying flat in the middle of the room?"

"Wally is on his own until I get back. He has to let his cast dry. He knows he must be still." He slipped on his Stetson. "Good day, Miss Marks."

The doctor strode off on those long legs of his and disappeared down the side road. Sylvia glanced back through the doorway at the man lying on the table in the middle of the other room. It didn't seem right to leave him. He couldn't look out for himself.

"You got anything to eat?" he called out to her.

She walked over to the table. He had a good twenty years on her if appearance counted. Thick white whiskers peppered his chin and his gray hair fell to his shoulders. A shiver ran through his body, big enough that she noticed it.

"Hey! Where are you going?"

She picked up what was likely his coat from a chair by the wall and laid it across his chest, tucking the collar snuggly around his shoulders.

"I'm hungry enough to eat a cow. Heard you brought some vittles."

"What I brought is for the doc."

"Then how about walkin' over to the restaurant and getting that Miss Sadie to make me a plate?"

She remembered the doc had mentioned eating there. "I only came to make payment for the doctor's help with my boy."

He pinched his mouth together.

It didn't sit right with her to leave this man on his own. He might get up and, after his injury, he could get dizzy and fall. That would mess up everything the doc had just fixed. "I think you better wait until Doc Graham comes back."

"The doc could be gone a long while. Babies take their own time in coming."

That was true. Tommy had taken nearly two days.

She touched the white cast tentatively. How long would it take to get hard? Mr. Brown's stubby fingers looked puffy compared to his other arm and hand. Was that normal? It might not bode well.

She looked around the room, finding nothing that she could use except for the pillow under the man's head. Doc Graham had grabbed his coat when he left or she'd have used that.

She searched through the cupboards along the long wall. In the third one, she found two blankets, refolded them and then positioned them carefully under the cast, making sure the man's hand was the highest point. Mr. Brown grimaced with the movement.

"How'd you come to get hurt?" Maybe conversing with him would take his mind off the pain. She didn't know if the doc had any willow bark tea and she wouldn't feel right using his kitchen to make something anyway.

"I got in a fight with a mean old mule at the livery."

She wiped off splatters of white plaster from the edge of the table. "I got me a mule myself. Her name's Berta. A body should know better than to fight a mule."

"That's easy for you to say, but I was only doing my job. Considering that I'm the one who is hurt here, I'd think a little kindness—maybe a cool cloth to my brow—a song…"

She stopped cleaning up. Was he teasing her now? "A song?"

A smile played about his whiskered face. "Well, food is higher in my thoughts just now."

"You don't give up when you set your mind on something, do you?" He certainly must be feeling all right if he wanted to eat. Maybe it wouldn't hurt. "Hold your horses and I'll get you a little something to fill you up."

She walked back into the waiting room, picked up the burlap bag and carried it to the kitchen. Rifling through a drawer of utensils, she found a bread knife. A few moments later, she returned to the exam room with a plate of bread slices smeared with honey.

She set the plate on his chest. "You can feed yourself with your good arm, I 'spect."

"It ain't gonna be easy. Will you...?"

She frowned. Just how much did this fellow expect? "I gotta clean up the kitchen."

"Don't rightly know how I'm going to manage. Crumbs will be everywhere. Might even stick to the cast. It could make the doc mad."

She dragged a chair up beside the man and sat down. Then she tore off a small piece of the bread, held it out until he opened his mouth and popped it inside. A look of satisfaction came over him as he chewed it up and swallowed. "Best darn bread I've ever had."

She nodded, mollified some that he thought so highly of her breadmaking.

"Ain't you that woman who lives out south of town?"

Well, there you go. Get comfortable and the next thing the rug would be pulled right out from under. She braced herself for his censure.

"Heard you was a healer."

She huffed softly. "If I was a healer, my Tommy wouldn't have needed the doc's help when he got hurt. The doc fixed him up good. Just like he fixed you up."

"Seems like your eyes light up whenever you mention Doc Graham."

"That's your imagination. Now finish this up." She stuffed the last of the bread into his mouth before he could say another word.

The front door opened and a breeze blew through the room. "You're still here?" Doc Graham said. He walked over and studied Mr. Brown and his cast. He wiggled the man's fingers. "How are you feeling now, Wally?"

"Better, since this nice woman has fed me."

"I'm surprised she stayed." He moved the plate of crumbs from the man's chest over to a side table and then shut the cupboard door she'd left open with a solid thump. "I see you made yourself at home, Miss Marks."

Was he accusing her of something? "He was shiverin' and…and someone had to be here."

Graham raised his brows.

She wasn't chastising him—well—maybe she was. A little. He shouldn't have left.

He frowned. "So you stayed to help?"

She hesitated. What had she done wrong? He wasn't happy about something and it seemed to be her fault. That had not been her intent when she started across the river. His cross attitude shadowed the entire day. She didn't analyze why it should bother her so. Most people didn't care for her intrusion, but the doc—she'd thought that he was different. Guess not. It would be best to leave. She grabbed her hat from the wall peg and slipped it on and then threw her heavy shawl over her shoulders. "I gotta go now. My boy will be missing me." She slipped outside and headed for her wagon.

Chapter Nine

After sending Wally Brown on his way, Nelson settled down to two slices of sweet brown bread and a thick slice of cheese. He took a bite of the bread, ready to wash it down with water, and stopped with the glass at his mouth. He'd never had such tasty bread—not in all the restaurants he'd frequented back in Boston. What had Miss Marks done to it to make it taste so good?

He wasn't proud of the way he had treated her. His words had been less than chivalrous. His thoughts had already been on Mrs. Blackwell as he dashed out of the office and he'd forgotten to elevate Wally's arm. Miss Marks had done exactly what was needed—finding something to support the arm and hand to keep the swelling to a minimum, and then getting him

something to eat. And on top of that, she had
cleaned up his mess in the exam room.

A thank-you was in order. And he should get
out to her place and check on her son's condition.

But the next day, he put Sylvia Marks out of
his mind. It was a wife he needed and he had
best be about it. He had only a month to decide
on and court a woman as stipulated by the Betterment Committee contract. At the end of a
month, when all the women lined up at church
with their chosen grooms, he intended to be one
of those men.

His stroll with Miss Vandersohn had been
pleasant until Wally had been injured. He should
call on her and inquire about her recovery. He
also needed to return her parasol.

"Are you fully over your ordeal from yesterday?" he asked her when she met him in the
hotel lobby.

She colored prettily, accepting her parasol
back.

"I'm much better, thank you. However, I am
mortified that you witnessed me in such a state."

"Please don't concern yourself with that. I see
such things on a regular basis. It's part of being
a doctor." He cringed. Telling her so this early
in their acquaintance might not be the best way
to advance his courtship.

"Yes…well, I'm sure your stronger constitu-
tion helps you manage it. Medicine is all so very

indelicate, isn't it? So…so *messy*." She wrinkled her lovely nose as she said the last.

He'd always thought human physiology and the healing of the body fascinating, but to say so would put her off. "Would you do me the honor of trying again? Perhaps supper tonight?"

She drew back a step. "I'm afraid that I must decline."

"Another time?"

She shook her head tightly. "Not ever."

Now he was the one to pull back. They'd gotten along well. This came as a surprise.

"You see—things would only end up as it did yesterday. I—I really cannot stand to be around sickly, needy people. What if I caught something?" She shook her head again. "It is all rather distasteful to me. And ugly. And messy."

He grew more annoyed with each word she spoke. Of all the selfish reasons not to help someone in need! "I'm sorry to hear that this is how you feel. I'll take my leave and won't bother you again." He tipped his hat and strode out the hotel door.

His shortsightedness embarrassed him. He should have stuck to his list of requirements for a wife—namely that she mustn't be too attractive. Miss Vandersohn—pretty *and* a prima donna were a terrible combination! She was the type that expected to be waited on when what he needed was just the opposite.

Surely among the brides-to-be he could find a better match. Someone who didn't mind shouldering a little responsibility for the good of humanity.

He would just have to keep looking.

Miss Penelope Pratt was unforgettable in that she was as tall as most men and thin as a beanpole. She was also older than any of the other women who had arrived on the train. She wore her black hair pulled back in a bun so tight that it tugged at the corners of her eyes.

She was in the bank, accompanied by Miss Simcock, when he ran into her. He waited for her to finish conducting her business and then approached her.

"Miss Pratt? Are you available for a stroll?"

The two women stopped abruptly. Miss Simcock giggled.

Miss Pratt looked down her long nose at him and then slowly nodded a composed, dignified greeting. "Certainly."

Miss Simcock appeared to deflate, whether because she had hoped to be the one asked out or whether she was relieved that she wasn't, he couldn't be sure.

"May we see you back to the hotel?" he asked her.

She shook her head. "I'll be fine."

He held the door for the ladies. Miss Simcock

turned left, back to the hotel, and he and Miss Pratt turned right and continued slowly down the boardwalk.

Miss Pratt didn't say a word as they walked past a dog and a few children playing in the school yard. The silence between them grew awkward. He hadn't expected this. Weren't most women prone to talking?

"Please. I urge you to speak freely. The one month that the Betterment Committee allows you to decide on a husband and a man to decide on a bride makes it crucial that we find out if we are compatible. That cannot happen unless we talk."

She came to a swift stop and pressed her lips together in a thin line. "That is a blunt way to put this highly uncomfortable situation."

He hadn't thought so. He'd simply been honest. "I tend to be direct."

He took the moment to assess her appearance. Green eyes, just like his, his height and a long, slightly curved nose. Egads! She could be his sister!

"Now what?" she asked, stiffening. "You look as though you swallowed your tobacco."

"I don't chew."

"I'm glad to hear that. I find the habit disgusting. Then what did that look mean?"

"I was noticing our…similarities."

"Oh, that." She raised her chin. "I noticed them immediately."

"Then *should* this move into a state of matrimony and *should* we have children—"

Her eyes widened.

"—their looks would be a foregone conclusion." It was an interesting possibility.

She frowned. "Perhaps as you suggest, it is best to be frank and let you know my thoughts on the matter of propagating. Your education may even allow you to comprehend what I am about to say better than the other men I have encountered here."

He wasn't sure what to make of that.

"I want to marry. Truly I do. I have no close family. I want a companion with whom to share my life." She took a deep breath and blew it out as if to steady herself. "However, I am not interested in the part of a marriage that happens behind the bedroom door."

If he had been walking, he would have stumbled.

"You are shocked."

"No…no…" *Yes, yes, he was!*

"Come now. I can see it on your face."

He swallowed—an attempt to absorb her statement politely and give himself time to gather his thoughts. "I have never heard a woman speak so plainly about such things."

"I will remind you that you asked me to speak freely."

He huffed out a breath. Could it be that he'd come across a woman who not only looked like him but who spoke and acted like him? "Perhaps I shall choose my words more carefully."

She bestowed a slight smile.

"Are you ready to continue with our stroll? We've only walked through half the town."

"As long as we understand each other."

They continued on their way.

It was disconcerting that Miss Pratt could be as blunt as he. Would such a trait be smart to have as a nurse?

"You've said the same thing to other bachelors?" he asked. He didn't want the entire town to be aware of any arrangements they might have that were of a private nature.

"No. The men I have met have all been much more forward than you. Each one found a way to take my arm or assist me in some way that required touching. When they did that, I immediately checked them off my list. I've spoken to no one else about marriage except you."

She kept a list? Another disconcerting thought. Their similarities were growing. "That is encouraging. But—am I so unlike them?" He wasn't sure he wanted to be all that different from the others.

She arched a thin brow. "As I said—you are

most direct. The others were still mentioning the weather while your conversation has already jumped beyond that to marriage. *You* are a gentleman. Your Eastern breeding is apparent in the way you speak and carry yourself. I would hope that means you keep this conversation we are having just between us."

She hadn't answered his question. Mayor Melbourne was a gentleman too, as well as Sheriff Baniff. And he could name several others who deserved that title. All were very different from each other, but he thought of them all as gentlemen.

"While we are on the subject, are there any other expectations you have of marriage?"

She shook her head. "No. I do find it interesting that you haven't taken me back to the hotel. You must still be considering me as a possibility, which is a pleasant surprise in light of what I just said."

More likely, it was because he was still in shock. He'd taken it as a bygone conclusion that if he married, he would have children. He wanted several. That was one of the benefits of wedded bliss. That, and the fact that he had vowed to be a better father than his own.

The distance from the boardwalk down to the road in front of Miller's Cabinetry Shop was particularly high. Considering what she had just said, he refrained from taking her elbow to assist her. He did offer his arm, but she didn't take it. He nodded toward the livery and began walking in that direction.

"I had expected children at some point," he admitted. "I will have to give your condition some consideration. I also desire a companion in marriage, but equal to that, or perhaps more so, I desire a nurse in my work."

He glanced sideways at her. His announcement hadn't shaken her nearly as much as hers had him.

"Go on," she said.

"I would like someone who will work beside me and help me run my office. This would entail having fresh bandages cut up, washed and rolled at all times. Watching over the patients that are in my office if I am called away on an emergency. Helping to make up medication, salves and tonics. All this would be in addition to cooking and cleaning and the general duties that wives do for their husbands."

She drew her brows together. "And what would you be doing while I did all this?"

He thought that was obvious. "Seeing to my patients."

"And in your free time?"

"I'll use my free time to keep abreast of the changes in the medical field. Reading, writing articles and taking an annual trip to Denver to meet with my colleagues."

"During which time, I would be required to remain here and keep the office in a state of tidiness?"

"I haven't thought that far into it, but that is the general idea. I suppose some years my wife might accompany me to see the sights of the city."

They walked silently past the livery to the railroad station, where she stopped once more. "You have given me a lot to think about."

"As have you." *More than you know!*

"I have no doubt that I could perform the duties you have mentioned."

"In return, you would have a roof over your head and a respected standing in the community and a lifelong companion." But he'd never considered that there wouldn't be touching, caressing or even a kiss now and then. His first words to her about what their children would look like sounded foolish now. Yet, perhaps, if he was honest with himself, it made sense. He certainly didn't know how to be a father. His had never been around much. The only hugs he'd received from his mother had been stiff and awkward. He had never seen his parents so much as hold hands. The marriage that Miss Pratt and he had just described to each other sounded a lot like his own parents' marriage.

The entire thing sounded like a business proposition. His initial excitement at the thought of abiding harmoniously had been squashed with pragmatism.

Well, wasn't that what he had originally intended? Josephine had made it clear he was not suitable marriage material. She'd called him cold. Nose in a book. Cared more for his patients than he did for her. He had hoped to move beyond that defining moment when she'd called off the courtship. He'd hoped for more warmth in a lifelong companion.

"I'll walk you back," he said, disheartened. "I think we both have a lot to consider."

They started back toward the hotel.

"May I see your office before returning to the hotel?"

"Certainly. It's only a few steps this way."

"*Everything* in this town is only a few steps away," she said flatly.

They turned down a side street and he pointed out his two-story office. It would be a breach of etiquette to take her inside with him, since she wasn't sick or in need of his professional services, so they stood before the house and he explained the layout inside.

"I use the parlor as my waiting area. The dining ro—"

"Doc!" Rollie ran toward him with his son Wiley gathered in his arms. "He's not breathing! Something is stuck down his throat."

"Inside," Nelson ordered. "Lay him on the

table." He took the steps two at a time and opened the door.

Rollie rushed through and laid his son on the exam table.

Wiley was limp, his lips turning blue and his face pale white. The hoarse wheeze of each breath filled the room as the child struggled for air.

"Do something, Doc!" Rollie cried out. "You gotta help him!"

Nelson turned Wiley facedown with his head and chest hanging over the side of the table. He pounded between the boy's thin shoulder blades with his hand. One. Two. Three.

With the third strike of his hand, something dark popped out of the child's mouth and landed on the floor.

Wiley coughed and sputtered and then dragged in a huge gulp of air. And then another. He started to cry. Big hiccups punctuated the space between his high-pitched wails. Sadie entered the room holding on to Wiley's older brother, Kade.

Rollie grabbed his son and held him tight as he mouthed a prayer of thanks. Wiley's cries gradually lessened until they were nothing but sniffles. Sadie and Kade moved in close, each of them stretching their arms around Rollie and Wiley. They all gathered in as much of each other as they could and held on.

There were tears in Sadie's eyes. Tears that, frankly, made Nelson marvel. Sadie hadn't been married to Rollie a year yet, and she'd taken on and loved the boys as if they were her own flesh and blood. There was something special in the family. Something Nelson suspected he would never know in his lifetime.

"Thank you, Doc." Keeping hold of Wiley, Rollie extracted himself from the other two and pumped Nelson's hand. "You come over to the restaurant and I'll fix you a big meal. Anything you want. Anytime."

"I'm glad I was here." He took hold of Wiley's hand. "And you, young man…don't scare everybody like that again."

A movement by the window made him glance there. Miss Pratt had come inside rather than head back to the hotel. She stood stiff and observant with a slight downturn to her mouth.

A better reaction than fainting.

She stepped forward. "How did this happen? Was he eating too fast? Not chewing his food?" Her tone filled with accusation.

Wiley buried his face in his father's shoulder.

"I snuck candy from the jar," Kade said. "I gave one to Wiley to keep him quiet."

"You chased me!" Wiley shouted.

"You said you were going to tell anyway!" Kade shouted right back.

"You mean your brother nearly died because you wanted a sweet?" Miss Pratt asked.

Kade drew back as if he'd been slapped. His lower jaw set in defiance. "I didn't mean to!"

From behind the boy, Sadie put her hands on Kade's shoulders, pulling him against her skirt. "Of course you didn't mean to. It was an accident."

She eyed Miss Pratt with a coolness Nelson had not seen before in the woman. Sadie had always been gentle, but now she looked like a cougar ready to defend her cub.

Rollie took Kade's hand in his and looked from Nelson to Miss Pratt. "We'll talk about this at home. Thanks again, Doc."

Together the family left his office.

Miss Pratt stared after them. "That boy is a menace! A thief! He nearly killed his brother and yet that woman had the nerve to be upset with me?"

"They had just been through an ordeal. Emotions, tension, all heighten at times like that."

"But what kind of a mother is she that she wasn't watching those boys more closely?"

"A good mother."

Miss Pratt gasped. "Well, you see now why I have no intention of having children. They are impossible to control. An unnecessary headache."

Her words, her attitude troubled him. She had

immediately sought to place blame—and worse, she had attacked a ten-year-old with her words. Neither were the best way to handle a crisis. He walked to the door and opened it for her. "I'll walk you back to the hotel."

"How can I be comfortable staying at the hotel now?"

She had brought it on herself. It was one thing to be blunt and give her honest opinion with him. It was entirely another matter for her to behave so with his friends and neighbors. "Give Mrs. Austin time to get over her scare. It will be better."

She swept past him.

At the door to the hotel, he stopped.

"Will we talk again?" she asked.

"Yes." But he knew talking wouldn't do any good. She wasn't the right woman.

Chapter Ten

Sylvia watched Tommy as he carefully stood, holding on to the back of a chair and the edge of the table for support. His headache and dizziness still plagued him, yet he kept pushing himself to do better each time he stood. He'd make himself stand longer with each effort. He took three steps now before falling back onto the seat. Tears brimmed in his eyes. He dragged his sleeve across his face.

Times like this, she wanted to take the pain away from her baby. It hurt her, deep inside, to know there was nothing she could do. If only his father was here to help. So many times through the years, she'd wished that. She never molly-coddled her son as Carl had accused, but the line between mothering him and being tough on him had always weighed on her. Of late, with his fall, it had become so much harder. Usually, she tried to err on being tough to make up for the fact he had no father to show him the way, but she was tired of having to be strong. She just wanted to be a mother to him—not both mother and father.

Tommy's thin little shoulders heaved as he released a sigh. "It's taking forever. I just want it to be over."

"I know, son. Doc said it was a bad injury—all the way down to the bone. It'll take time, but you are doing everything you can to help yourself. I'm real proud of you for trying so hard."

"Next time he comes, I want to show him I can do it on my own."

His words caught at her heart. He expected the doc to come back? Doc Graham wouldn't. She'd told him not to.

"I don't know that he'll be coming back. He's got other sick people to see. People a lot sicker than you."

Tommy scooted down in his chair and crossed his arms, his lower lip pushed out. "He'll come back. He likes me."

She couldn't give her son what he wanted. It was out of her power. She rose from the table. "I gotta see to the animals."

She used the outhouse and then saw to Berta, leading the mule into the shed for the night and giving her a scoopful of grain. She did the same for Penny, then sat down on the milking stool to milk her while she ate. She squirted the first milk to the side the way her mother had taught her to clean the stream. "You give good milk, my girl. Sure do appreciate your sweet butter and buttermilk." Sylvia started humming. She rested her head on the goat's warm back and relaxed into the milking, feeling Penny relax with her as the fullness in her udder lessened.

"Thought I'd find you out here."

Sylvia tensed. What was Carl doing here?

"Where's the boy?"

"Inside."

"Then we got a moment to ourselves."

"What do you want, Carl?"

"I came by the other night to see about things and bring you some venison. Heard a man's voice coming from inside your place."

Carl hadn't come in the evening for a long time. That alone put her on edge. "Tommy got hurt. The doc came to check on him."

"He stayed a long time."

Not...*what's wrong with Tommy?* But all about the doc. "That's none of your business, Carl Caulder."

"You keep forgettin' that I look out for what's mine." He shut the door quietly behind him. "The way I see it, Tommy bein' my kin and all, that makes you something too."

She backed farther into the shed, her nerves

tingly, and not in a good way. First the teasing in the mercantile and now this.

"Thought you were seeing a woman up by Fort Wallace. She might not like you stopping by."

"Verna up and married a soldier. Ain't seen her for three months."

Her insides tensed. "So here you are."

He smiled. "Here I am. And I could use some lovin'. It ain't no crime to be a little needy now and then. Figure you might feel the same way."

She blew out a shuddery breath. "You're wrong. I don't feel that way about you, Carl."

"Now, is that any way to speak to the man that brought you meat? You know I could bring a lot more than just meat. I could make it easier on you —if you'd just soften up to me a little like you did my brother."

He took hold of her upper arms, his fingers digging in. "You know no one else is going to take a second look at you. You're strapped with a boy no one will want. And you ain't the purty gal you once was."

A violent shiver stabbed through her center. Close like this, she could smell the liquor on his breath. "Get away from me, Carl! You been drinking again."

A muscle in his jaw worked. "Maybe I just don't want to see that doctor comin' round no more. I see that, and maybe something bad will happen to your Tommy."

Her heart nearly stopped. She pushed him away. "Don't you threaten me! Don't you ever do that! Your brother would beat you bloody if you hurt a hair on Tommy."

She stepped back and tripped over the milking stool, falling to the ground. Carl stood over her staring at her as if he wasn't sure what to do with her. Finally, he reached down, grabbed her arm and yanked her to her feet.

"Thomas ain't around anymore, Sylvie. You need to quit living like he'll walk through that door again, 'cause he won't. And I don't aim to hurt little Tommy. He's my kin after all. All I'd need to do is take him somewhere where you can't find him. Then maybe you will be the one coming to me for a change. All I want is for you to ask me if you need a man. Not some stranger who don't know you like I do. All I'm asking is that you remember that."

He stepped through the doorway and out into the yard. There was a muffled sound and then his footsteps faded away.

She stumbled to the door, knocking the pail of milk over in her haste, and raced to her soddy to check on Tommy.

"Who was that, Ma? I heard voices."

Relief hit her in waves. She shook uncontrollably as it flowed through her. For all his threats,

Carl hadn't entered the cabin. She dropped to her knees and hugged Tommy.

"What is it, Ma?"

"I'm just grateful is all," she whispered, too choked up to find her voice. She pulled back and held him at arm's length. "If I didn't know better, I'd say we had a guardian angel looking out for us tonight."

She let go and turned to start supper. As she picked up the heavy iron stew pot, her arm ached. She rubbed where Carl had grabbed on to her. It would hurt worse tomorrow. Carl would be bound to treat her better—more like a sister—if Thomas had married her.

She stared at Tommy. Her boy. Her beautiful boy so much like his father. Why hadn't Thomas taken the time to wed her proper and give his son a last name? Tommy deserved that. She deserved that too.

It was a thought she'd held quiet inside for some time, afraid that to admit it would mean she'd be a traitor to the man she had loved. Now something compelled her to whisper it out loud. "Thomas? You wronged the two you said you cared for the most. You wronged me and Tommy. And I can't ever forgive you for that."

Chapter Eleven

Enough was enough. Two bride assessments were all Nelson could stomach for one week. It shouldn't be so incredibly taxing looking for a woman who would make a good wife and nurse! Between his other patients and Mrs. Blackwell's frequent false labor symptoms, he simply didn't have the time to give to the endeavor.

The one bright spot had been Miss Marks's freshly baked bread and honey. He wondered what day of the week she usually did her baking. Perhaps if he timed things well, he could check on Tommy on a day that she might offer more of the heavenly stuff.

Friday, he finished the last of her loaf.

On Saturday, he felt the first tug of craving for the bread—a new sensation for him. To satisfy it, he walked over to the restaurant and ordered a plate of Sadic's special with an extra helping of sourdough bread. It wasn't the same.

Sunday morning broke sunny and clear, with a few white puffy clouds on the horizon. Connor Flaherty gave a soul-stirring sermon about the unconditional love extended to all believers. Nelson listened and thought it sounded real nice, but he had difficulty believing it. Not once growing up had he experienced anything close to unconditional love. Any mistakes he'd made, his parents had been sure to punish him. There were consequences, good or bad, to every move he made. Reverend Flaherty could drone on all he wanted, but Nelson wasn't going to jump on that wagon.

After the service, Mara Vandersohn and Miss O'Rourke were escorted by two men from town to a waiting buggy. With the large basket in the boot, it must be a picnic that was planned. Miss Pratt, Miss Weber and Miss Simcock were surrounded by others from the congregation, both neighbors and interested bachelors.

It made more sense to Nelson to wait until the men were back to work during the week and try then. Mayor Melbourne had refined the contracts of the women to stipulate that they had to converse for at least an hour with each of the bachelors who had paid to the Oak Grove Betterment Committee fund. That money had paid for the costs of their journey and hotel. Because of that, Nelson knew he still had time to meet the other brides. He only hoped he had better luck with one of them than he had with the first two.

"Doc! Doc! Hold up!" Josiah, the mayor, strode up to him. "I can't make it for our game today. I'm meeting with the new schoolteacher about a play area at the school."

"Then you forfeit?"

"Absolutely not!" he blustered.

Nelson chuckled. Josiah hated to lose anything. He wouldn't want to accept a loss of their weekly chess game. "Then what do you propose?"

"How about an early supper at the hotel and then our game? Say…four o'clock?"

"Sounds fine." He raised his hand in a quick wave and headed to his house.

At his door, he hesitated with his hand on the knob. Nothing and no one waited for him inside. With the spring sun shining warm and comfortable on his shoulders, it didn't make sense to sit in his study on a day like today.

He was restless. It wouldn't be long and his parents would arrive. That had him on edge. Or maybe it was the sudden freedom of the day when he was used to working constantly. All he knew was that he was at odds with himself today. He walked back down the steps and headed out of town.

Following the worn path made by the deer,

he came to the river. The water level was higher than last week and the current swifter, likely due to melting snow from farther upstream.

He walked along the bank. The ripples and eddies flowed beside him faster than his stride. Now and again the song of a meadowlark called to him. On the opposite bank, young cottonwoods sent branches out low over the water. Before he knew it, he was standing at the ferry and contemplating the far shore.

And thinking of Miss Marks…and her son… and her bread.

He needed to see how Tommy was doing. Sunday was not a conventional day to check in on his patients, but then Sylvia Marks was not a conventional woman. And it *had* been an entire week. It was past time that he checked for himself to see that Tommy's healing was coming along properly.

And he wouldn't mind a taste of her bread if she happened to have any. The thought made him smile.

He stepped onto the raft and untied the tether line with a quick snap. Then grasping the rope alongside the ferry, he tugged the raft along, hand over hand, until he landed on the opposite bank amid the tall grass and the cottonwood trees. He wound his way through the prairie grass, down a small dip in the land, and came to the Markses' house.

The soddy looked smaller and dingier than he remembered and the yard messier. The shed's door hung crooked on one hinge, with the other hinge long rusted and broken. A goat, tied to a clothesline, munched contentedly on a crop of weeds.

At fifty paces from the cabin, he called out.

The goat bleated in answer.

He strode up to the door and was about to knock, when laughter from inside the cabin stayed his hand. He stood there, undecided about barging in on their day.

Suddenly, it was quiet.

Then a rifle jutted out from the window. "Who is out there?"

"Dr. Graham. I came to see how your son is getting along."

"Oh." Miss Marks pulled the rifle back inside the soddy. A moment later she opened the door.

Her cheeks were flushed and her eyes bright. She wore a coarse brown skirt and cream-colored blouse. Her dark brown hair was tied back from her face in a single thick braid.

"Well…come on inside and see for yourself." She braced the door open with a hand-sized rock.

He ducked through the entryway as light streamed into the one room. In the daylight, he could see that the walls had been plastered inside with mud, giving them a smooth appearance and a soft gray color. The only wood in the room was the door and the mantel, and five beams to help hold up the roof.

The hearth had been swept clean. As a matter of fact, the entire place looked orderly and clean. Miss Marks rested the rifle on two iron pegs high across the mantel. Tommy sat at the table with a Bible open in front of him.

"How are you feeling, Tommy?"

"All right."

"Any headaches? Visual disturbances?"

Miss Marks chuckled. "You have to use simpler words with a seven year-old. Tommy is smart, but he still is learning."

She turned to her son. "The doc wants to know if things look fuzzy or blurry. Like—" She backed out through the door and halfway to the shed, then held up three fingers. "How many of my fingers can you see?"

"Three."

The boy didn't even squint. A good sign. "And no pain in your head?" Nelson asked. "Dizziness?"

Tommy shook his head—somewhat carefully, Nelson thought.

His mother walked back inside. "He gets dizzy, but each day it's less. Other than that, he is acting normal, Doc."

"May I check the lump you had back there?" Nelson asked. When Tommy didn't refuse, Nelson ruffled through the boy's hair at the back of his head and touched the cut. No further oozing. And the lump was gone. Satisfied, he took a seat at the table. "What about your leg? May I take a look at it?"

At Tommy's nod, Nelson lifted the boy's injured leg.

Tommy gasped, tensing his muscles, and gripped Nelson's forearm, his fingers digging deep.

Nelson hesitated, then lowered the leg. "This won't work."

Miss Marks hurried to her son's side. "How about you sit on the table?" She boosted her son up and then gently raised his foot to rest on Nelson's knee.

Mimicking her slower movements, Nelson rolled up Tommy's pant leg and carefully unwrapped the cloth bandage. When he pulled the wad of cotton material away, he noticed a sticky substance coating the entire area of the wound. "I thought I told you to keep this clean. What do you have here?" He sniffed his fingers to identify the odor.

"Honey," Miss Marks said. She stood with her arms crossed in front of her—a challenge for him to say anything against her work.

He tossed the bandage aside and leaned closer to examine the wound. Reddened, puffy edges had formed along the line of the skin break. But it looked like new skin forming rather than inflamed skin. He pressed gently against the edges. No pus. And no evidence of any forgotten sutures. Miss Marks had gotten them all out.

"It's healing well," he said with a grunt. "Which comes as a surprise, considering how dirty that shed roof must be. Stop using the honey on it. I told you before that honey will just draw bugs and who knows what else." It was a miracle that infection hadn't set in.

"But it helps—"

"Nothing was said about honey in medical school."

"My granny in Virginia used honey for everything. It's good for all sorts of things. Just like cider vinegar…"

He shook his head. "Have you noticed a foul odor? Any discharge?"

She frowned. "Like I told you at your office, it's healing fine."

Gently, Nelson moved Tommy's foot this way and that, making sure he had good movement in his ankle. That was his main concern now. "Have you put any weight on it?"

"It hurts," Tommy said.

"I expect it does…and will for a time to come."

"He kind of hops around on his good leg, favorin' the other," Miss Marks said.

Nelson rewrapped Tommy's ankle and then lowered his leg gently to the floor. Seven days was enough for the skin to mesh together. "You have to start using the leg, even though it hurts."

"You said he had to rest." There was an edge to her voice. "So I've been making him rest. Do you know how hard that is for a boy his age?"

"I only meant for two or three days."

Her brown eyes hardened. "Then you should have said so."

She paced the short length of the room, her stride short and fretful.

He frowned. "If you remember, I was the one being held at gunpoint."

She stopped moving and glared at him, her hands clamped into fists. Then a moment later her lower lip trembled. "I did the best I knew how and you are telling me I did something wrong?" The sheen of tears came to her eyes. "Doc Graham—have I crippled him for good?"

He suddenly realized his mistake. He remembered saying something about the need for the wound to heal correctly when he'd been here before. She was frightened for her son, frightened that something she'd done or not done had done permanent damage. He had handled it roughly. He hadn't meant to strike fear in her or Tommy.

He stood and took her hands. They were small

against his larger palms. "Miss Marks... Sylvia," he said, hoping to calm her. A tingle of awareness rushed up his arms.

Unexpected. Startling. His pulse jumped.

Immediately, he let go, yet the sensation lingered.

Her eyes widened. "Doc..." She stepped back.

"I—uh—don't want you to think that," he said, gathering his thoughts. "You've done a fine job with Tommy. You're a good mother, Sylvia, but from now on, he must use his leg so the new tissue will get used to stretching. How about we give it a try?" he said, turning from her to her son. "Boys heal real fast. Did you know that? Faster than grown-ups do."

His words didn't have the effect he'd hoped they would. Tommy hung on every word, but his mother was still obviously frightened and believing the worst.

Then a determined look came over her face. "Come on, son. We've got to start right now." Sylvia hooked her arm under Tommy's armpit. "Doc? You want to take his other side? That way he will feel stronger by our caring on each side of him."

He liked the way she'd put it—as though by sheer strength of will, her love would somehow communicate itself through to Tommy and give him strength. He'd certainly never felt anything like that from his own parents.

He matched her position on Tommy's opposite side. The boy weighed hardly more than Nelson's microscope. He held up the bulk of Tommy's weight so that the boy's first step wouldn't hurt too much. Being bigger and stronger than Sylvia, he also wanted to lighten her load.

"Go slow!" Tommy said.

"Slow as a sunrise," Sylvia said softly.

Nelson looked over the top of Tommy's head, trying to figure out what she meant by that. She was calming down now that she had a new purpose. She watched her son's movements intently, every now and then biting her lower lip. Wisps of dark hair framed her face. She fascinated him although he didn't know why. There was always something new and different about her every time they were together. Something that made his life richer.

"Now lean into it a bit," Nelson said, returning his attention to Tommy. "With your full weight, each and every time. No skimping."

"Ah!" Sylvia wilted suddenly, her face contorting with pain. She rubbed her upper arm.

Nelson straightened. "Miss Marks?"

She took three deep, fast breaths.

"Sylvia?"

She glanced up, her eyes glistening with tears she held in. "Sorry. Got a bruise there a few days back." She repositioned Tommy's hold on her. "Let's try again."

The way she explained it bothered him, but he returned his attention to her son. "Get going, Tommy."

Tommy slowly took another four steps.

"Very good," Nelson said. "Rest a minute and then one more time."

Tommy took a shaky breath and then nodded. They repeated the moves and then helped Tommy sit back down. He beamed up at them. "I did good, didn't I?"

"You sure did," Sylvia said, a soft, proud smile on her face.

It transformed her. And it dazzled him.

She glanced over. "Why, Doc Graham! Is that a grin on your face that I'm seeing?"

Immediately, he relaxed his face. "Are *you* having visual disturbances, Miss Marks?"

Her smile widened, and a dimple appeared in her left cheek. "Well, I must be."

She turned back to her son. In that moment, with the sunlight streaming in the window behind her, he figured it out. It wasn't that she was a striking beauty, although she was quite comely. It was the love on the inside that shone out and brightened everything and everyone around her. That was what called to him.

He tore his gaze away and back to Tommy.

"Keep practicing. Add two more steps each time you get up. You'll do that for me?"

Tommy jutted out his chin, the motion reminiscent of one Nelson had seen in Sylvia. "If you stay and help."

"Uh…" Nelson stumbled with his thoughts. He'd *like* to stay and help. He liked being here. But there was a difference between a visit as a doctor to check on the boy's health and a visit as a friend. That was an invisible line that he usually didn't cross. "You are in very good hands. Your mother makes an excellent nurse."

He paused, shaken by his words. He'd said that to bolster Tommy. He'd wanted the boy to look to his mother for direction, but that made the words no less true. Sylvia Marks had done well with her boy. She had done very well with Wally and Miss Vandersohn too.

"You mean that, Doc? You think I'd make a passable nurse?" Sylvia asked.

For the first time since he'd known her, she sounded unsure and tentative—nothing like the woman who had held him at gunpoint. "Yes. More than passable."

He didn't know what to make of this side of the woman. The more he knew of her, the more enchanted he became. Each new thing he learned was incongruent to his original assumption. It was easier to keep her pigeonholed in a neat little box as an eccentric, backwoods woman—someone who regular society tolerated but essentially had passed over.

He was finding that she wasn't anything like that at all.

Chapter Twelve

Sylvia jumped up quickly. "Might you stay awhile? I could probably rustle up some coffee."

She swallowed hard, already regretting the words that had rushed out of her. Of course he couldn't stay. He was much too busy of a man to spend an afternoon with two near strangers. There were others who needed him, others he would surely rather be with than her and Tommy. What was she thinking by trying to keep him here any longer than a minute? That Tommy was as important as those others? That she was?

She near held her breath, waiting for his answer. It came to her then that she wanted him to stay more than just about anything else. He talked to her—and really listened to what she said, like her thoughts were important. Tommy too. He made her feel good—whole. Even when they argued—like over the honey.

And she wasn't even going to consider what had happened when he took her hands. His touch had done things—calmed her, steadied her and warmed her all at the same time.

"I suppose you have other people to see today," she said. "People who are ailing. I— We don't want to keep you."

He studied her with those deep green eyes of his. He was so smart and had such an important calling. Why would he want to spend any more time with her and Tommy?

"You don't happen to have any of that dark bread, do you?" His voice was deep and measured.

"The molasses bread? Sure. I got some." She held her breath. Would he stay?

"So that is what makes it sweet."

She nodded. "It's the sorghum."

"Do you smear that on wounds too?"

"Oh, it's not the same as honey!" Then she realized that his eyes were twinkling. He was teasing her! She was caught with a fit of shyness as her cheeks warmed.

It had been a last-minute thought to grab that loaf and take it to him. She'd wanted him to have the honey. She'd teased him about using it to sweeten himself, but it had been in her mind that he could use it in his doctoring. It hadn't occurred to her that he wouldn't even believe it could be of help. Sometimes she just didn't know what to make of him.

He slid back into the chair, looking a lot like Tommy did when he was expecting cake.

She couldn't keep down her smile, so she turned toward the hearth to hide it. Looked like she had a guest! Something that hadn't happened in a long, long time. Her insides suddenly had butterflies flying every which way. She pressed her hand against her tummy to quiet them. Taking a match from the tin box on the mantel, she crouched down at the hearth and started a fire. Then filled her pot with water and a handful of chicory root.

"What was all the laughing going on as I walked up to your door?"

She rose up. "Oh, we were playing our Sunday game. Since we don't go to church, I try to teach Tommy what he's missing right here. When the lesson is done, we play a game to help make the learning stick."

"I can't remember a time that my mother played a game with me. Or my father, for that matter."

Her heart clutched. What was there to say to that? Even her own mother had turned a rope now and then so that she could jump with her friends. "Maybe she was too busy with cooking and cleaning and all."

"We had two maids, a cook and a butler."

She couldn't imagine having that much help around. "Well, it sounds like you could do with learning a game or two."

"I play chess. Matter of fact, I have a standing appointment every Sunday afternoon with the mayor to play chess with him."

"That so? But you're here today."

"He postponed it until later."

"Well, I never played that myself, so I couldn't teach Tommy." She turned to her son. "Why don't you show the doc the game we were playing and explain it to him? Might be you can beat him if you try hard."

While her son did as she asked, she pulled the molasses bread from the pantry cupboard and cut it into thick, hearty slices. Then she walked out to the well and drew up the crock of butter she'd made for the week. She set everything on the cutting board and carried it over to the table.

When the doc took a bite of her bread, a look of pure contentment passed over his features. It caused a warm, contented feeling to rise up in her. And seeing how much Tommy enjoyed the doc's company made that feeling grow.

Doc Graham was a handsome man. She liked his strong forehead and the way his dark mustache and small beard were trimmed. But most of all she liked his eyes. Not that they were a pretty, deep green, the color of a Virginia pine—

although that was nice—but that they saw beyond the surface of things. And they were kind.

The thought made her consider the last time
she'd been in town. What was that woman doing
helping in the doc's office when she couldn't
stand the sight of someone sick? Sylvia hadn't
said anything to the doc, but she sure didn't care
for that woman. Whoever she was had com-
plained and spoken ill of the doc and then the
entire town of Oak Grove as Sylvia helped her
across the street. Then, once she had emptied
her stomach in the umbrella stand at the hotel,
she'd given Sylvia a mean look, wrenched her
arm away and tromped up the stairs to her room
with a big flounce of her skirt. Sylvia hadn't
been expecting a thank-you, but that look had
been enough to make a body's soul wither.

The pot was steaming over the small fire now.
Sylvia grabbed a towel to protect her hands from
the hot handle and poured two cups. Tommy had
eaten his portion of bread and now continued the
game on his slate by himself.

"Doc, how come that woman was helping
you with Mr. Brown?" she asked, setting the
pot back over the hearth.

"Miss Vandersohn is one of the women that
came West to be a bride. We were taking a stroll
together when Wally got hurt."

Her stomach did an odd flip. That was right.

He'd said he was looking for a woman who could cook. She sat down at the table. "How many women answered the call?"

"Five this time."

"That's a good number. Should make five men real happy."

A pang of envy stung her conscience. One of those men would be the doc. He'd make a good husband despite what he had said, even if he did put his doctoring first. A woman would be blessed to be a constant in his life. A heavy weight sank inside her at the thought.

Once, she had dreamed of a proper marriage where she and her husband would work hard to make a home together. But when Thomas up and died before wedding her, leaving her in a family way, Carl had said no man would take on a fallen woman and someone else's brat. She'd had her one and only chance.

She would have welcomed a man to help share the good times and the rough times. She had always expected to work, but not like she was doing now. Some days she was bone weary with it. She hoped those women fared better. As for her? She'd had to put those dreams away.

"Has Miss Vandersohn recovered?"

He snorted. "Undeniably. And she made it very clear that she would not accompany me on a stroll anytime in the near future."

She couldn't help it—she grinned, unaccountably relieved. "I had a feeling that might happen."

He took a gulp of his coffee. "It's probably for the best. I don't believe she had the necessary fortitude to be a doctor's wife."

"That does require grit on a woman's part," she said matter-of-factly. "Well, you got four more chances to find a bride."

"To be exact—two. Miss Pratt is too much like me. I think we would get on each other's nerves within a fortnight. And another woman giggles nervously at every turn. I'm not sure that her condition is curable." He leaned forward, closing the space between them all to a more intimate distance. "Imagine her helping while I perform surgery, only to have her burst into a fit of nervous giggles."

She struggled to stifle her smile. "That might scare the poor person you're trying to help."

"Exactly." He pulled back and took another bite of bread.

My, it was nice to hear him talk on and on. His voice was so rich and low that it mattered little what he said. She just liked the tone. "Sounds like you're having a trying time finding a cook and a bride."

"None have worked out so far." He let out a long breath. "I joke about it, but I am probably hoping for too much. I like my choice of career.

But the fact is, it's a huge responsibility to be the sole person taking care of the ailments and broken bones of such a vast area. I'm challenged by it…and humbled by it at the same time." His gaze deepened, as though he was looking inward. "There is something rewarding about knowing my patients and understanding their family situations. It's like being invited in to be a member of their family for the most critical moments in their lives."

Her breathing stilled on his words. She'd never had a man speak to her so. Never had a man share a piece of himself like the doc was.

"Of course," he continued, suddenly breaking the mood he was in, "in your case, you didn't exactly invite me."

She giggled and then cupped her hand over her mouth, remembering what he'd said about the woman who giggled all the time. "No. That definitely wouldn't be called an invitation."

The doc laughed at something Tommy did in the game. He didn't seem to realize he'd turned her world on its ear with what he'd said.

The afternoon wore on until the shadow of the shed fell on the cabin and a swirl of cooler air blew inside. The doc looked up from the game the same moment that she did. "It's getting late. I should go."

A pang of disappointment shot through her. Of course, he had to get back. It was just that it had been a day she'd never forget. She was sure Tommy felt the same way. Reluctantly, she rose to her feet.

"I expect it's time I see to Berta and Penny." Maybe doing her evening chores would help put her feet back on the ground after the past few hours.

The doc raised his brows. "Berta and Penny?"

"Well, you've met Berta, my mule. Penny is my goat. You enjoyed her butter on your bread."

"Ah, yes. She greeted me on my arrival. She makes good butter."

Why did he keep looking at her like that? As if he was pondering something about her. She had caught that same stare two other times through the afternoon. It made her feel all tingly inside. She wasn't sure that was a good thing to be feeling about any man. She'd learn from experience that they were hard to trust. The doc, however, seemed different than any she had ever met before.

"Could you help Tommy walk one more time?" she asked. "He did real well with you on one side and me on the other."

He nodded. With their help, Tommy took four steps before asking to stop.

"Try it again before you get in bed tonight," he ordered and ruffled her son's hair.

Then he shrugged into his fancy coat and hat and ducked out the door.

She still found it hard to believe he had stayed all afternoon. They walked, side by side, to the edge of her yard, which skirted the vast prairie and the dirt road. The sun hung low, casting an orange glow on the rolling fields. "I want to thank you for paying so much attention to Tommy. He sure liked playing that game with you."

He studied the shed and then the soddy in that quiet way he had. "How do you manage to live way out here?"

"I have good neighbors down the road a ways—Julian and Adele DuBois. They've been a lot of help to me and Tommy. I manage."

"It would be easier for you in town."

"I'm not welcome in town. Tommy either." A familiar lump formed in her stomach. She hated to talk about that part of her life. It was personal. Seemed her one wrong choice would haunt her forever. It was Thomas who had failed her, yet she would bear the weight of it.

"You saw," she said. "And you probably heard...that first day at the mercantile." She was aware the Gallaghers were quick to gossip about most anything.

"Sylvia...I don't know what happened in your past, but you can't let it hound you the rest of your life. There are a lot of new folks in town. And more coming every day."

"Like those women who want to be brides?"

"They'd give you a chance. I would if it were up to me."

Didn't he know it hurt her to see those women and their hope when she had none? Didn't he understand? In the end, it was safer not to feel anything, safer to stay tough. Then it wouldn't hurt so much to be snubbed. "They would only find out about me. That woman in the mercantile would see to that."

"Mable Gallagher?"

She swallowed. "Her or Carl."

The concern on his handsome face made her insides shake. Like he cared something for her and Tommy. He might think he was helping, but she couldn't let herself get soft and think that others would welcome her. It just wasn't so. The few times she let her guard down, something always happened and it made everything worse.

She looked over the prairie toward the setting sun. He had ruined a perfectly wonderful day.

"Sylvia."

At his voice, she looked down and concentrated on the dirt on the toes of her shoes. It helped to hold back the sting of tears. "I know things ain't perfect here, Doc, but I'm doing the best I know how raising Tommy. I know what those kids at school would call him. I couldn't stand to have him hurt like that. We are better off on our side of the river and away from all them people. Now, I don't want to hear any more about town."

"Fine. No more talk of town. But I want to see your arm. The one with the bruise."

Her breath left her. If he saw the bruise, he would know it wasn't from any old bump. Carl's fingers had left a recognizable imprint.

She covered the spot on her arm, shielding it from his view, even though she knew her long sleeve hid the purple-and-yellow skin. She backed up a step. "I don't need doctoring."

His gaze held hers. Serious. Determined. "Let me see."

He wasn't going to let this go. At the thought, she went numb inside. Better to be numb than to feel anything.

Slowly, he moved away her hand that shielded her injury. Then, ever so gently, he rolled up her sleeve.

At his touch, she crumpled. He was so tender, so cautious. She looked away, struggling to hold back the burning of unshed tears. He'd see. He'd know. And he'd be disgusted.

Her sleeve was high enough now. He turned her arm, checking the whole of the bruised area. Then he lowered her arm, pulling the material back down over it without saying a word.

She shrank on the inside. What must he be thinking?

"This has nothing to do with a fall or stumbling against anything."

She couldn't bring herself to look at him. She didn't want to see what was there on his face.

"Are there any more bruises?"

She shook her head.

"Is this a…gift…from Caulder? He did this to you?"

"He don't know his own strength sometimes."

"This has happened before?"

Anger. It was anger she heard in the doc's voice, but it wasn't directed at her. She raised her gaze to his. "Not for a long time. He only came back around last week when you saw him in the mercantile. Before that, he was gone for three years. He's Thomas's older brother. We came out here together, the three of us, from Virginia. Carl helped Thomas build this soddy, but mostly Thomas did all the work."

"What happened to Thomas?"

"At the last, we put on the roof and the DuBois boys came by to help. They asked if Thomas and Carl wanted to head south with them to join a cattle drive the next day. Thomas had never been on a drive before but figured he'd be back in a few months and have enough money to see us through our first winter. I asked him to wait a day, to go into town and see to a wedding first like he had promised my ma and pa and his parents too, but he was in an all-fired hurry to meet up with the DuBois boys. It didn't help that Carl was egging him on."

The furrows deepened between the doc's brows. "He never came back?"

She nodded. "Adele came by to stay with me a spell after that. I think she felt responsible in a way, since it was her sons who had asked Thomas to join up with them. She's the one who recognized I was carrying Tommy and came by to help again when my time came."

"I'm glad you weren't alone." His eyes still sparked with anger.

"Tommy looks a lot like his father," she said, proud of that. "Thomas was good and smart and...kind." She rushed to say the last. She didn't want the doc thinking that she would ever give herself to someone like Carl.

"But Carl was jealous that I chose his brother over him. He came around after Thomas died and learned I was in a family way. He thought I would fall all over him, wanting to give my baby the Caulder name quick before Tommy was born. But I couldn't do that. Carl always has been a mean one when he drinks. He would have been mean to me and mean to Tommy."

"I take it that Carl didn't like being rejected."

"He talked it up all over Oak Grove, letting people know I was never married and that my baby was a..." She wouldn't say the ugly word.

"Since then, I don't go into town much. Something bad always happens when I do."

"What made Carl come back a few days ago when he gave you this?" He indicated her bruised arm with his chin.

"He brought some venison by the night you were here fixing Tommy and heard your voice inside the house. He thought…" The implication was uncomfortable. The doc wouldn't think of her in that way. No man would. She hurried her words to get past the painful thought. "He came back two days ago to ask about you. I told him the truth—that you'd come to doctor Tommy— but he didn't want to believe me. Like I said, Doc, he's a mean one."

The doc's face was ruddy with anger. "Did he…?" He asked, his voice hoarse. "Sylvia, tell me right now. Did he force himself on you?"

She shook her head. "No. I haven't been with any man but Tommy's father."

He visibly relaxed, his shoulders resting down and his expression calming.

It was awkward talking about this with Doc Graham, but the things he asked, and the way he asked…maybe he did care for her a little.

"Well, now that you know everything, you can see how it ain't fittin' for you to come by anymore."

"Because of Caulder?"

"You'll only rile him more."

"I'm not afraid of him. In fact, it makes me want to stay. You need protection out here."

She shook her head. "It's not that. I'll figure out a way to take care of Caulder if he comes by again. It's you. You're gonna upset a heap of people if they find out you came out here to visit."

"I didn't. I came to check on Tommy's recovery."

She blew out through her nose. "And stayed a mighty long time. As much as I like the company and grown-up talk, Doc, people ain't fools."

"Some are. The next time I see Caulder, I won't be so easy on him. He has no business hurting you or trying to force you to do anything you don't want to do."

Even though she liked that the doc wanted to protect her, she had to figure things out for herself. She couldn't depend on any man. They had always disappointed her in the end.

"You been calling me by my given name. Been a long time since anyone did that." And she surely liked it, but that was neither here nor there. He shouldn't keep doing it.

"Maybe it's because I had a good time today and I'd like to return. I happen to like your name. And I wouldn't mind if you called me Nelson."

She sucked in a breath of the sweet, clean air. He was getting more personal by the minute. He might have discovered more about her and her situation, but that didn't mean they could be real friends. The kind that visited back and forth. She had had a wonderful day up until he'd asked her about her bruise. Even talking about that had opened up something between them, like opening the window to let the fresh air flow in and sweep out the bad. But he couldn't come back.

"You call me by my given name when I'm in town and people could think there is something more between us than a checking up on Tommy. If you're wanting to marry one of those women from the train, you should be spending time with them, not me and Tommy."

"I want to come back one more time. Just to make sure Tommy is progressing."

She would surely enjoy that, but his coming here and stirring up things better left buried was a worry. Tommy already looked to be attached to him more than was smart. Her boy had hung on his every word the entire afternoon. Better to stop things now. "No need to do that. I'll let you know if Tommy has a problem."

He stood there, obviously ready to argue his point.

And she was getting irritated. She plopped her fist on her hip.

"Some people don't have the good sense to know when a visit's over. Now, the light is fading and I got chores to attend to before dark."

She spun away from him and didn't look back as she stomped toward the shed.

Nelson's chest tightened with pent-up frustration as Sylvia stormed away. She didn't realize the danger she was in staying out here on her own, or if she did, she was being too darn stubborn to accept any help.

It had been a surprising day. He actually enjoyed it very much despite one certain woman's penchant to be so independent. Yet he admired her for that too. Wasn't that exactly the way he had thought when he left his home in Boston? He'd make things work no matter what. There was no alternate plan for him. But for Sylvia, surely there had to be an alternative.

He made his way back across the river on the ferry, his thoughts of Sylvia, and thoughts of Tommy, swirling inside like the eddies he saw in the river.

How in the world did she and her son manage so far from town? It couldn't be an easy life, yet he'd not heard one complaint from her lips. She and Tommy had so very little, and yet they both seemed happier than he had ever been at Tommy's age. His cheeks hurt from all the unaccustomed laughing he had done that afternoon. As different as he was from them, he had felt very comfortable and had a good—no, *wonderful*—time.

He'd never played a game with either of his parents. Over the years, he got along with his mother better than his father, but still she was always distant and, in his mind, cold toward him. He would have thought that was how all parents were if he hadn't come across, among his schoolmates, mothers who were more like Sylvia.

He'd never been comfortable around members of the opposite gender. He supposed that the all-boys school he'd attended had something to do with that. He'd never had a chance to practice speaking to girls other than at chaperoned dances and then it had been awkward. Much like those dances, the forced "getting to know each other" strolls lately with the women from the train also sapped his energy.

Yet an afternoon with Sylvia had flown by faster than a minute. She was easy to talk to. Open. And he didn't have to mold his responses based on some written etiquette code. She took his words at face value and didn't twist them this way and that, as more sophisticated women had a penchant to do.

His parents' train was due in four days. What would they say if he suggested a game such as the one he had played with Tommy and Sylvia? It might be fun to see their reaction. Then again...he might be setting himself up for one more disappointment. Growing up, they had most often answered his queries with a resounding "no." It didn't matter what he did to try to engage them in his life. They simply weren't interested. Why would the silence that had settled between them for the last four years make this visit any different?

Why were they coming at all?

Darkness fell as he crossed the railroad tracks and started up Main Street toward his house.

It was only as he was letting himself in his front door that he realized he'd forgotten about the early supper and chess game he'd promised to the mayor. Guess that meant he was the one to forfeit this time.

He smiled to himself, thinking of his afternoon, thinking of Sylvia.

It had been worth it.

Chapter Thirteen

The next afternoon he called on Katie O'Rourke. He'd heard good things about her from a few of his nosier patients. Miss O'Rourke had the start of lines near her pale blue eyes and a more generous girth than the other brides. He was immediately drawn to her pleasant smile and outgoing personality. He invited her to dine with him in the hotel's restaurant.

"I'm surprised you asked for me, Dr. Graham. I imagined that you would be interested in a younger woman. After all, your first choice was Mara. She's the youngest of us from the train."

"There is something to be said for life experience in a good marriage, Miss O'Rourke. You and I are likely close to the same age and have far more in common."

Rollie brought in two bowls of cabbage soup

and two plates of scalloped ham and potatoes. He set them down before Nelson and Miss O'Rourke. "Hello, Doc. Ah…Miss Katie…I would appreciate your opinion on the meal."

Nelson raised his brows. Miss Katie, was it? It wasn't like Rollie to solicit anyone's opinion, especially when it came to his wife's cooking. Ever since Rollie married Sadie, he had said that she could do no wrong.

"Oh, Katie here is a fine cook," Rollie said, catching Nelson's expression. "She's been teaching Sadie and me some secrets from her native Ireland. I wish she had been here for Saint Paddy's Day."

Across from him, Miss O'Rourke smiled. "You're too kind, Mr. Austin. I'm sure this will be delicious."

"Well, I'll be waiting to hear your thoughts." And with a quick rap on the table as goodbye, Rollie headed over to another table to speak with another couple.

She could cook! That was good news for Nelson's purposes. He settled back to enjoy his meal, his opinion of Miss O'Rourke rising steadily.

"What is it you did before coming to Oak Grove?" he asked halfway through his soup.

"Ach. I suppose you might think that I was married before, seeing as how I'm older than the other brides, but I haven't had the pleasure."

"It was on my mind," he admitted. "I find it refreshing that you don't make excuses. Sensible."

"Well...it is what it is, isn't it?"

She took a bite of ham and potatoes before continuing, "Ye see, I took care of my parents. First my ma fell sick, and it became my duty to do the cooking and cleaning and tending to my sisters. Then, a year after she passed, my da had an accident on the river. He needed my help after that."

"What about your sisters? Did they help?"

She shook her head. "They married off as fast as you can say Christopher Columbus. First Bridget and then Susan. I'm glad of it. They have bonny husbands and they are happy."

Another mental check went down on the positive side of his list. She thought of others before herself, and she'd cared for a sick mother and ailing father and hadn't minded her duty. "Miss Katie," he said, "the fact that someone hasn't snatched you up bewilders me."

A becoming blush rose up her apple cheeks. "It's hoping I am that I'll never have to care for another sickly person again, unless, of course, it was my own. You see—I like to be out of doors and I've had so little chance to do that. A garden of my own to tend on my own little patch of land, and cooking what I grow. Could anything be better than that?"

Oh no. That didn't sound like the life he had envisioned. "What about helping your husband?"

"I suppose it would depend on what he did. For instance, I do like animals, you see. And as I said—growing things. Anything that is out of doors."

"Well, what if he was a doctor?"

Her eyes widened. "Are you asking me for my hand?"

His heart nearly stopped. "No, no!" he said quickly. "Of course not. It's much too soon."

"Well, then, just what is it you are saying?"

"I'm obviously not doing a very good job of making myself clear. I meant to say, or to ask…" He was stumbling about like a fool! He took a deep breath and began again. He leaned forward. "I would expect my wife to work with me. In my office. Doing things such as a nurse would do."

She snatched herself back from him as if burned. "I'm sorry, Doctor. I've done my duty as a daughter and I hope never to look on another hurt or dying man or woman in my life. It's my heart, you see…"

"No. I don't see," he said perhaps a little too crossly. "You are experienced. You are obviously well suited for the type of work."

"But I couldn't bear to go through it again. Every person I tended would remind me of my ma or my da. I…couldn't." The last was said in a whisper as if she was remembering more than she wanted. Her eyes filled with tears. She stood. "I won't be misleading you to think that I would."

Others in the restaurant were watching the drama with growing interest. This was not how he anticipated the afternoon going. "Please, Miss O'Rourke. Sit down again. I would have you finish your meal."

She stood there a moment, undecided.

"Believe me, I do understand. I'm disappointed, for myself, but I completely understand your position." It was obviously too much for her gentle nature.

"Are we to be friends, then?" she asked, her voice uncertain.

"That would suit me fine. A person can't have too many friends."

"To be sure," she said, gave a relieved smile and slowly sat back down to finish eating.

Nelson lay back in the barber chair while Otis Taylor wrapped a steaming hot towel across his jaw and up the sides of his face. He closed his eyes and sank into a state of semi-bliss as he relaxed and let the peace and quiet of the early Thursday afternoon take him.

Last night's vigil at the Whistle Stop Saloon had drained him of energy. Around eight thirty, Chris Sanders, owner of the saloon, had rushed to his office yelling for help. An altercation between two foolhardy cowhands had turned dangerous. Tempers ignited between men too young to respect the life they'd been given or anyone else's and too prideful to back down. A week's pay, cheap liquor, gambling and guns had been more than they could handle and one man had been shot. Unfortunately, no matter how hard Nelson had tried to help him, the bullet to the man's liver had been fatal.

The bells above the door tinkled.

"Well, hello, ladies," Otis called out. "What can I do for you?"

Nelson raised his head slightly and opened his eyes.

"We're looking for— Oh! Is that the doctor? Hello, Dr. Graham." The woman, a strawberry blonde with freckles, covered her mouth with her hand and giggled. She blocked his view of the second woman who had entered the shop after her.

It was a rather undignified pose to be in for meeting them. Nelson maneuvered his chair back to a sitting position and stood to acknowledge them properly. Well, as properly as he could, considering he had a wet towel on his face. He swiped off the towel and bowed slightly.

"Have you met Miss Simcock and Miss Weber?" Otis said.

The one woman let out another round of giggles.

"Only at the town hall meeting. Are you ladies getting to know Oak Grove?" he asked.

They nodded in unison.

"We won't keep you," Miss Weber said, leaning slightly to see him around Miss Simcock. "We're here to learn about the quilting club that Mrs. Taylor is hosting tonight."

"She's upstairs," Otis said. Then he walked to the base of the narrow stairwell and yelled up. "Martha! You've got company!"

Mrs. Taylor appeared at the top of the stairs. "Miss Weber! I am so glad you have come! I hear that the quilts you brought are exquisite. Come on up. You too, Miss Simcock. I keep my supply of material and notions up here."

Nelson settled back into the barber chair with the thought that he was right to steer clear of Miss Simcock. That giggling would drive him mad after only a few hours. Whether it was from a condition or from simply being irrationally happy, he could not abide it. Perhaps she would calm down once she married. He, however, would not be the one to witness that.

Otis lathered up Nelson's face. Overhead, the muffled voices of the women talking created a pleasant sound.

"Heard what happened last night, Doc," Otis said as he used a straight-edge razor to shave

Nelson's whiskers. "A shame to lose a life in such a way. Mayor Melbourne's plan to bring women here to settle this town down makes more and more sense."

"Mmm." He didn't answer because to do so might cause Otis to nick his jaw.

A few moments later, Otis handed him a towel to wipe off any stray soap. "Done."

Nelson got up, smoothing his palm over his trimmed hair and then his chin. At the same time, the two ladies descended the narrow stairs. He nodded to them and watched them leave.

"Either of them catch your eye, Doc?" Otis asked when the door had closed behind them.

Unfortunately, no. He didn't say it out loud. The only woman occupying his mind of late was Sylvia Marks and he didn't know what to think of that. Something about her appealed to him— an openness, an honesty that he hadn't seen in the others. There was something special about her. Something hardy and strong and clean.

"Not at the moment," he answered Otis. "At the moment, I am concerned with only one woman."

Otis grinned. "Which one might that be?"

"My mother. She is arriving on the afternoon train today, along with my father."

"I don't recall ever meeting them. First time here, ain't it?"

Nelson nodded. "And likely the only time."

He paid for his shave, grabbed his Stetson and walked out the door.

He strode down the main street of town toward the small train station. The wind off the prairie whipped his coat and kicked up the ends of his string tie. He'd dressed in his best. His parents would expect that. And he'd stocked his kitchen pantry with more food than it had ever seen.

After he had their things removed from the train and carried to his house, he would take them to Austin's restaurant for an early supper. After that? He had no idea—he'd never had the privilege of a visit from them before.

He heard the train whistle blow and picked up his pace. They would expect him to be standing there, ready to help them, even as the train pulled into the station. He would hear of it if he wasn't in full view through their window. It irked him a bit. He'd always done what he could to encourage their regard, and yet they barely noticed him. He would probably end up doing a number of things they disliked on this visit, simply because he didn't know much about their preferences.

He stepped up to the flat platform at the depot and looked down the tracks. As the locomotive chugged around the last bend, smoke billowed up from the smokestack, which the brisk wind immediately whisked away. The engineer put on the brakes, causing a loud ear-grating squeal as the train slowed and then came to a stop.

He checked the row of windows in the first car, and then the second. Finally, he saw her, in the center of the second passenger car. The windows were dirty and dusty, and her image blurred. She wore a large-brimmed black hat, decorated with a gigantic black bow. Instead of looking eagerly out of the windows like the other passengers, she looked down to her lap. With the dirty windows, he couldn't see far enough into the train to see his father. If her note had given him a queasy premonition, her attitude now increased it a hundredfold.

When the last of the disembarking passengers had passed by, she stood, glanced out the window at him without any expression on her face and moved to the front of the car. A second later, she appeared on the steps.

In black. She was entirely in black—not just her hat.

He did not see his father.

A weight, the size of Kansas, formed in his gut.

"Hello, Mother." He moved forward and offered his hand, helping her descend the last and largest step to the platform. He swallowed. Then through the netting of her hat, he gave her an awkward kiss on one cheek.

There was nothing he could say. The ground

had just dropped out from under him. His father was dead. He should feel something, yet his insides felt numb. There would be no chance to find out what had gone wrong between them and no chance to fix it. No chance to make amends. Ever.

"Hello...Nelson."

She was thinner than when he'd last seen her, with a few more lines on her face. Yet even with the sadness that overshadowed her, she was as beautiful as ever.

"I'll get your things." He escorted her to the area where they unloaded the trunks.

"I brought only one bag," she said. "I—I wasn't sure how you would take the news I have for you. One bag seemed sufficient."

"Which one is it?"

She pointed. "There. By the gray trunk."

He picked it up, took her arm again and led her down the steps to the road.

Walking past the livery and the blacksmith shop, the sound of iron striking iron suddenly stopped. He caught Brett Blackwell's questioning glance. Nelson shook his head. Now wasn't the time for introductions. After he and his mother passed by, the noise started up again.

"This is it," he said a few moments later as they walked up to his front steps.

She paused and gazed up at the fairly new

two-story house. Without a change in her expression, she then continued up to the front door.

He remembered his first thoughts on getting her letter and how he'd hoped for more of a reaction at seeing his first home, his first office. Circumstances had changed drastically since that day.

Inside, she removed her hat pin and hat, then searched for a place to set them. He took them from her and set them on her bag, which he'd left by the door.

She stared at the entry and at the row of four chairs against the wall. "You use your parlor as a waiting room?"

"Yes. And the dining room is where I do my exams. The light is better in there." He indicated the adjoining room. He didn't want to talk about his office. Not now. He wanted to know more about his father and what had happened. "Tell me about Father."

"He passed peacefully in his sleep," she said in a controlled voice. "The funeral was well attended. A few cousins came on the Graham side."

"When?" he asked.

"Three weeks ago."

He counted back. She had known when she sent the letter and yet hadn't mentioned it!

"I wanted—no—I *needed* to tell you in person." Her lower lip trembled.

He strode to her and helped her to a chair.

He was crushed. Even with his father's funeral, he'd been excluded. His cousins—people he'd seen only four or five times over his entire life—had attended, yet he'd not had that moment to say goodbye to his own father.

He crouched at her knee and looked up at her face. "I could have come, Mother. I could have helped. Why didn't you send for me?"

She loosened the drawstring on her satchel and withdrew a lace handkerchief. She dabbed at her eyes. "I know you would have come. I—I wanted you to be there too, but it wasn't possible."

"Why not? A telegram, Mother! A simple telegram and I would have come!" Frustration at her, at the situation, at his father, speared through him. He'd never understand his family! Never! He stood and stormed across the room. He raked his fingers through his hair and stared out the window, trying to control the rage that engulfed him.

There had been other times in his life when they had disregarded his feelings. He'd tried at first to limit his expectations, thinking he wanted too much. With that, however, he had learned that hope couldn't be snuffed out so easily. Over the years, he'd struggled to manage his anger at being forgotten and ignored, to tamp it down and control it. This, however, was the worst. He felt betrayed. His own mother could have sent for him—wanted him there according to her own words just now—and yet hadn't. There had to be a reason.

He turned back to her. "Tell me why."

Her shoulders heaved with a soft sob. "Please—"

So, there *was* a reason. "Please what? I don't understand any of this! You treat your cat with more deference than you do me."

She fretted with her handkerchief, balling it up and then stretching it back out.

"You might as well answer me. I won't let this go, Mother."

"Because…you are not a member of the Graham family."

He froze. He hadn't heard correctly. He was sure of it. He turned to look at her. Sitting there in the chair, she looked smaller somehow—frail—when he knew she wasn't frail at all. "What did you say?"

"It was my husband's wish at the end, that you not attend the funeral. It was his last mean wish."

Her husband—not *his father*.

"Ellison made many demands throughout our marriage that affected you. The first, however, affected you the most. He would marry me and give you a name, as long as I never told you or anyone else about the circumstances surrounding your birth." She sniffled. "When he fell ill, he reminded me, once again, of the promise that I had made. I begged him to reconsider, but he was adamant and would not lift it. Finally, a month before he passed away, he relented and said that once he was gone, I would be free of my promise. In return, he did not want you at his funeral."

Memories shifted as he remembered them not from his once childish point of view, but from that of an adult. Birthdays forgotten, holidays ignored, trips made with only his mother. "That answers many questions I've had, Mother. You were a dutiful wife."

"I've tried to be a good mother too. As much as Ellison would allow."

The walls were closing in on him. He had to get out—out of the house and out of the town. He had to think, had to adjust to what she had said.

"I'll show you to your room."

"Are you sure you want me to stay here?"

"You thought I would throw you out? Have you stay at the hotel?" he said irritably. "Of course you will stay here. I don't hate you, Mother. I simply find that I don't know you."

He ignored the hurt he saw in her eyes. He carried her traveling bag upstairs to the north room. She followed more slowly.

"Make yourself comfortable. Fix some tea if

you would like. I don't have a maid, so you will have to do it yourself." He knew he was being inhospitable. He didn't care. She had hurt him deeply and he wanted to strike back. Before he said anything more harmful, he had to distance himself from her. "I'm going for a walk."

And with that he spun on his heel and left.

He strode south behind the row of buildings, crossed the train tracks at the station and continued across the field. He tried to purge any thinking, any memories from his mind. All he wanted was to move, to work his muscles to their limit and by doing that to stoke the sudden confusion and anger that boiled inside him like a cauldron ready to explode. Let it explode. Let it.

He ran. He followed the trail, familiar now, along the riverbank toward the ferry landing. He ran until his muscles screamed for him to stop, his arms pumping, his face layered with sweat. Yet the thoughts still came. Thoughts of birthdays, Christmases, holidays—all spent in the dormitory, while the other boys returned to their own homes. The loneliness that he had endured. The wondering why his parents never wanted him to come home. He thought about his grandparents, and the similar traits that had carried down to him—all from his mother's side. No wonder. He also thought long and hard about his responsibility to carry on the Graham name. It was something he had always assumed he was supposed to do. Father—Ellison—had never spoken to him of it. Now he knew why.

He came to the landing and stopped, bending over at his waist, his hands on his knees, to drag in great gulps of air. How did this new information change things? He snorted. He had to be in shock, and yet here he was thinking like a doctor, already trying to analyze himself. He'd told his patients that sometimes life was just messy. How ironic. He hadn't thought he was talking about his own tangled life.

He stared across to the ferry landing on the opposite shore. Beyond the young cottonwoods, only a short half mile, was Sylvia's home. He couldn't see it from where he stood, but in his mind's eye he visualized the times he'd spent there. He'd been content and happy in that hovel of a house, but never in his own while young. Sylvia gave Tommy what Nelson had never had—unconditional love.

Swiftly on that thought came another. Were Sylvia and his mother the same except for the paths they'd chosen? Realizing she was with child, Sylvia could have married Carl but had chosen to raise her son on her own. Why had Mother married Ellison and did the man know that she was with child at the time? Or did that bit of information come later?

Mother's choice should have been infinitely better. Ellison had money. He wasn't physically mean, but he'd withheld his love and forced Mother to avoid her own son, in his own way punishing them both. Neither woman had had great choices upon discovering their conditions, but between Tommy and himself, he wondered, given the choice, if he would have chosen Tommy's lot over his.

Other sons might worry, at a time like this, about their inheritance. He didn't want any. He didn't expect any either. A man who couldn't give love, even to the woman he married, was not a man who would give his fortune to a son who was not his.

He had so many questions. He wondered about his father—his real father. Who was he? Did he know he had a son? Was he alive now? What did he do? Did Nelson have half brothers or sisters somewhere?

He turned around and stared across the tall prairie grass toward town. The cross on the church steeple was the only thing visible from this distance. Oak Grove had been his new beginning when he settled here. It was proving to be a good decision. Now he knew that he'd never go back to Boston. He'd never return to the mansion that wasn't ever a home to him.

He started back to town, his thoughts slowly becoming cohesive again. He and his mother had a lot to talk about, but things wouldn't all be answered in one conversation. He was glad now, that she had come to tell him in person. The truth answered so many questions and generated even more. He could handle the truth. For the first time, he understood what he was dealing with.

Twenty minutes later he walked through the front door of his house. Mother was in the kitchen, the teakettle whistling. She ignored it when she heard the door close and came to stand in the hallway, her hands clasped in front of her.

He took off his hat, slipped it over the peg and walked to her. In a move that was at once awkward and at once necessary, he enveloped her in a hug and held on.

At first her shoulders were stiff, but then slowly she circled her arms around him. And then finally, finally, she gave in and gripped him too. Her body shook with quiet sobs.

Still he held on.

And the teakettle whistled.

Chapter Fourteen

Sylvia glanced back at her son in the wagon bed. Tommy was having a hard time of it. The road to the DuBois farm had many ruts and every jolt of the wagon jarred his injured ankle and his head. Although he didn't cry out or complain, his face was white and strained. She couldn't take him to town with her. He'd never be able to handle a longer ride.

She reined Berta down the dip to the small creek and then back up the other side.

When Sylvia stopped the wagon in front of the house, Adele walked out her door. Sylvia explained her situation and Tommy's injury and asked if he could stay there until she got back from town. Then she hiked Tommy onto her hip and carried him into the house.

Once back in the wagon seat, she handed

down a crock of buttermilk. "That's likely the last of it. Miss Penny is drying up. Is there anything I can bring back for you from town?"

"Two large spools of strong white thread for my loom."

"I'll see if the mercantile has it," she said as she unwound the reins from the brake lever and made to leave. "You all right, Adele? What are you rubbing your knee for? Need some liniment?"

The woman straightened. "Achy is all. Rain's coming."

Sylvia couldn't see a cloud in the sky, but she trusted Adele's rheumatism. The woman always seemed to know things before they happened. "I won't be long."

Sylvia wondered briefly if Doc Graham had liniment that would work better than her homemade kind. Seemed they both had different ways of doing things. She gave a nod to Adele and reined Berta toward the river.

Forty-five minutes later, she maneuvered her wagon over the train tracks at the crossing and into town. She couldn't keep herself from glancing down the side road to Doc Graham's house when she drove past. Wonder what he was up to today. Tommy asked about him almost daily since the doc had made his visit and, truth be told, she wondered about him too. Daily.

She'd like to think that it was the things he'd said about being a good nurse. His words had filled her with pride—way too much pride most likely as it would come to naught in the end. But still, she'd felt a little stronger, walked a little taller in remembering it.

But mostly she thought about the way his green eyes twinkled when something amused him and how tender he'd been about the bruise on her arm. And his big strong shoulders. She thought about that a lot more than she should.

At the hotel, she slowed to make a wide turn and stop the wagon right in front of the mercantile. Halfway through the turn, a couple stepped off the boardwalk without looking. She pulled back on the reins. "Whoa! Berta!"

Doc Graham stopped suddenly and grasped the arm of the finely dressed woman to hold her back. He tipped his hat. "Miss Marks."

"Doc Graham," she answered. Seemed strange when no one else ever bothered to greet her on the road. Good thing he hadn't called her by her given name like he had on Sunday. That would have surely had eyes turning.

From her high seat, she waited as they crossed the road and then stopped on the hotel's boardwalk. That couldn't be one of the brides that he'd told her about, could it? Envy over the woman's pretty dress and bonnet slammed into her. She had never owned anything so fine. Dark green piping and stitchwork fancied up the front of her silk shirtwaist and showed off her trim waist. Then her green-and-white-striped skirt flared out in a perfect circle. Sylvia thought of her own clothes. She had two dresses to be exact. The brown one for workdays and the blue one for coming into town. When she plowed her small field in back of the house with sorghum and winter wheat, she even wore Thomas's old overalls and his boots stuffed with rags so they would stay on her feet.

The more she looked at the woman's dress, the more the acid of envy ate at her gut. She would never have such a dress. She squeezed her eyes shut tight. No point in looking any longer. When she opened them, the woman was gone and so was Doc Graham.

She circled Berta around to the front of the mercantile and climbed down from the wagon, searching the road once more for any sign of the doc. She was anxious to tell him how well Tommy was doing on practicing his steps.

When she didn't see him, she gathered her basket of eggs and jars of sorghum molasses from the back of the wagon and carried them into the mercantile. Last, she brought in a crock of Penny's milk. It took three trips with Mable Gallagher watching her closely each time she entered and left the store. The woman didn't lift a finger to help her. Not once.

"Last batch of eggs were cracked and no good," the woman said.

"All of them?" That Carl Caulder had been at fault, swinging the basket the way he had.

"All but one. I will take a dozen of these in replacement to make your account tally properly. And if that's your goat's milk in that last crock, you can march it right on back to your wagon. We get our milk and butter from the Gibsons' dairy farm now."

She tried not to take Mable's caustic ways to heart. The woman preferred money for her goods, not bartered items, and treated customers accordingly. A few years back, Mable had delivered a scathing lecture on that very subject out on the boardwalk. Seemed like everybody stopped to listen. Since then, Sylvia had learned it was better to keep her mouth shut.

"Go ahead, then," she said, "And take six more eggs for the inconvenience it caused you. I'll see if Mr. Austin will want the goat's milk."

"Oh, he gets his milk from the dairy now too. His wife, Sadie, prefers that for cooking."

Mable was just full of cheery news today. Sylvia walked across the room to the area that held material and sewing things. First off, she wanted to see if she could find the thread that Adele had asked for. She searched the bins, dismayed at first to find several skeins of black thread but no white. Then, as luck would have it, she found the last white skein. Adele wanted two, but this would have to do for now.

She also decided to get chalk so that Tommy could use his slate more often. Usually, she tried to conserve his pieces of chalk, but since he couldn't move around much because of his injury, it would help to occupy him.

While she collected her items, the door opened a number of times. She kept her nose to her business, uneasy that the store was more busy than usual. She'd chosen Wednesdays for her weekly trip into town particularly because it had always been the quietest day. Guess that was changing with all the women arriving on the train. That meant a good opportunity for the Gallaghers and their mercantile to make a heap amount of money as the women set up their new homes.

Two women entered the store together and struck up a conversation with Mable. They were close to Sylvia's age, although she had never seen them before, so she suspected that they were the Betterment Committee's brides. Mable acted all sugary sweet to them, just like she did if the mayor or the banker came into the store. As the woman chatted, completely ignoring her and talking on and on about the fashions back East, Sylvia became painfully aware of her place as an outsider.

They weren't leaving anytime soon and she

had another stop to make at the blacksmith shop. After waiting a goodly time, she squared her shoulders and marched up to the counter, laying her items out. "I'm ready, Mrs. Gallagher."

The two ladies stopped their chattering and turned to stare at her. Guess she was a sight. She'd worn her best blue dress. It was clean, but she knew the hem was frayed and one button was missing on the bodice. Instead of Thomas's work hat, she had worn a bonnet. It was a simple cloth one that matched her dress. Adele had made it for her.

"Hello." She smiled tentatively.

Mable pursed her lips, making it clear that she did not appreciate the interruption. She set her glasses low on her nose and looked over what Sylvia wanted to purchase. "I cannot sell you that," she said and picked up the white thread, tossing it to the side.

The one thing that Adele had asked of her! "Why not? It was in the bin."

"I promised all the white thread to Mrs. Taylor. She is busy making dresses for the weddings that are coming up. There will be five weddings and so she needs enough thread for five dresses."

"Surely she doesn't need all the white thread," Sylvia said. "When are these weddings to take place?"

"You would know if you attended church. They will happen on Sunday in two weeks' time."

The two other women watched the exchange with interest.

"I have ordered more," Mrs. Gallagher said. "It will be in at the end of the month."

"Maybe Mrs. Taylor would gladly give up one."

"Well, that's not really my problem now, is it? You'll have to take that up with her yourself. I promised all the white thread to her and *I* keep my promises."

The way she said the last inferred that Sylvia *didn't* keep her promises. In front of customers! Sylvia's cheeks burned with humiliation.

She waited while Mable tallied up the bill. Once her account was square, she took her supplies out to the wagon, including the goat milk. Again, it took her two trips in and out of the mercantile. As she was leaving for the last time, Mable called out to her.

"If you expect to see Martha Taylor now, you won't find her at home. On Wednesday afternoons, she closes her shop and rides out to visit the Cresswells at their farm."

It seemed Mable enjoyed delivering bad news. It reminded her why she hated to come into town. She always left in a sour mood.

At least Brett had always been cordial to her. She drove down the road and stopped at the blacksmith's shop. The large door stood open, and although his fire was hot, he wasn't inside. She decided to wait. When ten minutes had passed, she finally walked next door to the livery.

Wally Brown was cleaning the dirt and rocks from one of the stable horses' hooves—a tricky maneuver considering he still wore his cast. The once white apparatus was now dingy and dirty.

"How do, Mr. Brown," she said.

He dropped the hoof to the ground and straightened. "How do yourself, Miss Marks. What can I do for you this fine day?"

His kind welcome smoothed over her recent encounter at the mercantile. "I'm looking for Mr. Blackwell to fix my mule's harness."

Wally stepped outside and eyed the ragged tear in Berta's leather harness. "I'd fix this for you easy enough without my cast, but I don't think I can as yet. You'll find Mr. Blackwell at his house over yonder."

"Thank you for your help."

She walked around the side of the livery and over to the two-story house and knocked on the door. A second later it swung open and two wide-eyed boys stared up at her. "You ain't the doc," the taller one said.

"Of course not. Why would I be?"

"Ma needs the doc."

"Hurry!" A woman's voice called out from

somewhere deep inside the house. "Hurry!" The last sounded like a sob.

Sylvia's pulse quickened. What was happening? She rushed past the boys and up the stairs. The woman sounded like she was in wretched pain. Sylvia took one look and by the woman's swollen stomach realized what must be happening. She'd been in the same place seven years earlier. "Mrs. Blackwell? I'm Miss Marks, come to help. Though most folks call me Sylvia."

Mrs. Blackwell looked up at her, a sort of helpless, hopeless fear in her eyes. "It's too soon!"

Sylvia swallowed, fearful too, but knowing she had to be strong and sure for the woman. That was how Adele had treated her at Tommy's birth. "Well, then, we'll do the best we can and the good Lord will handle the rest. Now, let's see what needs a-doin'."

The woman looked uncomfortable, lying catawampus in the bed. Sylvia helped her straighten out and then eased her forward while she stuffed the pillows behind the woman's back for more support. "How close are the pains?"

"I don't know. Too close. My name is Fiona."

Sylvia smiled. "Nice to meet you, Fiona. Has your water broke yet?"

A tear squeezed out of Fiona's eye. She nodded, her lower lip trembling. "Just now. That's why I know it's time. Brett went for Doc Graham."

"I saw the doc not too long ago on the street. I'm sure your husband will round him up and get back here as fast as he can."

"Is Ma goin' to be all right?" the taller boy asked from his stance halfway up the stairs. He looked unsure as to whether he should come closer.

"What's your name?" Sylvia asked.

"Wyatt, ma'am."

"Well, Wyatt, I'm going to help your ma until the doctor comes. How about you watch out for him at the door with your brother? Let me know as soon as you see him coming."

The boy nodded and then, as his mother whimpered, he skedaddled down the stairs.

Sylvia found some folded sheets in the cabinet in the hall and brought them back into the room, closing the bedroom door behind her. She rushed to the bed as another pain gripped Fiona.

"You did better that time," she said, hoping it encouraged the woman.

"It helps, knowing you are here. I didn't want to be alone, but I had to be strong in front of my boys."

"I'll look out for them once the doc gets here." She folded the sheets and pushed them under Fiona so that she'd have a dry place to lie. Then she poured some water from the pitcher and handed her the glass. "Here. Sip this."

After Fiona had had a drink, Sylvia set the

glass aside. By Fiona's breathing, another pain was already building. Sylvia dipped a cloth into the water and wiped it over her forehead and cheeks, pushing back the strands of hair that clung to the sweat on her brow. "That's better. This baby will come into the world and see her mama looking pretty as a peach."

Fiona gripped Sylvia's hand as the pain worsened. When it passed and she'd relaxed, she smiled up at Sylvia. "You said 'her.' Do you think she will be a girl?"

Sylvia offered another sip of water. "That's what you want, ain't it?"

"Yes, although I suspect Brett will want a son." As Fiona said the word, she closed her eyes. "It's all happening so fast. I don't know how you came to be here, Sylvia, but thank you."

Heavy footsteps sounded downstairs and Sylvia started to rise. "That must be the doc now."

Fiona gripped her hand harder. "No. Stay. I—I want a woman with me. Someone who understands."

"But—your husband—"

"I'm here," Brett said, rushing to his wife's side. "I brought the doc."

Sylvia glanced over her shoulder to find that Nelson was already there. Both he and Brett looked surprised to see her. She didn't figure explanations were important at the moment. "Her water broke, Doc. And she says the pains are coming closer. They look to be strong."

"If you will move aside, Miss Marks, I will examine her."

"I want her to stay," Fiona said. "I want her to stay with me."

Sylvia moved back, unsure what she should do. She wanted to help this woman in her time, but she didn't want to be in the way. "I—I could watch the boys, if you wish."

"No," Fiona ground out as another pain gripped her middle. "Here. I want you here."

Brett Blackwell's face drained of all color.

"Brett, don't you dare pass out on me!" Nelson said. "Sit down!" He looked directly at Sylvia. "Close the door. Mrs. Blackwell doesn't need an audience."

She jumped at the order. He meant for her to leave? She glanced at Fiona. Her eyes were closed, but she had said she wanted a woman with her. Sylvia understood about that. It was how she felt when Tommy was born.

Conflicted as to whether to stay or go, she walked to the door, where the two youngsters peeked in with wide-open eyes. They looked to be close to Tommy's age. "Come on, boys. We'll get things ready for your new brother or sister."

She took them downstairs to the kitchen. She learned their names—Wyatt, the older one at eight years, and Rhett, who was six—and sent

Wyatt out to pump a bucketful of water from the well. She sat Rhett down at the table and gave him the chalk that she'd bought for Tommy, telling him he could draw on the tabletop. It wasn't a fancy table and she figured she could wash off the chalk pictures easy enough. It would give both boys something to do while things were happening all around them. When Wyatt returned with a full bucket, she set a pot of water on the stove to warm and filled the tin pitcher for coffee.

All the while, she listened for the squall of a newborn and sent up a prayer for a healthy baby and mother. She wanted to be with Fiona, but after all Nelson had done for her and Tommy, she also wanted to do as he asked.

Ten minutes later, Brett thundered down the steep stairs. He might be a huge bear of a man, but at the moment, his face was a greenish pasty white and he looked like a feather might knock him over. If he passed out, there would be no helping a man his size and it would scare the boys.

"Oh, my, Mr. Blackwell! Sit down!" She pulled out a chair for him. "I'll get you a cup of coffee."

He sat down but waved off the offering of coffee. "I don't feel gut."

She slid into the last chair at the table, watching him closely. "I see that."

He placed his big paw of a hand on her forearm. "Doc Graham vill take gut care of my Fiona. I vill see to the boys."

Did he mean that she was to leave? She swallowed. "All right."

"My wife asks for you. She says she needs you there."

Her heart thudded in her chest. Tears welled and burned behind her eyes. No one besides Tommy had ever needed her before. "Well, of course. I'll go up right now."

She poured the hot water into a bowl and carefully carried it up the stairs. Birthing was a messy business and eventually something or someone would need a good washing. She balanced the bowl carefully on her hip as she entered the room and then shut the door behind her.

Nelson gave her a quick nod as she pulled up a chair to Fiona's side. The woman looked spent, but when Sylvia took her hand, Fiona gripped it hard and smiled a tired smile up at her. "How is Brett?"

Sylvia leaned forward. "He made it downstairs to a chair. He's a bit shaky. But he's watching the boys—" She hesitated, then smiled. "Or maybe they are watching him."

"My Brett is a good man."

"Yes, he is," she murmured, marveling at how calm Nelson was. They were both good men. "We are here for you, Fiona. You've done it twice before, right? Your body knows just what to do." She chuckled. "Guess that's why it's so anxious to get going. You can do it."

"All right, Mrs. Blackwell," Nelson said. "If you feel the urge to push, go ahead. Nice and easy. Your baby is almost here."

Fiona arched her head back, straining, and then brought her head forward with the effort of pushing.

A thin, reedy cry split the air.

"Oh! Oh!" Fiona cried out. "Let me see! Let me hold it!"

Nelson cleared the mucus from the baby's pale face with a towel and then placed the infant on Fiona's abdomen. Quickly, Sylvia covered the baby with a cloth and began rubbing the moisture away. She stopped when she dried between the baby's legs.

"Why, Fiona, look! Look! It's a girl!" Sylvia cried out. "You did it! You have your girl!"

"And she is a big one for being a month early," Nelson said. "Looks like she will do fine. Baby girls tend to be fighters."

Fiona gathered her daughter to her, holding her close as tears leaked out of the corners of her eyes. Wonder and awe filled her gaze. "A girl! Who would have thought I'd have a daughter?"

It had been a long time since Sylvia had seen such love in a mother's gaze, but she knew how it felt. It was the same as when Tommy was born. It reminded her of the love she'd felt for her tiny son.

She took away the damp blanket and snuggled another dry one around the baby. "I'm glad to see you prepared for all this with all these cloths and fine blankets. Why, just look at her! She's already peeing! Don't that beat all?"

She grabbed another blanket and discarded the soiled one. "What name have you chosen for her?"

Fiona looked at Sylvia through her tears. "I was afraid to hope for a daughter! I thought choosing a name would ensure that I had a son, so I didn't choose."

"Well, it looks like you and Mr. Blackwell have some deciding to do," Sylvia said.

"Miss Marks, would you hand me that empty basin?" the doc said, indicating a bowl on the bureau. "Push once more, Mrs. Blackwell. A gentle push is all…"

Sylvia hurried to give it to him, watching with awe as Fiona expelled the afterbirth and then fell back onto her pillow. She took the basin from Nelson, covered it with a cloth and set it aside.

"This birthing is a messy business, ain't it? I'll have you cleaned up in no time. Here, take a sip of water. You look done in. Pretty—but done in."

She used the water she'd brought up the stairs to wash off every bit of Fiona she could and then found the woman's hairbrush on the bureau and brushed her hair back while Fiona held on to her new daughter and counted her fingers and toes and marveled at her nose and her delicate ears.

When Fiona settled onto clean dry sheets and began to nurse the baby, Sylvia suddenly felt as though the woman's need for her had dissipated. She backed up to the door.

"Thank you," Fiona said. "Having you here eased my fears. You've been a big help."

"I was glad of it. When I had my son, my neighbor came to be with me. We women, we have to help each other in times like this."

"Ahem." Nelson cleared his throat. "If you are ready, we will get Mr. Blackwell."

Fiona nodded.

Nelson stood and stretched his back. His gaze sought Sylvia's and held. "Why don't you do it?"

Her? He wanted her to do it? It would be an honor to tell Mr. Blackwell and the boys. She hurried down the stairs, knowing they were all anxious to hear the news.

She told Brett Blackwell only that his wife and baby were doing well, not whether he'd had a girl or boy. She figured that was Fiona's gift to him. She did hold the boys back for a minute so that the man could have a moment with his wife and new baby alone.

"Can we go up now?" Wyatt whined.

"It's time, I reckon."

As the boys scrambled up the stairs, making a beeline to their mother, they passed the doc on his way down. Nelson stopped at the bottom of the stairs with the table separating him from her. He had a strange look on his face as he addressed her. "Mrs. Blackwell urged me to thank you for her again. Between her cooing over her daughter, she is singing your praises."

Sylvia was still glorying on the inside. "It was a wonder. A new life. I was glad to help, glad to be a part of it."

"I believe you were." His green eyes captured hers. "I must ask, Sylvia… Have you ever done this sort of thing before? And I'm not talking about with your sheep. I'm talking about with women."

She shook her head. "Did I do something wrong?"

"Not at all." A smile spread across his face. "You were extremely helpful. I'm just astounded it came so naturally for you."

She shrugged as if it was a small thing. It wasn't. Inside, all that she'd seen, all that she'd done and the words Nelson said to her swirled together in an exhilarating state of fulfillment. "I'm just happy the baby and Fiona are fine. That's the important thing."

She looked about the small kitchen. Maybe she should make more than just coffee. "Seems like she's got plenty of help now, unless I could get her something to eat."

"That isn't necessary. Fiona expected Hannah White to be with her in her time. She wants me to inform her now. Hannah lived here for a short time with the Blackwells and knows her way around this kitchen."

"I wish I had known. I would have fetched her."

He shook his head. "No. You were the best thing for Fiona. You are what she needed."

His words made her glow on the inside. "I'm glad," she whispered. She'd done a good turn. She'd been useful. That meant a lot to her. Wouldn't Tommy be excited to hear the news!

The doc slipped his coat on and then collected his hat from the shelf near the door. "It was fortunate for her that you came by. Why did you, if you don't mind my asking?"

"Oh, that! Seems like a long time ago now. Clear on the other side of a life coming into the world!" She knew she was rambling a bit. Maybe a little giddy with all she'd seen and done. "I needed to see Mr. Blackwell about Berta's harness. I came looking for him. Guess I'll let it go for another week or so. He won't be wanting to do any work for a while. Not with a new baby."

He waited at the door. "Walk with me, won't you? We will inform Mrs. White and then I have something for you at my office."

"For me?" she asked, to be sure he hadn't misspoken.

"Well, actually, it is for Tommy."

"All right, then."

He held the door open for her, making her feel just like a princess. She knew it didn't mean anything. He probably did that for all women. But it had been a long time since anyone held a door for her and it was real special.

But then, as she passed by, he tugged her shawl up closer around her neck, brushing the skin on her neck. "The evening has a chill to it," he said.

Her heart skipped a beat. It was like lightning sizzled beneath his touch.

Chapter Fifteen

He was in shock. That was all there was to it. With no training, no preparation other than having had a baby herself, Sylvia had known instinctively what to do for Mrs. Blackwell.

Beside him walked the best assistant he'd come across. And, surprisingly, after a Sunday afternoon of games at her house, someone he considered a friend.

Two weeks ago, he would have scoffed at the idea. The difference in their social standing would have made friendship unlikely, if not impossible. Most people wouldn't look beyond the fact that Sylvia was a poor, unwed mother. They might have even considered her dangerous, since one of his first meetings with her involved her waving a firearm. To that, Nelson now had to add that she was intelligent, hardworking, kind and even fun.

They stopped at the Whites' home and he informed both Teddy and Hannah of the changes at the Blackwells'. That done, he and Sylvia continued to his office. He left her outside while he retrieved the crutches that he'd had Jackson make for Tommy. He carried them down his front steps and handed them to her.

"I'd hoped to get these to you sooner. However, my mother arrived and I couldn't get away."

Her eyes grew big as she turned one over in her hands. "It's mighty nice of you, but I can't accept these."

He'd been afraid of this. "Why not?"

"I can't pay for them."

"I'm not asking you to. They are a loan. When Tommy is done with them, you must bring them back to me. There will be other children who will need crutches in the future."

"Well…"

"Sylvia. He'll go farther using these. One day, he'll realize he doesn't need them anymore and then you can bring them back. Now, where is your wagon? At the livery?" He started that way.

She hurried to keep up with him. "In case you forgot, he's my son. I'm the one who decides things for him!"

"I'm his doctor. That trumps."

He knew his strides were too long for her,

but the day had been an eye-opener for him in more ways than one. What he thought he knew about her had been challenged time and again since their first meeting. She surprised him. Over and over.

Besides being weary of her stubbornness just now, he had also been in the mercantile with his mother and witnessed her embarrassment. He was angry at himself for not saying something, for not standing up for her, but he'd fully expected her to stand up for herself the way she always did with him. Instead, she had let Mrs. Gallagher cow her. After seeing that and then to be confronted with her efficiency and calmness as she took charge at Mrs. Blackwell's delivery of her baby—well, the whole of her simply equaled more than any of the parts taken separately. People had misjudged her.

He cared about her. And he didn't like others belittling or judging her. She deserved a chance at life that wasn't just about existing. She was smart and full of common sense. He didn't want others brushing her off as insignificant. He especially didn't want her to believe that about herself. She was so much more.

"All right! All right! Have it your way!" came her breathless cry behind him.

He stopped and turned around. Twenty feet away, Sylvia had doubled over, clutching her side as she laughed. "Wait! Wait! I got a hitch in my git-along. I know you mean well, but you sure have an irritating way of showing it."

She looked funny bent over like that, and besides that, her laughter was contagious. When she caught her breath and straightened, her face was flushed and her eyes sparkled. He struggled to hold in a smile. Did she have any idea how vibrant she looked at that moment?

"It's right there." She pointed to her dilapidated wagon in front of the smithy.

He settled the crutches into the back next to her other goods.

"Where is Tommy?"

"He's staying with my neighbor."

"Then how about having supper with me? It's the least I can do after all your help with Mrs. Blackwell. You could meet my mother."

The joy left her eyes, as well as the sparkle. "That ain't such a good idea. It's best that I get back home."

He grabbed his hat from his head. He really wanted her to stay. She deserved a moment of rest. A moment where someone did something for her for a change. "Sylvia—just for a short while."

She cocked her head, a furrow between her brows. "You shouldn't call me that. Not here on the street."

After all they had been through together, the fact that she challenged his desire to use her given name struck him as ludicrous. "After being kidnapped, isn't a first-name basis what comes next? I'm sure there is an etiquette book on the matter."

"Now you're just teasing me." She let out a huff. "Guess you have a point there with the kidnapping and all, but..." She looked down at the dirt. "And I don't mind so much. But—it ain't right. It ain't proper. People would think..." Her voice trailed off.

He stepped closer. "People would think what?"

"It just ain't a good idea is all."

"Look, *Sylvia.*" He raised her chin with his fingertips and stared into brown eyes so dark and stormy and pretty that they took his breath away. "I happen to care about you and what happens to you and your son. You are letting a fraction of the people of this town dictate your life and the others you close out and don't let in. If they knew you like I do..."

She puffed up like an angry hen. "How do you know anything about me? You haven't been here long enough to know what it's like to have people look at you like you don't count."

He wanted to hold her. His fingers itched to draw her to him and hold her until all the fight and all the pain drained out of her. "Let me help you. You are letting them have too much power over you. I don't like to see you hurting!"

She jerked from his touch. "Then leave me

be about it! Words hurt!" She glared at him, her fingers curled into fists.

"I know they do. Even lack of words hurt and that's something I've had to live with a good deal of my life."

"Then can't you see? I don't want people saying things about you that ain't true."

He didn't care about himself. He was worried about her. "Me? That's not going to happen." He frowned. "You don't mention yourself."

She lowered her gaze to the ground. "Folks already got that part set."

He didn't like hearing her put herself down. "Mrs. Blackwell didn't make you feel that way."

"She's new in town and don't know…"

He'd had enough. It was a simple thing. He'd had dinner with Miss O'Rourke without trouble. It would be the same with Sylvia. If she just pushed back a little…gently…the whole town would come to embrace her. "Come to the restaurant. Take the first step. I'll be with you."

She stared at him and for a moment her face filled with longing. "I'd surely like to have a meal at a fine restaurant. It'd be something." She looked down at her hands, her cheeks flushing. "More'n that, it'd be something going in there with you. I'd be proud to be on your arm."

Her soft admission stirred something deep inside him. "I'd be honored to have you accompany me." Did that mean yes? Was she wavering?

She let out a sigh and then climbed into the wagon.

"Sylvia? What are you doing?" He moved closer.

"Thank you for inviting me. Like I said, it'd be something."

He frowned and covered her hand that rested on the brake lever with his own. He didn't want her to go. Not yet. Not like this.

"You gotta understand how things are. I don't belong here."

"You do as much as anyone. You deserve happiness, and help with Tommy, and a kind word from Mrs. Gallagher."

She went still. "What do you know about Mrs. Gallagher?"

"I know it wasn't right how she spoke to you today."

Her eyes widened. "You were there? You saw?"

"I should have said something. I'm sorry I didn't."

She let out a shuddery breath. "You were there?" she repeated. She untied the reins from the brake lever. Tears pooled in her eyes. "I gotta go. Get up, Berta. Let's go home."

Adele had been right when she'd said rain was coming. No sooner had Sylvia collected Tommy than the sky started spitting. A steady drizzle

commenced on the ride home and she had to pull
the tarp over them at the last. She unhitched the
wagon and settled the mule in the shed while
outside the weather brooded with its rumbling
thunder and darkening sky.

Why was it, when a body had a good and a
bad thing happen, it was always the bad thing
that claimed residence inside and blocked out
the good? It was just like the dark clouds that
blocked out the last of the sun the way Mrs. Gallagher's hurtful treatment blocked out all the
good that had happened with Fiona.

But nothing could block out what had happened with Nelson. He'd been proud of her! She
could see it in his eyes and feel it inside herself.
Her heart had near pounded out of her breast.
In all her life that had never happened. He made
her feel strong, and courageous, and full of hope,
as if nothing could keep her down. And he'd
done it with just a word, just a glance, just a
touch. She had wanted to say yes to his invitation in the worst way.

She leaned against the wagon, put her forehead in the crook of her arm and gave in to the
turmoil happening inside her. The day had been
surprising in so many ways. Nelson cared about
her. And he had caressed her. His hand had lingered on her neck. Even now her skin tingled
as she thought of it.

A longing welled up inside that she knew she

had no right to. Her insides curled in on her as she thought of his handsome face and his strength. It had been a long time since Thomas held her, but she remembered how it felt. To have a man like Nelson care for her the way a man does a woman was beyond any commonsense hope at all. For that feeling to grow into love was too far a leap for a woman such as herself to imagine. She would be content with his friendship, his kindness and nothing more.

On the roof overhead, the rain pounded harder. Lightning crackled and lit up the sky outside, the bright flash illuminating the yard. Berta stomped and brayed, and the rooster crowed. Sylvia gave Tommy the crutches, threw the tarp over their heads and rushed across the yard to the cabin.

Chapter Sixteen

The rain kept on for days.

The yard turned to a soupy, muddy mess that Sylvia had to traipse across twice a day to see to the animals—her two sheep, Penny the goat and Berta. She was glad that she'd bought extra oats the last time in town, since she wasn't turning them out to graze. The chickens squawked and flapped their wings frantically whenever she entered the shed, as if she could do something about the weather even though they were the driest of the lot, roosting as they were atop a few high stacks of straw.

And still the rain came down.

She played games with Tommy until her eyes crossed. He practiced bearing weight on his injured leg several times a day and walked with the help of his new crutches. Every day he went a little farther, refusing to let go of the crutches, and she began to worry that he'd forget how to walk without them, which was probably a sign she was worrying too much and needed a heavy dose of sunshine.

She set out buckets and pans to catch the muddy drops of rain that tunneled through the sod roof. Sturdy beams supported the sod overhead, but even so, this was the third roof that she'd had to put over the beams. Once the weather cleared, this one would require patching. She only hoped the roof would hold and not come crashing down in their sleep.

They were making pancakes for supper on the fourth day of rain when Tommy yelled.

"Ma! Look!"

A pool of water moved over the threshold and spread ominously toward them both, flowing into the dips in the dirt floor.

"Get away from the door!" she cried out, afraid he'd slip and hurt his leg further.

Fear sprang into his eyes. She'd have to calm her voice so as not to scare him. Quickly, she rolled up the braided rag rug and set it on her bed so it wouldn't get soaked.

"We can't stay any longer. We gotta get out of here. Get your coat on." She shrugged into Thomas's long leather one. She'd given up wearing his boots two days ago when the mud had sucked them off her feet while she'd crossed the yard. She grabbed her money sock and stuffed it in her pocket.

The water kept coming. It flowed toward the hearth at the same time that she realized the fire there still burned. She grabbed a pan half-filled with muddy water from a leak in the roof and doused the fire. She picked up Tommy and set him on the table. "Ready? Climb on my back and hold on tight. Don't let go of your crutches."

Once she had a solid hold of him, she opened the door and waded across the yard toward the shed. Tommy clambered up into the wagon while she hitched up Berta. She set a board from the wagon bed to the ground and led the goat up it without any trouble and handed the lead line to Tommy. The sheep were another matter. Try as she might, the sheep balked and jumped off the ramp to the ground each time. They were too big for her to pick up and set in the wagon, so after several attempts, she gave up. She gave them both a huge scoop of feed.

"What are you doin', Ma?" Tommy asked.

"They'll have to be on their own for a few days, until we can come back."

"Will they be all right? What about the coyotes?"

"They won't be worrying about finding food." She searched the shed one last time before climbing up to the wagon seat. "Hang on tight now."

She snapped the reins and drove Berta out into the storm.

The DuBois farm was farther back from the river and usually weathered a downpour better than her place. The road was treacherous, with the mud sucking at the wagon wheels. As she approached the creek, her heart sank in her chest. The dip that separated their two homesteads had turned into a raging river. She stopped the wagon and stared at the expanse of water that separated her from the road on the far side.

The wagon shifted, sliding sideways.

"Hold on!" She grabbed her son, steadying him.

Again, the wagon shifted and then started to settle. They couldn't stay here! They'd slide into the water and be stuck for good!

Handing the reins to Tommy, she climbed down and grabbed Berta by the bridle, tugging her around, forcing her to struggle out of the soft ground. Mud squeezed through the holes in her boots and inside between her toes. She only hoped no snake came calling. That'd be more than she could handle.

Finally, she got everything turned and climbed back into the wagon. What to do? The only way now to higher ground was to get across to the other side of the river and away from the buffalo wallows. She reined Berta toward the ferry crossing.

When she arrived, she said a prayer of thanks that the ferry was on her side of the river. Then she stared in shock at the rope that spanned across to the other side. Usually, it hung four feet above the water's surface. Now it dipped with but a few inches at most between it and the river. Her heart hammered inside. It would be dangerous to cross.. but more dangerous to stay on this side.

She climbed down and led Berta carefully onto the wooden ferry. The large raft heaved and shuddered with the rush of the river. Was she a fool to try this? Or more a fool not to? Berta brayed and she jerked her head up, her eyes large and frightened.

"There, there, girl. We'll make it. Just you stay calm."

She called over the mule's head to Tommy. "Lie down in the bed. Hang on to that goat and the wagon too, tight as you can."

She worked the loop of the tether line over the stump to free the raft, a difficult thing with the water tugging and pulling at the ferry every second. It was a wonder that the ferry hadn't broken loose and traveled downriver on its own, before this.

Immediately on being freed, the current ripped the ferry away from the shore. She gripped the line hard, struggling against the pull of the current as they neared the center of

the river. The water raced faster here than near
the shore. Debris washed from the banks and
rushed along helter-skelter in the water, coming up against the ferry, pushing and shoving it.

Her arms ached. The rope rubbed her palms
and fingers raw. The wind and water whipped
and tossed the small raft like a toy. They were
almost there—only two feet from the bank—
when a young, uprooted sapling rushed toward
them. She yelled at Tommy, "Hold on!"

The impact jarred the raft, yanking the rope
from her hands. At the same time, the goat
pulled from Tommy's arms. "Penny!" He started
after her.

"No!" Sylvia screamed and scrambled toward
him. Just as she grabbed him, the raft heaved
up violently and spilled them into the water. She
fought to keep Tommy's head above the water
while fighting the current. It wanted to suck her
and her son back toward the center of the river.
Finally, her feet scraped against the bottom.
She grabbed the wet weeds that grew along the
bank and pushed Tommy up toward the higher
ground. He struggled up the steep slope and
turned, waiting for her.

Her arms were so tired and the coat she wore
had filled with water and tugged at her. She
slipped her arms from the sleeves and let the
water carry it away, only to realize too late that
her money was in the pocket. She gripped the

grass along the bank and tried once more to pull herself up. Her feet kept sliding backward and getting mired in the mud.

"Ma!" She heard Tommy cry out. "Ma!"

Chapter Seventeen

The spring rains hammered Oak Grove. At first, Wally Brown, and even the mayor, had downplayed the amount of rain, explaining that farmers and ranchers could use a soaking now and then. The crops would be better for it come planting time in a few weeks.

Nelson was concerned for Sylvia and Tommy until someone told him the DuBois farm was on the highest land in that area. He remembered Sylvia talking about the family there. She might not leave her homestead for her own sake, but he had no doubt she would go there if there was any doubt of Tommy's safety.

Things between him and his mother had settled into a stiff formality. He needed to talk to her, but he kept putting it off. For someone who prided himself in facing things head-on, this was one area where he hesitated.

On the afternoon of the fifth cold day of constant rain, he returned to his office after checking on Mrs. Blackwell and her new baby. He met Miss Pratt at his door. She followed him up the steps to the porch, and once she was under the overhang, she shook out her umbrella, in her zeal, forcing the droplets all over him.

"You said you would visit. I've come to question your absence."

Her usual blunt manner once again. "I've been busy. You probably heard that my mother is visiting."

"I thought that might have something to do with it." She sighed. "Well, I had to get away from the hotel for a spell. Mr. Austin has given his empty rooms—the last four in the hotel to families who could not return to their homes because of the flooding. The entire hotel is rank with the odor of wet, dirty clothes."

That bothered him. He should go out to Sylvia's place and check on her and Tommy. He needed to know they were all right.

He opened the door for Miss Pratt as it seemed she was determined to visit. Hopefully, his mother would awaken from her nap upstairs and curtail any length of stay longer than thirty minutes. He shrugged from his coat and hung it and his hat on the wall peg. A shiver coursed through him. "I could use a cup of tea. I'll make us both one."

A rumbling cough sounded from the direction of his exam room. The office had been empty when he'd left for the Blackwell's home.

"Excuse me. I need to see who is here."

He left her, not caring that he'd been abrupt. Actually, he was happy for the interruption. He heard the front door close with a decided click as he headed into the other room. Josiah sat in a chair by the wall.

"What can I do for you, Mayor?"

"This cough has kept me up for the past two nights."

"A common occurrence this time of year." He examined the mayor. When he went to get a bottle of tonic for the man, he realized he had run out of stock. He searched his inventory for a substitute, sliding bottles and jars aside, and then spied the honey from Sylvia. He measured a few ingredients into a portion of the honey, then put the pot on the stove.

After a few minutes, the mayor walked into the kitchen. "You and Miss Pratt? She didn't sound happy with you as she left. I believe that was just short of slamming the door."

"After a few conversations, I've decided that Miss Pratt and I do not complement each other well."

"Then I'm afraid you better work fast, Nelson. Since you've discounted Miss Simcock, the only woman left is Miss Weber and she has a swarm of admirers. The one thing on your side is that she is so busy helping at the hotel with the influx of people that she hasn't had a chance to narrow down her choice of suitor."

Why did the thought of another round of questioning and getting to know one more "bride" sound so unappealing? Miss Weber might make a great helpmeet, but after three unsuccessful attempts, he wearied of finding the right woman to fit into his life.

"I'll let the tonic cool. Then I'll bottle it for you," he said. He moved the pan of medicinal syrup off the stove. "Miss Pratt said the hotel is filling with people whose farms are flooded."

Josiah coughed. "It's bad. Worst I've seen since moving here. I may have to open up the new town hall as a shelter if more families come in from their land."

"Where are their farms?"

"On the south side of the river."

His chest tightened. He should have listened to what his gut told him and checked on Sylvia and Tommy two days ago. Instead, he'd let the words of others lull him into inaction.

He bottled the tonic for Josiah and sent him on his way. Then he took the stairs two at a time and knocked on his mother's door.

She answered, holding a ball of yarn and knitting needles. "Has Mayor Melbourne gone? I wasn't sure if I should sit with him when you aren't here."

"Yes. He's gone." He glanced beyond her at the rumpled bedcovers. She wasn't sleeping well. "I'm sorry if it was awkward for you. I don't expect you to manage my medical business. You are still getting over the loss of your husband."

"We still haven't discussed that. We need to."

"Not now. I'm heading out."

She glanced out the window. "But it will be dark soon!"

"Suddenly worried for me, Mother?" He couldn't resist the barb.

Her eyes filled with pain and then shuttered down.

Remorse pinched him. "People are hurting from all this rain and the river is up. There's someone I need to check on." He turned from her and headed down the stairs.

In the livery, he saddled his gelding, mounted and urged the horse into a gallop toward the river. The rain had let up in the past hour, which made the going easier, although the ground was still soft. At the river, he slowed. Across the expanse of water, one hundred yards away, the opposite bank had disappeared and vast fingers of water stretched across the land.

He rounded the bend that sheltered the ferry landing.

It was completely gone.

Chapter Eighteen

Nelson woke at first light. Restless dreams had plagued him through the night. He'd returned to town after finding the ferry landing gone and alerted Sheriff Baniff and the mayor. He'd also let Jackson Miller know. The carpenter would want to get started on another landing as soon as possible. Once the water receded, the farmers and ranchers staying at the hotel would want to get back to their land to see what had become of it and their livestock.

He parted his bedroom curtains. Bright sunlight streamed through the window. The clouds were gone.

He dressed and descended the stairs. A group of men planned to ride out this morning and check the damage. He would go with them. Sylvia was uppermost on his mind. He hoped she was safe and warm at the DuBois place.

His mother came down the stairs. It was unusual for her to be up this early. In Boston, she usually had tea and toast in bed before she started her day. Her long, dark hair, streaked with a small amount of silver at her temples, fell down her back in a loose braid and she still wore her robe. She filled the teakettle with water and set it on the stove. "You're up early."

"Couldn't sleep. I...have a patient, a young boy. Guess I'm worried about him and his mother."

"Surely his father saw them to safety, dear."

He met her gaze. "No father. No husband. Tommy's fatherless."

Like me.

He didn't say the words, but the accusation hung between them with the same force as if he had. His mother clamped her mouth shut and turned away from him. Her hands shook as she readjusted the kettle over the burner plate. A moment later she walked from the kitchen.

He blew out a breath. He was taking his anger out on her, when he didn't know the whole story. He hadn't let her explain past that first horrible day when she'd first arrived. He followed after her. "Mother—"

She took hold of the front doorknob.

She wasn't going to run out into the road in her robe, was she? "Mother! Stop!"

She did stop. Fast. She nearly tripped over a body lying on the porch.

Nelson grabbed her arm to steady her. He peered over her shoulder at the boy sprawled across the three steps to his porch. It was Tommy and he was deathly pale.

Nelson's gut clenched. "Get a blanket, Mother. Please."

He crouched down. "Tommy! What happened? Where's your mother?"

Tommy moaned.

Nelson gathered him in his arms. Tommy shivered violently and curled into him. Nelson had to get him warmed up.

"Here," his mother said. She hadn't left to get a blanket. Instead, she had removed her robe and now pushed it around the boy.

He was shocked. And gratified. "Get inside, Mother. I don't want you sick too."

He started for the exam room and then thought a bed made better sense. Carrying Tommy upstairs, he laid him down in his own bed. The boy had lost one boot. Nelson removed the other one and then removed the boy's damp shirt and pants. He piled the blankets on top, tucking them in all around.

Tommy moaned and slowly opened his eyes.

"Where is your mother?" Nelson asked.

Big tears gathered in Tommy's eyes. "I couldn't get her to move."

Nelson took him by his small shoulders. "Tell me where she is. Where did you leave her?" She would never leave her son on his own like this if she had one ounce of strength left in her. He was sure of it. His heart pounded. She could be hurt. Or worse. "Talk to me, Tommy. I'll go get her. I'll get your mother."

Tommy's chin trembled. "The river."

Please let it be this side. "I'll go."

Tommy's expression calmed. He turned into the pillow, grasping it with his small hand.

Nelson's mother entered the room. She had taken a moment to dress.

"This is my mother. She'll look after you. Stay here! Do you understand?"

Tommy gave a slight nod.

"Please be careful, son," his mother said quietly.

Nelson raced down the stairs, grabbed his coat and hat, and rushed out the door, heading for the livery.

A dun-colored horse stood tied to the railing outside—saddle and all. He undid the tether and mounted.

"Wait, Doc!" Wally ran out from inside the stable. "You can't take that one. That horse is for Mr. White."

"I can't wait. Miss Marks is missing. I found

her son on my steps just now." With that, he reined toward the river. "Teddy can use my horse." He kicked the horse into a gallop.

He kept his eyes peeled for any sign of Sylvia along the trail. The soggy ground and mashed-over prairie grass would surely offer up a sign of her. She might be at the river, but she could have moved. Not knowing frustrated him beyond rational thought. He had to find her! Tommy needed her! He…he needed her!

The thought settled inside. He needed her. He couldn't analyze his thoughts now. He couldn't think. All he could do was answer the pounding need inside to find her.

At the river, the water rushed by, but telltale signs told him it was now receding. Mud and brush from farther upstream lodged against small stubborn outcroppings of the bank that had refused to wash away in the deluge.

He let out a shaky breath. Tommy's ankle wasn't completely healed. How had the boy managed to cross the river and make it into town? That miracle was Nelson's only hope that another had happened too—that he'd find Sylvia alive.

He turned the horse downstream. They passed the ferry landing and traveled farther, continuing to search. Sylvia might be difficult to see if she was covered with mud. If she wore that drab brown skirt of hers—and it hadn't pulled her under the water—she'd be doubly hard to spot. He vowed to himself that when he found her, he would burn that skirt and get her one that was as bright as her spirit—something yellow or pink. And he wouldn't let her talk her way out of accepting it.

He heard a high-pitched cry. Inhuman, yet vaguely familiar. It sounded again This time he recognized it. The bleat of a sheep or a goat.

He dismounted and rushed to the bank's edge. There, half submerged in the water, was Sylvia. She lay on a sandbar with her goat lying against her side, its tether rope tangled around her arm and upper body.

He scrambled down to her and dropped to his knees. "Sylvia!" He shook her shoulder. There was no response. He put his ear to her chest and heard the steady, slow beat of her heart. He felt the rise and fall of her chest as she breathed.

Her skin was ice-cold except for the side that the goat had snuggled up against—a miracle in itself. The goat's warmth had probably protected her from further exposure to cold.

He untangled the rope from around her, deeply aware of how pale she was. Her skin had a blue cast around her fingertips and mouth. "You stubborn, stubborn woman!" He wanted to berate her for waiting until the last minute to leave her land, for scaring him nearly to death, for any number of things. Instead, he gathered her to him and held her tight. Thank God he'd found her. She was numbed with exposure, but alive.

He buried his face in the crook of her cold neck and breathed, wanting his warmth to transfer to her. He marveled in the steady pulse he felt against his lips.

She tensed and then shuddered.

He drew back.

She stared at him, unfocused and bewildered. "Nelson?"

The pounding in his chest settled to a slower rhythm. "Yes."

"You sure are a fine dream," she said on a sigh. Her eyes closed again and she relaxed into his arms.

"Just like a woman to faint when I want her help," he said, his voice gruff. He meant it as a joke, remembering for a moment Miss Vandersohn. Sylvia was so very different. Sylvia wouldn't *allow* herself to faint—not until she was sure Tommy was safe, not until Miss Blackwell's baby was delivered and both mother and baby were safe, and not until Wally Brown was looked after. And here the woman had fainted. In his arms.

Staring down at her, he didn't care what she did, only that she was alive. He hugged her to him once more.

Then he gathered her to him once again, trying to breathe his warmth, his strength into her. "Oh, Sylvia. What am I going to do with you?"

The goat, freed now, ran up the bank and bleated in answer.

Nelson shrugged out of his coat and wrapped it around Sylvia, then scooped her up into his arms. He settled her onto his horse and then mounted, pulling her back against him. She relaxed, her head resting against his chest as she exhaled— a sound that was at once contented and trusting.

He'd never heard anything so beautiful.

Surprisingly, the goat followed them all the way back to town.

"Catch the goat," he said as Wally came running out of the livery to grab the horse. Nelson dismounted and carried Sylvia to his house, surprised to see Miss Pratt open the door for him and Miss Weber standing in the parlor.

"Miss Pratt? If you would be so kind as to turn down the covers in the room upstairs—"

Her eyes widened in shock. "Surely—"

"Sylvia is getting heavier by the moment," he said, interrupting her.

Miss Pratt bustled up the stairs.

He followed, depositing Sylvia on the bed.

"Really, Dr. Graham. You must realize how inappropriate this is." Miss Pratt pursed her lips.

"I don't see a problem. My mother is here.

The hotel beds are all occupied and, considering the height of the river, they will be for some time. This is the most logical place for Miss Marks to stay. She needs to have her wet things removed immediately. Warming her is of the utmost importance."

Miss Pratt's mouth fell open. "Surely you aren't suggesting that I participate in this? It would be tantamount to saying that I approve she stay here!"

"Then I thank you for your help." He unwrapped his coat from Sylvia's shoulders.

"I saw her eyes open. She's listening. Surely she can remove her own clothes."

He straightened and turned to the woman. "She's exhausted. She held on, all night as far as I can figure, to a piece of timber and a goat, in order not to be washed away downriver. Her energy is spent. She deserves our help, not a lecture!" His voice grew louder with each word from his mouth.

As he moved to the end of the bed to remove her shoes, Miss Weber came to the doorway with a tray. "I have a hot cup of tea for her, Doctor. And there is one on the stove for you as well."

"You can set it there," he grumbled, with a tilt of his chin indicating a bedside table. He turned back to Sylvia and removed one of her stockings that had fallen around her ankle.

Miss Pratt huffed.

"You can either help or leave, Miss Pratt. I won't have you standing there making noises as I work. This woman needs to get warm."

She spun on her foot and headed down the stairs.

He reached for the other stocking, the top past her knee. How that had managed to stay up at all was an ironic mystery. He would have to remember to tell Sylvia. She'd find it funny—or perhaps odd—later on.

Miss Weber reached out with her hand and stopped him. "I'll do it, Dr. Graham. And I'll sit with her for a while."

He wanted to stay but understood the wisdom in her words. "I do need to check on my other patient. Tommy will want to know that I found his mother."

Miss Weber smiled gently, understanding in her eyes. "I'll let you know when she awakens."

He stepped across the hallway and opened the door to his bedroom. Tommy lay snuggled down in his bed, fast asleep. Nelson's mother rose from her chair at the boy's side and came to the door, a finger to her lips.

"I gave him a few bites of porridge, then he fell asleep and hasn't woken again. He will need a bath when he wakes. The poor thing is filthy from head to toe."

Nelson wanted to check Tommy's wound but

thought for now sleep was more important. "He injured his ankle a few weeks ago. He probably had to stumble along, and even crawl now and then, to get here."

"Were the crutches you had in the hallway meant for him?"

Nelson nodded. "I'm sure they are lost to the river now."

She turned from him to take her seat again and keep watch.

He had to make things right. He took a deep breath. "Mother, what I said before… It was rude. I was angry."

"You still are."

"You're right. We should talk about things."

"I'd like that. Whenever you are ready."

His conscience eased at her words. The pressure inside that had been there since he'd learned of Ellison's passing lessened. He nodded.

Chapter Nineteen

~~~

Sylvia awoke in a strange bed, a strange room and a strange house. A woman she didn't recognize sat beside the bed, her head resting against the straight-backed chair. Her chestnut-brown hair was swept back and fashioned in a pretty knot, with the ends of a plaid bow at her nape, dangling over her lace collar. The young woman watched her steadily through wire-rimmed glasses.

"I'm Victoria Weber. How are you feeling?"

"Tommy?"

"He is here, and recovered from his ordeal. He will be glad to see you awake." She stood. "I promised the doctor that I would let him know when you woke."

"Nelson?" she asked quickly and then tried to

bite the word off. She should have said "Doc."
She felt her cheeks warm.

Miss Weber smiled. "You *are* feeling better."

"But—where am I?"

"At Dr. Graham's."

The implications of that troubled her. She remembered a dream about him. Had there been a kiss? The memory of him holding her, burrowing his face in her neck, came back full force. Had that really happened? "How long?"

"Since early this morning."

She turned toward the window. Pink-and-orange clouds streaked across the sky. The sun was setting.

"Do you remember what happened?" Miss Weber asked.

"Some."

"I'm sure it will come back to you. I'll get Dr. Graham. You just rest."

The woman left, leaving the door ajar. Sylvia heard voices that sounded from far off. Downstairs? Footsteps sounded—a step and a shuffle, step and a shuffle. She struggled to sit up, surprised at how difficult it was to move. Her arms—every part of her body—felt heavy and sore. Halfway through her struggle, the door burst open.

Tommy rushed in. "Ma! You're awake!" He lunged for the bedframe, grasping it for support, and then climbed up onto the high bed, crawling to get to her.

She circled him with her arms and hugged him tight.

He grimaced.

"What is it?" she asked, immediately loosening her hold.

"I made it all the way here, Ma! I scraped my knees good, but I got here."

She smoothed back the hair from his brow. "All the way from the river with your sore leg? That's a wonder, Tommy! I'm so proud of you. You are one strong boy." She hugged him to her again. Tears welled up and spilled from her eyes. He was safe!

"Well, it is good to see you awake," Nelson said.

He stood in the doorway looking tired and worn and very dear. His thick dark brown hair stood on end, tousled as though he'd run his hands through it every which way, and there were shadows beneath his eyes. His clothes were rumpled and caked with mud—a complete mess.

She wasn't sure what from her memories was true and what was a dream. Heat rose up her cheeks. Guess she'd just better keep still about any of it. One thing she was sure of—*he* was the one who had found her. *He* was the one who had brought her here. "Hello, Doc."

He came to the side of the bed and brushed

the hair from her forehead. "You sure gave us a scare. Let me help you sit up."

He took hold of her under her arms and dragged her up to a higher sitting position. Then he wedged an extra pillow behind her back. It seemed he held on to her longer than was necessary. She didn't mind a bit.

As he backed away, she realized that she was clean and clothed in a soft ivory nightdress. Where had that come from? And where were her clothes? Her cheeks flamed more. No one had ever taken care of her, except when she'd had Tommy. That had been a long time ago. And that had been Adele—a woman she knew.

Miss Weber came into the room. "Sadie brought a crock of soup over from the restaurant. I'll run downstairs and get a bowl for you."

Sylvia nodded in mute amazement.

"Miss Weber is one of the women from the train. She's been a big help."

She should be happy about it. He needed to find a good woman to help him in the office and this Miss Weber seemed to be making herself at home. She swallowed. "I guess she's the one who cleaned me up and gave me this soft gown. She seems real nice."

"She is nice."

Sylvia pressed her lips together. "Well, then. Looks like she might be just what you need."

"Could be," Doc said. He looked at her kind of funny, like he was perturbed with her.

That look had an awful lot of longing in it. Thomas had looked at her in just such a way a long time ago. So long ago now that she had buried it deep inside. It had hurt to think on things that it conjured up, things she knew were over for her. The look in the doc's eyes brought it all back and made her yearn again for things. She drew in a slow, deep breath to quiet her insides and lowered her gaze to Tommy. She kissed the top of his head. "You smell all soapy clean, son. Somebody got you to take a bath after you already had one in the river?" She said it teasingly. She ran her finger under the strap of his new suspenders. The shirt he wore, however, wasn't new. "These aren't your clothes."

"Doc Graham got them for me!"

"Mrs. Blackwell lent them," Nelson said. "Wyatt has grown out of them and Rhett hasn't grown into them yet. She is happy to let Tommy use them."

Sylvia swallowed. "That's real kind of her. I'll make sure to thank her."

Miss Weber entered with a tray and a bowl of soup upon it. Tommy moved off the bed, and she placed the tray on Sylvia's lap. Her stomach rumbled at the scent of rich chicken broth and noodles.

"Sylvia? How do you feel?"

He'd used her given name right in front of Miss Weber! "Plum tuckered out."

"You've been through a lot. You will stay here for tonight."

"Oh, Doc!" She nearly spilled her soup. "I can't do that! It's stopped raining now. I can go home…" She frowned, remembering suddenly that with the ferry gone, she couldn't get back across the river. "I'm not real sure how at the moment, but I'll figure something out."

"No. You'll stay here. Tommy too. As long as you need to until you have your strength back."

She glanced at Miss Weber. What must she think! "Doc—it ain't proper."

"There's no room at the hotel. It's filled with others, just like you, who had to escape the flooding. I wouldn't want to leave you alone there anyway. You need looking after. For one night, anyway." His expression softened. "Perhaps you have forgotten that my mother is here. That should satisfy your worries."

She nodded. "Guess there's no place for me to go."

"Then it's settled." He motioned to Tommy to scoot from the room. "Miss Weber? Will you take Tommy downstairs? I'll bring the tray when Sylvia is finished."

"Certainly."

Sylvia reached to hug her son. That done, she sank back against the fluffy pillow. The sound of Miss Weber's footsteps faded down the stairs with Tommy's awkward gait that favored his injury.

"You are mighty bossy, telling me where I must stay."

He shrugged and sat down on the bed beside her. "I'm the one who found you. Besides that, I'm your doctor now and doctors do get bossy when their patients don't have the common sense to follow orders." He took her hand in his and covered it with his other hand.

Her breath caught as tingles raced up her arm.

"I thought you'd drowned," he said, his voice hoarse with concern. "I thought the river had taken you."

This was a side of the doc she'd never seen before. He'd worried for her that much?

"I'm here. I'm safe. 'Cause of Tommy getting to you and then you coming for me." With her free hand, she reached for him, wanting to ease the worry and the tension she sensed in him. "I'm gonna be fine. And I thank you from the bottom of my heart for coming to find me."

He caught her hand and brought it to his lips.

The tray on her lap tilted and the bowl of soup started to slide. She drew back quickly, grasping the bowl. "Guess I better be still."

He smiled. "I rode out yesterday afternoon to collect you and Tommy. I got as far as the ferry landing and realized it was gone. The water had spilled over the banks on your side of the river. I hated myself for waiting so long to check on you. I knew, deep down, that you wouldn't leave your land until the last possible moment." He swallowed. "I hated not knowing whether you were safe."

"It wasn't your place to—" She stopped at the frustrated look he gave her.

"Don't tell me I shouldn't have worried. You're stubborn to a fault about that land of yours. What finally made you leave?"

"Well...the water came under the door. I figured it was time to get out."

"You couldn't make it to the DuBoises'?"

"Not with the lake between our farms."

He raked his fingers through his hair.

"What is it?" she asked. She took his hand. "What is it?"

He stared at her hand holding his, then raised his gaze to hers. "I never want to feel that helpless ever again."

Guess there wasn't a need to say anything to that. He was a man used to being in charge, used to bossing people around and fixing their ailments. It humbled her, that he cared so much for her and Tommy.

He picked up her spoon, dipped it into the soup and brought it to her lips.

"I can feed myself."

"I know." His eyes were saying a lot more than his response.

She took the spoon into her mouth. The soup was tepid. It probably tasted wonderful. She couldn't much tell with the way he looked at her and stole her breath away.

She didn't trust herself with him so near. "I'll do it. You need to sit over there." With her chin, she pointed to the chair by the window.

"I'm too close?"

"Yes," she whispered. And too handsome, and too charming, and too… She squeezed her eyes shut. She couldn't *think* with him so near.

"All right. You've been through an ordeal." He handed her the spoon back and then he stood. "You scared the life out of me. Never, ever, scare me like that again." He leaned down and kissed her forehead.

Something fluttered in her chest. "I have a feeling that you don't go around kissing your other patients."

He stepped back from the bed. "You're right."

"Son?" An older woman stood at the door. She had dark hair with silver streaks running through it, pulled up and back in a simple knot at the back of her head. Small black shiny earrings decorated her earlobes.

"Come in, Mother. I'll introduce you."

She carried herself stiff and proper as she stepped into the room. Sylvia thought she was beautiful and elegant all at once. Her embroidered black silk dress rustled as she moved to the side of the bed. "I thought I'd better check on things. You've been up here for a while."

The doc's mouth tightened.

"I'd like you to meet Sylvia Marks, Tommy's mother. Sylvia, this is my mother, Mrs. Judith Graham."

The woman spoke, her voice cultured and low and...cold. "Miss Marks. A pleasure."

Sylvia dipped her head. "Hello, ma'am."

Nelson looked from his mother to her. "In the morning, Miller and a few others are heading downstream. They want to find any...animals that got caught in the river, and get an idea as to the extent of the damage."

She was pretty sure when he said animals that he also meant people who had lost their battle to the river. She could have been one of them—Tommy too—but for him.

"Maybe you'll come across my mule."

"I'll look for her." Nelson sent Sylvia a small smile. "We will leave you to your soup. Get some rest."

He ushered his mother out and then closed the door as they both left.

That woman didn't want her here. Sylvia could sense it as sure as Adele could sense the rain.

She looked down at her soup. A minute ago,

she'd been hungry. No longer. Yet she hadn't eaten in more than a day. She took a sip, the taste of the salty broth registering.

She had a lot to muddle through.

The things Nelson had said just now. She knew he could charm the feathers off a bird if he had a mind to. She swallowed as another thought came to her—or love from a woman who had had too little of it. It would be so easy to lose her heart to him. Too easy.

Maybe she already had.

She drew in a shaky breath.

He had made it clear more than once that he was looking for a wife from among the women from the train. Someone pure and sweet and honorable. Someone like Miss Weber. She was perfect for him. Not someone like her.

But the way he'd acted—it was more than just being kind, more than being a little worried. He'd come for her in that terrible storm. She covered her face with a hand, remembering the look in his eyes. The dreams that she'd had—of him holding her with strong arms, murmuring against her hair, breathing against her neck. They were glorious dreams, but they were only that—dreams. Yet she wanted to feel his arms around her and feel him press his mouth to hers the way a man would do with a woman he loves. She yearned for it and she was fearful the whole of it had shown on her face and trembled, unspoken, in the air between them.

She felt what was left of her heart slipping away to him, piece by piece. Her chest ached from it and yet she couldn't help it.

She loved him. She loved him something fierce.

Yet she wasn't right for him.

The sooner she got back to her side of the river, the better it would be for both her and Tommy.

Nelson stood on the opposite side of the closed door for a full minute, battling with himself to keep from striding right back in there and kissing her proper. That was what he wanted to do. The thought shocked him. He was in totally unfamiliar territory. He had always felt protective of Sylvia, ever since first meeting her in the mercantile when she'd looked like a cornered cat facing off against a large mongrel dog. Even the kidnapping hadn't changed that desire to protect her. But of late, something stronger, something deeper had woven into his feelings for her.

The chaste kisses weren't something he had planned. He had been overcome with relief for having found her, for the fact she was alive. That, and that she looked utterly beautiful sitting there in his home, in his guest bed.

He ran a hand through his hair. He could

make all the excuses to himself that he wanted, but it didn't change the fact that he wanted more of her. Possibly—all of her.

He headed downstairs.

"Nelson?" his mother called from the parlor. "It's dark, and Miss Weber must get back to the hotel."

"Of course. I'll escort her back."

"She's been quite helpful. Perhaps you might take her to supper as a way to thank her? I don't mind fending for myself tonight."

He nodded and walked past her into the parlor, where Miss Weber gathered her things.

"You've been a huge help today. I am indebted." He opened the door and stepped out onto the porch with her.

While they walked, he asked her about herself, where she came from, her family. He was careful to avoid the large puddles of mud as he assisted her from the boardwalk down to the street in order to cross over to the hotel.

At the door, he paused. "May I take you to supper? It's the least I can do after all you've done for me today."

She didn't answer immediately. She searched his gaze. "I'd enjoy taking a meal with you. Truly I would. But I don't think that I'm the one you want to be with just now."

She was astute or somehow he'd given himself away. "Miss Marks and I are good friends. Nothing more."

"You mean Sylvia, don't you?" Miss Weber said. "I'm quite tired. I think you are too. Why don't you ask me again in a day or two, if you feel inclined? And you don't owe me a dinner for helping today. I was happy to be useful. Good night, Doctor."

"Good night." He waited until she had entered the hotel before heading back to his home. Things might have been different if he'd come to know her first. Perhaps he should have gone through the list of women from bottom to top instead of the other way around, but it was too late now. Now knowing Sylvia as he did, his affections were for her alone.

At his house, he stepped into a darkened parlor. He walked back to his study as a thought came to him. He removed the paperweight and picked up his list, scanning it quickly. He let out a long, slow whistle. Miss Weber had managed to pass all his requirements with a perfect score. She was even willing to wash Sylvia's and Tommy's ruined and mud-caked clothes. He'd been the one to prevent that. He wanted to burn them.

He should get to know her. It was the logical thing to do. It made perfect sense.

Slowly, he crumpled the note and tossed it on his desktop.

She wasn't Sylvia. And only Sylvia would do.

"You didn't stay for supper?" his mother asked when he entered the kitchen.

"Miss Weber declined my invitation." He looked about the room. "It's quiet. Where is Tommy?"

"He wanted to be with his mother. I went to collect her tray and she was fast asleep with her son snuggled in beside her."

Disappointment washed over him. He'd wanted to see them again before they went to sleep for the night. At least he'd had a good look at Tommy's wound. The dunking in the river hadn't hurt the new, granulating tissue. He'd done nothing more than wrap the ankle back up with clean bandages.

"Thank you for your help today," he said.

"You bolted down the steps and were gone before I could blink." She brought two steaming bowls of soup over, one for each of them. "I heated this back up. There is plenty for the both of us."

He sat down at the table. "I wish I had some of Sylvia's bread to go with this. She makes something called molasses bread."

"Son." His mother reached out to palm his cheek.

He flinched. She had never done that before. Ever. The last time he'd touched her had been the day she arrived and told him the truth about his father.

"Be careful. It is obvious to me how you feel about Miss Marks. There is more there than a professional relationship."

"You haven't cared about what I do for years," he said.

"That's not true. I have cared."

He tried to stay detached, calm—the same way that she had been toward him his entire life. "You sent me away when I was Tommy's age and conveniently forgot about me. You've abdicated any right to have an opinion on how I conduct myself."

"Your father—" She stopped at the warning look he tossed her.

"My father?"

She shoved aside her bowl, the only evidence that she was agitated. "Ellison provided for the both of us. You were fed and clothed and educated. You never wanted for anything."

"You didn't know what I wanted." She had effectively silenced him after a few years of ignoring his pleas. He'd given up. She didn't seem to realize that.

"He gave you what a father should—a name and, with that name, respect."

"Is that why you married him? Was he aware that he was getting two for the price of one when he said his vows? That you married him for his money, his name and respect?"

She raised her chin. "You say those words as if they are poor reasons to marry."

"No. Not poor reasons, simply not the only reasons."

He was letting his anger get the better of him. He had never understood his parents' relationship. He had a vague memory from childhood of them embracing, but from the time they sent him away to boarding school, they'd never had any physical contact in front of him.

He stood and walked to the window, staring out into the darkness as he gathered his thoughts. "What happened, Mother? Tell me what happened to my real father and why you didn't marry him."

She was silent behind him. He thought at first she wasn't going to answer, but then he heard a strangled noise and turned to her. Her face was buried in her hands, her shoulders shaking.

Was this a play for his sympathy? Then, disgusted with his cynicism, he withdrew his handkerchief from his vest pocket and held it out to her. "Here. Take this."

She raised her head. Her eyes glistened with tears and her cheeks were wet with their trails.

He tossed the cloth on the table in front of her.

Slowly, she picked it up. "Your father—your *real* father worked for the Revenue Cutter Service. He was a liaison between that part of the government and the Lighthouse Board." She dabbed at her eyes. "He was an officer. We were introduced at a dance organized by the military there on the Cape."

"Go on."

"I—we—fell in love."

"That night? Or did this happen over a period of time?" It was a mean, sarcastic thing to say.

She looked at him evenly. "Over the course of the next year."

He slid back into the seat across the table from her.

"His name was Charles Gunders. He traveled a lot for his job, and each time we were apart, the deeper our love for each other grew. When he asked for my hand at Christmas, I agreed immediately. We planned to wed in the summer. I was ecstatic. I thought he was too." She looked down at the handkerchief that she had worried into a wrinkled mess in her hands.

"What happened?"

"There was trouble at a shipping channel up north. Something about a new line of buoys being installed. He was there a long time." She hesitated. "Then I received a letter. He wasn't coming back. He'd had a change of heart. After that, I heard that he had asked for a transfer and moved to the West Coast."

Nelson inhaled. "So, he left us."

She nodded. "Not you. He did not know about you."

"What about Ellison?"

"His family and mine were neighbors. I knew him growing up. He always felt something for me, but I—"

"I understand. You did not return the sentiment."

"Ellison came home from the university to celebrate his graduation. I…encouraged his affections and we wed."

"Without telling him about me?"

She sighed. "I was afraid to tell him at first, but I couldn't go through with it. I told him a month before the wedding. He wanted to marry me despite my condition." She met his gaze. "Ellison did love me."

"Then it worked out well for you." His jaw was tight.

She nodded. "For a while. But as you grew older, you looked more and more like Charles, your real father. Even your mannerisms mimicked his. It bothered Ellison more and more. You see, I couldn't give him any children of his own."

"So he sent me away." It explained so much.

"He was hurting. He couldn't stand to look at you—or me. He forbade any contact with you."

"That's why he didn't want me at his funeral—or in any other part of his life.

"And why he didn't want me going into practice with old Dr. Harney when I came home from medical school. He didn't want a constant reminder of me so close." It cleared up a lot of his misconceptions. "Tell me. If Ellison was still alive, would you have ever told me?"

She shook her head, her chin high. "I promised."

"If something had happened to you, I would have never known the truth."

His mother paced the length of the room, her steps and manner agitated. "He tried, Nelson. He really did try at first. And, in the end, he stood by his vows and took care of both of us."

He stared at her, his thoughts in turmoil.

"It's important that you understand this. The Graham name is respected everywhere. I want it to stay that way."

"I haven't done anything to dishonor the name."

"But you may be about to."

"What do you mean by that?"

"I happened to see the paper you have on your desk. The one where you list the qualities you want in a woman that you marry. It wasn't idle scribbling. You are considering marriage, aren't you?"

"Yes."

"The...woman you have upstairs...is not suitable to bear the Graham name."

He had suspected that would be her attitude. "That is my decision to make. Not yours."

She stiffened. "Well. Think long and hard before you let anything progress."

He turned away, weary and tired of the conversation. "I'm going to bed. Good night, Mother."

Chapter Twenty

Someone knocked on his bedroom door. Now what?

Nelson rubbed the sleep from his face and sat up. Daylight streamed into the room. "Be right out." He dressed quickly and opened the door.

Tommy stood there. Someone was banging pots and pans in his kitchen.

"What is it?" he asked.

"Ma wants to know where her clothes are. I told her that you burned them, and she is madder than a wet hornet."

He looked across the hall and saw that Sylvia's door was wide-open and that her bed was made. Guess he hadn't thought much of the repercussions. All he'd wanted to do was get rid of the muddy, wet rags. She was probably making breakfast in her nightgown. Wouldn't a chance visitor or patient find that vision interesting!

The image amused him, but it also brought back the things his mother had said last evening. He had to agree with one thing—what he was thinking and feeling was heading into dangerous territory.

What could become of them? Really? They were two such different people. Much too different to meet somewhere in the middle. For them to be together, one of them would have to jump the proverbial river and he didn't see that happening. Sylvia had made it clear that Oak Grove and the folks who lived here did not suit her. And he certainly could not move his office out of town and hang his shingle on her shack. It was too far for people to come when they were ailing. He would be out of business in a fortnight.

All that might be true, but it still didn't overshadow the fact that he had fallen for her. What he would do with that, he wasn't sure, but at least he would be honest with himself. There had been too many secrets in his life. His feelings for Sylvia wouldn't be one of them.

The aroma of bacon and eggs and fresh coffee drifted up from downstairs. Nelson sat down on the top stair. "Hop on. We'll face her wrath together."

A grin lit Tommy's face. He whooped and

then climbed on to ride piggyback down the stairs.

"It's about time you got up," she said when they entered the kitchen. "Sit. Is your mother coming?"

He hadn't checked, but her door had been closed. "No." He deposited Tommy on a chair.

"All right, then. I'll hold some food back to keep warm for her. Help yourself to some coffee."

He was surprised that she hadn't started right in berating him about her clothes. The shapeless nightgown that she wore covered every inch of her down to her bare toes. He poured cups for the both of them. "Looks like you are back to feeling like yourself."

She scooped up fried potatoes and eggs and bacon onto three plates and brought them to the table. "Hungry as can be." She sat down with them. "Thank you. I'll be forever grateful that you came looking for me yesterday. And that you took care of Tommy and me."

"Friends do things like that."

She smiled slightly. "We can't be friends. You know why."

"I know what you told me. Doesn't mean I agree with it."

She huffed. "Now who is being stubborn."

He grinned. Then he took a bite of food. "You look fetching today." She did. Her hair was soft and shiny, a dark chocolate waterfall down her back. Everything about her was totally inappropriate and fascinatingly pretty.

That dimple appeared on her left cheek. "Good thing you think so, because unless you bring me a needle and thread and some material, this is what I'll be wearing until I leave."

"I've given that some thought," he said, more serious now. "I have a few errands to do this morning. I need to stop by to see Mrs. Blackwell to check on her and her baby. With all that was going on yesterday, I neglected that."

"Do you know what she named her baby?"

He shook his head. "While I'm out, I'll stop by Miller's and ask if he'll make another set of crutches for Tommy. He can measure him this time and get the correct size."

"Doc? About some clothes. I can make my own. If you will bring me back some material and needle and thread."

"I thought I'd leave that up to my mother. She would be better at picking out a suitable fabric."

"Oh, no! I don't want to bother your mother."

He had a feeling he knew why. Sylvia was very sensitive of others' feelings. She must have noticed his mother's reticence toward her.

"And I'll keep a tab here of what I owe you. The honey will be coming soon."

"Do you think I expect you to pay me back?"

"No," she said after a moment's hesitation.

"I know you don't expect that. But I can't accept charity."

He wasn't going to argue with her. He was simply going to stop by Mrs. Taylor's and have the woman come by to take measurements for a new dress. Sylvia might balk, but he would give her no choice. He wanted Sylvia to have something nice. She deserved it. Tommy did too.

"I'll be back in an hour. If someone comes to the door—" He thought for a second and then felt a smile tug at his mouth. "Let Tommy answer it. And you hide."

His errands took longer than expected, and when he returned to his office, he was surprised to hear voices coming from the exam room.

Abigail White, Teddy's sister, was sitting on the exam table, her sleeve rolled up past her elbow on the right arm and the rest of her arm buried in a bowl of mud. Her cheeks had mud plastered on them too, and her left eye was slightly swollen. She was sniffling, while Miss Weber and Sylvia stood on each side of her, both speaking at once in calming tones.

"What happened?" he asked.

Abigail straightened. "Oh, Dr. Graham. I'm so glad you've come!"

She sounded miserable.

"I found a leak in the back of the newspaper office," Abigail said. "You know that small room where we keep the old editions of the paper?

Water covered the floor. They're all ruined! All destroyed! So much waste!" she continued, moaning as she spoke. "So much important information—all lost."

Her distraught answer wasn't what he wanted. He reined in his frustration. "What about *you*?"

"Me? Oh, I don't know. I'm upset, of course. And Teddy will be furious when he finds out."

Nelson took a deep breath. This was wholly unlike Abigail.

"She bothered a beehive," Sylvia said. "Got stung a few times. Just little ol' honey bees. Not those big hornets. I figured egg whites or mud was the best thing for her to take out the sting. It's what I always use when I get stung while gathering honey."

"Good thinking," he said, stifling a smile. Apparently, Sylvia was completely recovered from her own ordeal and was up to helping others again. "There sure is plenty of mud around."

Sylvia exchanged a look with Miss Weber that said, *See? I told you.* "Got any other ideas that will help fix her up? Have you got some willow bark tea back in that kitchen?"

"Not that, but something that works as well or better. How long has the mud been on?"

"An hour at least," Miss Weber said. "We've had a lovely chat."

"Is the swelling around that eye going up or down?"

Miss Weber and Sylvia drew closer to Abigail to decide, peering down their noses until they were only inches from the upset woman. "Down," they answered in unison.

"Then I prescribe you clean it off once you are home, Miss White. I'll prepare a paste that you can apply should the pain return." He headed to the kitchen, where he kept his powders and pestle and mortar. While he worked, he half listened to the chatter between the three women, enjoying the lively discussion and the fact that Sylvia was taking an active part.

When he returned, he handed Abigail a piece of newspaper, the paste folded inside. "Here you go. Simply smear it over the stings if they start to bother you again."

Miss Weber threw her shawl over her shoulders. "It's time I got back to the hotel myself. I just came to see how Miss Marks was feeling today."

He saw them to the door.

He turned to find Sylvia cleaning up the mess that the mud had made on the exam table and then crouching to clean a few spots on the floor. "You're wearing a dress!" It was a pretty lavender spring dress.

She popped up quickly. "Miss Simcock had one I could borrow. She thought we looked to be about the same size."

"It's becoming. The color I mean."

She flushed a pretty shade of pink and smoothed the skirt. "It's called gingham. I've never had anything so fine. I feel like I should curl my hair and set a bow in it like Miss Vandersohn."

"As long as you don't faint like her, I think that's a fine idea."

Her eyes sparkled.

"Did Miss Simcock fix your hair too?"

She touched the neat little bun at the nape of her neck. "I did this part. I figured since I was in town I should clean up some. I...don't want people talking poorly of you or your office with me here."

"I wouldn't let them."

She glanced away.

Had he rendered her speechless? That was a new development.

"You can be charming, Doc. When you have a mind to be."

She didn't know it, but she could too. "I have something to show you and Tommy." He'd checked on her goat while he'd been out. She didn't know about Penny.

"That'd be fine, excepting that Tommy ain't here. He's out behind the hotel. The Austin boys and the Blackwells are practicing roping a stake out there."

Nelson couldn't imagine Tommy being up to

playing physical games with his injured ankle. "How did he get over there?"

"We got a surprise visit this morning from Maggie Miller. She said her husband had made two pairs of crutches of different sizes. These are bigger, and a bit harder for Tommy to use, but he's managing."

"It sounds like Tommy is fitting right in." Would that change her attitude about people here in town?

"I know what you're thinking, but I never saw him so hopeful as when those other boys asked him. I didn't have the heart to tell him no."

"No. Of course you couldn't."

"Should I call him back so you can show us whatever it is you want to show us?"

"I'll show you both later." He went back into the kitchen to clean the pestle and mortar.

"Oh, I can do that," She jumped up and reached for it. "I need to earn my keep."

He didn't let go. He meant it to tease her, but she quickly let go.

"I'm just not used to being idle."

He watched her clean the few things from breakfast while he leaned against the hutch, purposely close and purposely in the way. He liked having her here. Everything about her fascinated him. He liked the curve of her cheek and remembered how soft her skin was against his lips.

He moved closer. "Is my mother upstairs?"

"No. She went out right after getting dressed. Didn't even have breakfast." Her small hands flew over the tabletop and side table, cleaning as she went, and then suddenly she stopped. She faced him. "She doesn't like me to be here."

"Did she tell you that?"

"Not in words."

This was his house and he wouldn't have his mother upsetting Sylvia. "It has more to do with me than you."

"It doesn't matter. The end is the same."

"I don't know that she likes anyone or anything right now. She came for a visit to let me know that my father passed away."

"Oh!" Sylvia's face filled with compassion. "No wonder she acted strange toward me."

She dried her hands on a towel. "Was he ill?"

"For a short while before he passed. His death was expected. She is still trying to adjust."

"I am so sorry. Were you close?" she asked cautiously.

He puffed out a breath. "No."

She waited for him to say more.

"A few things she said have got me thinking." He took her hands. "About Thomas."

She stiffened. "Thomas? Why?"

"Much like your loyalty to Thomas, Mother has been very loyal to my...father." He still had trouble calling Ellison that now that he knew the truth. It would have been different if the man had cared about him and acted like a father. But since his mother had asked him to keep the secret, he would. For her sake, he would honor her wishes. Revealing the truth now, after so many years, would benefit no one.

"How did you come to be way out here in Kansas in the first place?"

"Well," she said slowly, "Thomas and I grew up together in the hills of Virginia. We went to the same small school and our families went to the same country church."

"I take it Carl was around too."

She nodded. "Boys in the hills started working in the coal mines when they were fifteen. Carl and Thomas hated being under the ground, always in the dark. That Tom—" she smiled softly, remembering "—he sure was a hard worker. Always had ideas running around in his head. Always full of new ways to do things.

"Thomas fancied me from the start and I felt the same way about him. He hated working in the mine. He talked Carl into throwing in with him. They bought Berta and a wagon and had enough saved up for a parcel of land once we got here. We planned to marry in the spring and leave right after."

"What happened?"

"The preacher sent word that he'd taken sick and asked us to wait for the next preacher to come through. That might have been two weeks or two months, Thomas and Carl didn't want to wait that long to head West, so we said our vows to each other as proper as we could in front of my ma and pa and Thomas's mother and an elder from the church."

"But no parson?"

"Tom promised my ma he would grab the next parson we saw and get married proper. He even put back enough for a plain gold band at the store."

He glanced at her hand.

She rubbed the finger a gold band would have been on. "He sold it once we got here. He bought wood for the roof beams. Said it was more important to have a strong house that would last. Then we had to get our seeds in the ground right away else we wouldn't make it past the first year." She shook her head. "Seemed like it was always something."

"Then he left on the cattle drive."

She nodded. "In his mind, we were already married."

"I can see how he would think that." But he couldn't believe Thomas would leave her to fend for herself. It was reckless and careless. Anything could have happened to Sylvia while he was gone. "He shouldn't have left you on your own."

"I managed. I moved in with Adele and her husband for a time. That's how she came to know that I was in a family way. By the time her son came back with the news that Thomas had died on the trail, I could feel little Tommy kicking and a-moving inside me."

She spread the towel out to dry on the back of a chair. "Thomas was the only man I ever loved and he gave me Tommy. And Tommy is the best thing that ever happened to me."

He snorted softly, amazed that she could be so content when she had so little. But then, she'd known true love. He never had that, and because of it, he'd never found contentment.

There was much more to her story that she had left out. She hadn't said a thing about the way she was treated in town. Here, she'd been loyal to one man, a man she had loved her entire life up until he died, and because of jealousy, his brother had been the one to ruin her in the eyes of the town.

Sylvia and his mother had both been in the same situation—carrying a baby and having no father to help raise it—but the way they had handled it was decidedly different. The contrast in the way he had been raised compared to Tommy was like night and day. He'd grown up with money and comfort and loneliness. Tommy had grown up with nothing, but love.

More and more he was realizing what he had missed growing up. Maybe it was because he was thinking of marrying and starting a family

of his own. Maybe it was because he was afraid
he would end up with the same type of family
that he'd grown up in. He didn't want any part
of that. He wanted to do better. He needed to
do better.

"You're being mighty quiet," Sylvia said,
watching him closely.

He looked, really looked at the woman before
him. She deserved so much. And he wanted to
give it to her, if he could. He loved her. And if
he had any say in the matter, he wanted her to
love him back, freely and without reservation.
That was the one thing he'd missed his entire
life and somehow he knew that she was the one
woman who could give it to him.

He had to figure out a way to make her a part
of his life.

"Come on," he said, holding out his arm for
her to catch on to. "Let's collect Tommy and
show him that surprise. You'll both enjoy it."

She couldn't begin to describe the feeling she
got, walking beside Nelson. She felt pretty in
Miss Simcock's lavender dress, with her hair
done up fancier than usual. She wanted to keep
a hold of his arm the entire time. He'd been a
gentleman to offer it. But she'd released it as
soon as they walked out of the house.

She guessed she was confused after the way
he'd acted last night. That little kiss he gave her

was innocent enough—but she had still tingled all through her insides as if he'd pressed his lips to her mouth and not just her forehead.

It had started off a passel of dreams. Dreams she had no right to, but she couldn't seem to stop them. She'd slept all day yesterday, exhausted from fighting the river, and then she'd tossed and turned all night, exhausted from trying to shut out the image of him carrying her back from the river and then sitting there beside her on the bed. It was getting harder and harder to keep her thoughts and her dreams straight. They were all mixed up and too wonderful to try to straighten out.

Behind the hotel, they watched Tommy try his arm at lassoing the post. He did well for not being able to trust that one leg. It took him ten tries, but he finally got the rope to land over the post. He grabbed his crutches, beaming up at her and the doc.

They headed to the livery. When Tommy's leg got to hurting him, the doc picked him up, easy as you please, and carried him piggyback to the big wooden doors.

"You go in first," he said to Tommy. "See if you can figure out what's special."

He waited with her outside. Suddenly, they heard a big whoop from Tommy.

"Ma! It's Penny! It's Penny!"

She rushed in and there was Tommy, kneeling down and hugging that little goat. Sylvia's happiness just about spilled over.

"She is plum happy to see you too!" she said. She looked around the livery for her mule. "Is Berta here too?"

"No," Nelson said. "I thought we could take a buggy ride tomorrow and look for her. That will give the ground more time to harden." He studied the goat. "Does she need milking or anything?"

"No. She was close to drying up. I think the job is done now."

"Does that mean no more butter or cheese?"

"Not unless I breed her again. I'll have to think on it. First, I need to get back to my land and see what I have left to work with." She didn't want to trouble him with her worries, but she had the chickens and sheep and a mule to find before she could think about breeding Penny.

"So, you are set on going back?"

She tilted her head and looked up at him. "It's where I live."

"You could think about staying here in town."

"I know you mean well, but a little rain ain't going to change my mind about town." She had to keep telling herself that it was just his way. That he'd do the same for any other stranded person, but it was getting harder and harder to believe it with all the little things he was doing for her.

They walked back to his office while Tommy hobbled off as fast as he could on his crutches to play with his new friends. Nelson had a few people waiting on him in the parlor, so Sylvia searched about for something to keep her occupied in the house. She wanted to be near in case Nelson called out and would like her help. It hadn't escaped her attention that Mrs. Graham had not returned yet to the house.

She wandered into the room he used for an office. He had some mighty big books on medicine. She opened one and couldn't pronounce half the words. It didn't seem fitting to move or organize anything in a man's study. A glass paperweight covered a crumpled piece of paper. She smoothed out the paper and realized it was the list he'd told her about.

Curiosity got the better of her and she looked over his writing. It wasn't the easiest to read, but she managed. A chuckle escaped. No one woman could be all this! He was sure to be disappointed. That thought sobered her. Nelson deserved a good woman by his side. How she wished it could be her, but she didn't see herself in half the qualities on his list.

The front door opened and closed. The pronounced feminine clips of his mother's footsteps came down the hall.

"Mother? A word?" Nelson called out.

Hurriedly, Sylvia replaced the paper and the

paperweight and scooted into the kitchen. She breathed a sigh of relief when she realized that the woman hadn't caught her snooping. She was sure Nelson's mother would have considered that one more mark against her.

Looking at the row of cupboards, she had a thought. If Nelson was set on getting a wife, she guessed she could at least make sure he had the necessary staples. She'd make a list of what was missing here in the kitchen. She dragged a stool over to a cupboard and started cataloging the items inside.

"What do you think you are doing?" he said.

She startled. Then turned to see him, his mother and Fiona in the doorway.

"Do you know that you have medicine and food all mixed together, Doc? It's a wonder you don't poison yourself making dinner. How do you find anything at all in here?"

"I get by. No one has died yet."

"Now, there's a fine way to go about it."

He grinned. "You really don't know how to relax."

She came down from the short stool and dusted off her hands. "Oh, I'm no good at relaxing unless I have needles and yarn and then I guess that's still doing something. How are you getting along, Fiona? How is your daughter? What did you name her?"

Fiona laughed. "One question at a time! I'm

fine now. We decided on Cordelia, although I think she will have to grow into her name. I left her with Hannah. You remember Hannah?"

She nodded. "Sure I do."

"If you like to knit or crochet, I know that Mrs. Gallagher at the mercantile has a new assortment of yarn just in. I'm on my way there now. Would you like to go?"

She'd like more than anything to get some yarn, but she remembered her last stop at the mercantile. She wasn't ready to face Mable Gallagher again, especially in a borrowed dress. Maybe when she had her own clothes back, she'd feel stronger. She still had that pretty blue one back at her place if the rains hadn't ruined it. "Thank you, but I'll stay here. I have plenty to keep me busy."

Fiona left with Mrs. Graham, and the doc went into his study.

Sylvia climbed back on the stool to finish organizing the pantry, but it seemed some of the light had gone out of her day. She was happy for Fiona, but with each passing moment, she dwelled more and more on her own predicament. She had no doubt that the soddy would still be standing when she returned, but how was she going to cross the river with the ferry gone? Would there be any chickens left or would the foxes and coyotes have found them? And what about her sheep? She was overwhelmed with the complications. It could be that her one and only asset was a goat!

She finished in the kitchen and walked back into the parlor. She crossed her arms and stood there, staring out the window as the sun dipped closer to the horizon. The sun shining through the lace curtains dappled the skin on her hands and arms. Her mind was a muddled mess with all her thoughts and she was tired of thinking on her problems so much. She couldn't figure out a solution to her dilemma and she had to— Tommy depended on her.

"There you are," Nelson said, coming into the room.

She didn't turn toward him but kept looking out the window. Here she was feeling sorry for herself when he'd been nothing but kind to her. "I finished in the kitchen. You now have a pantry *and* an apothecary cabinet."

He stepped up to her side. "Thank you."

"I also made a list of things you need. I figured—whichever of those gals you decide on for a wife would probably appreciate having a few staples."

He touched her shoulder. "Sylvia…what's wrong?"

She sniffed and then she turned to look up at him, her emotions raw and too near the surface to contain. "I'm frightened. Really frightened."

He drew her to his chest.

It was the one thing she needed—his strength, his support, for just a moment, just enough to gather herself back together again. She leaned into him. The feel of his strong arms around her made her knees weaken. If only she could stay here forever.

Tears burned behind her eyes. "I keep pondering things and I can't see my way to any answers. I'm so used to taking care of everything, especially Tommy. And I don't know that I can now. With no mule, no sheep and likely no chickens, how will I make ends meet? What's to become of me and Tommy?"

His palm was warm on the back of her neck. She heard the *thump, thump, thump* of his heart, so strong, so steady.

"I don't have any answers for you. Not if you won't give the people here in Oak Grove a chance to get to know you and see for themselves what I see in you."

She squeezed her eyelids harder together. "What could you possibly see in me?"

"That's easy. I see a woman who cares more about others than she does herself. Maybe too much. You care so much for your son that you were willing to kidnap me. What would have happened if I was a different type of man? What if you had gotten hurt? Then what would have become of Tommy?"

"It was a crazy thing to do. But I had to do something. I couldn't bear to lose my boy."

He rubbed the back of her neck. Small, round, soothing strokes. A touch that said he cared about her.

And the things he said out loud! She'd never heard such words before. Calming words, words that built her up, like she was something special. His voice rumbled through his chest.

"You even care about the man who gave you Tommy. You don't ever say a negative thing about him despite how he left you. What he did wasn't right."

"He thought it was. Thomas couldn't help that he died."

"I know. But he should have found a way to make it right with you back in Virginia with a preacher and your family all around. You deserved that. You deserve so much."

"Well, I'm partly to blame. I should have held myself apart." She swallowed. "Thomas was a good man for all his faults."

"Not good enough for you."

She didn't know what to say to that. The doc made her feel precious.

"Things will work out," he said, and he bussed her hair with his lips.

She wasn't feeling all that sorry for herself when he did that. Instead, she was noticing a warmth spreading through her that tickled all over. She shivered against his vest.

She looked up and found him searching her face, his own expression troubled. He moved closer—hesitated just a moment—and then closed the space between them, kissing her soft and gentle on her mouth. She loved the soft feel of his lips on hers, the safety of his strong arms holding her close, even the tickle of his whiskers on her upper lip. For a moment, she allowed herself to relax and kiss him back. It would be so easy to be like this forever.

Pleasure rose up inside her that made all the hairs on her head tingle. He cupped the back of her head with his hand, smoothing the hair there just under her bun, and pulling her closer against him. Her blood raced through her, excited to the point it made her tremble.

This is what got you into trouble in the first place, a voice inside told her. She broke off the kiss and pulled back slightly, her heart beating too fast.

"I found this for you at Mrs. Taylor's," Mrs. Graham said from the front doorway.

Sylvia covered her face with her hands. She'd let things go too far! Her face had to be red from what had just happened and his mother had probably seen the entire thing! Now the woman would surely think poorly of her.

Nelson, however, didn't move away. He

turned to acknowledge his mother but kept his large hand splayed on the small of her back.

Sylvia stepped away from his touch.

Holding herself as stiff as a board, Mrs. Graham entered the parlor, carrying a folded length of material and a smaller package wrapped in a muslin cloth and tied with a string. She walked into the parlor with a frown on her face as she looked from her son to Sylvia. "This should be enough for a dress."

Sylvia took the material from her and unfolded it. It was a sturdy mustard-colored cotton. She'd hoped, foolishly, for something with a pattern. Perhaps a gingham check like the one she wore of Tessa Simcock's.

"It should hold up well," Mrs. Graham said.

"With the work that's ahead of me, I'll need something serviceable and strong. This will do fine. I can't be wishing for anything that will fall apart after a season." She turned to Nelson, who had remained quiet. "Looks like there's enough here to keep me busy until I can get back on my side of the river. Maybe even enough to make a shirt for Tommy if I cut it carefully."

He pressed his lips together, enough that it was hard to remember how pleasant they'd been to kiss.

What had she said that had bothered him? Was it the way she had acted at seeing the material? He didn't think her ungracious, did he? She stroked a wrinkle from the material and tried to hold back the sudden prickle of tears. He was so good to her, she didn't want to upset him.

Mrs. Graham turned to her son. "Mr. Miller stopped me as I passed by his shop. He wants to speak with you."

"I'll go see him." Nelson shrugged into his coat and hat and then focused his gaze on her. "When I get back, we can all have supper at the restaurant."

The restaurant? She wouldn't be comfortable there! Didn't he understand that? What was he trying to do? She opened her mouth to tell him so and then remembered his mother standing there. To decline his invitation would sound ungrateful.

She was trying to come up with the right thing to say when he walked out the door.

Mrs. Graham held out the other package. "You will need this too."

Sylvia took it from her and untied the string. Inside the rolled-up cloth were scissors, needle, thread and six buttons. "Thank you, Mrs. Graham."

Mrs. Graham pursed her mouth. Her eyes weren't soft and green like her son's eyes, but a hard, steel gray. "I don't want your thanks. I want you to get busy and make your dress so that you will be able to leave as soon as possible."

Sylvia sucked in a breath. She gathered up

the sewing items and material. She'd work on the dress in her room, where she wouldn't be a bother to anyone. "I plan to leave as soon as I can get across to my land."

"Then we understand each other."

She lifted her chin. A glimmer of rebellion sparking inside her. "The doc don't seem to mind me being here."

"He is vulnerable just now."

The doc? Vulnerable? "You mean because of his father?"

"I see he has shared things of a personal nature with you."

She turned toward the stairs. "He considers me a friend." Funny, she was the one who had always tried to fight that. Now she was waving it like a banner.

"I'm afraid that you are not a suitable friend or otherwise for my son."

The words hurt like a slap to her face. Sylvia stopped with her hand on the banister and turned back to Mrs. Graham. "You don't know anything about me."

"Mrs. Gallagher informed me of plenty when I stopped in for the material."

Mrs. Gallagher again. Sylvia's chest tightened with pain. She hated that she'd let this woman hurt her. Even if her home was filled with water and snakes to the brim, she couldn't wait to get back there. Anyplace was better than here with this woman. Anyplace was better than town.

She picked up her skirt and hurried up the stairs as fast as she could.

Chapter Twenty-One

The next morning, Nelson dressed and stepped from his room. Sylvia's door was still closed. It had been ever since yesterday when he returned from the Millers'. He hadn't been able to entice her out of her room to go to the restaurant. He'd taken Tommy and his mother out to eat and then brought back a plate of food for Sylvia and left it by her door.

He crossed the hall in two steps and removed the towel from the plate. Half the food was gone. At some time during the night, she'd eaten a little. He knocked on her door. "Sylvia? How are you this morning? Are you feeling better?"

"Yes."

He waited for more elaboration. None came.

"Tommy and I are going to look for your mule

after breakfast. Would you like to ride out to the river with us and help search?"

"Yes."

It wasn't like Sylvia to be so subdued. It bothered him. Something had happened when he'd left her alone with his mother and neither woman was talking to him about it.

He'd thought about that kiss all night. By morning he'd made up his mind. The list be damned. It didn't matter what was written there. He wanted her. Her past didn't matter. It was a future he wanted with her. And he meant to speak to her about it today. Somehow, he would convince her that she was welcome—in town, in his home and in his heart. If he had to go forward patiently in small increments, then that was what he would do.

Considering her attitude over the past twelve hours, Nelson had expected some silence from Sylvia during the carriage ride. When she climbed into the buggy, refusing his help, and made sure that Tommy sat between the two of them, he knew whatever bothered her still plagued her. But something was up with Tommy too. Nobody was talking.

He stole a glance at her. She sat straight and proper, holding the side handle with one hand and her other arm around her son. Her hair was braided into a pretty knot in the back. He hadn't thought about her lack of a hat. He'd have to remedy that once they were back in town.

"When I stopped in at the livery this morning, Wally mentioned that a group of men left early to look for the ferry. They hope to find it salvageable. Maybe Miller can repair it rather than build an entirely new one. It would save time and lumber."

"Why do they have to build it anyway?" Tommy asked. "I don't want to go back. I like staying in town."

It was the first time that Nelson had ever heard the boy whine.

"Well, of course we have to go back!" Sylvia said irritably. "What about the sheep? What about our chickens?"

"Well, what about my friends?" Tommy said. "I want to play with them. It's more fun staying in town."

Sylvia squeezed her son. "That's just because it is a change for you. We don't belong here. Doesn't make any sense to get too used to things."

Nelson focused on the road, but his thoughts mulled over her words. Something had happened to solidify her resolve to go back to her land. How could he make her see that she'd be safer in town and hopefully, one day, happier?

Suddenly, her attention riveted ahead as

they approached the river. "Look how high the water is!"

She looked over Tommy's windblown hair at Nelson. "I don't know that I'll ever trust that river again. It never came up this high before. I thought our place was safe. Guess now I'll worry every single spring and every time it rains hard."

It would be on his mind every year too if he couldn't convince her to leave her land. He clamped his mouth shut to keep quiet. Arguing with her only made her dig in her heels more and he didn't want to say anything in front of Tommy. But he would have it out with her— eventually. He would find out why she was suddenly so intent on going back to her home.

He pulled the buggy up to a stop at the ruined ferry landing.

Miller was there and had already started repairing the ramp and dock. A wagonload of new lumber stood to the side of the trail and a new coil of rope lay in the grass, ready to be strung across the river. When Miller saw Nelson, he put down his saw and walked over. "Hey there, Doc."

"Any predictions on when we will be able to cross the river?"

"The river is down a foot from two days ago. Still a strong current. I'd say another two days, barring any rain, should make it safe. Usually, it isn't all that deep here—no more than three or four feet at most."

Nelson huffed. "Except in the spring when it rains. I can't even see where the landing was on the opposite bank."

Miller nodded. "The water is covering it. Miss Marks, I don't see how you and your son survived the crossing."

Sylvia stared at the expanse of water. "I don't know either. Guess I got an angel looking out for me."

"I wonder how the DuBois family and some of the other folks who stayed on their land are doing," Nelson murmured.

"No telling," Miller said. "I'll have this landing done by nightfall. Hopefully, the others will find the ferry downstream and not too damaged."

Nelson hoped they found the ferry, but he hoped it wouldn't be too soon. He still needed time to change Sylvia's mind about staying. "We are headed that way now, looking for a mule."

They spent the next few hours searching for Berta without any luck. Finally, he turned the buggy around and they headed back to town. Tommy seemed to be the most discouraged of the three of them. Nelson bumped the boy's small shoulder gently. "Maybe Berta is smarter than all of us and she is back in her shed, stealing all the grain and oats you had stored up."

When they jumbled over the railroad tracks and entered town, the boy perked up. At the livery, almost before the buggy stopped, Tommy climbed down and hobbled off on his crutches to find his new friends.

"That ankle of his will be stronger than before with all his moving," Nelson said.

"He's getting harder and harder to pin down!" Sylvia said, her gaze lingering at the door where Tommy had disappeared. "I'm glad he's getting along with those other boys, but it will make it that much harder on him to leave when the time comes."

Nelson wrapped the reins around the brake lever. The sweet smell of hay lingered in the air.

"He will be back soon."

Sylvia looked at him askance. "Why?"

"All his new friends are in class this morning." Which meant he had better say what he had planned and be quick about it.

He climbed from the buggy and then reached up to help Sylvia down. She held on to his shoulders. Her hands lingered even though her feet were on the ground.

"Doc—" she said cautiously. "By that look on your face, you got something on your mind."

Her eyes were big and brown and luminous.

"We were interrupted yesterday. That's what has been on my mind."

He pulled her against him and kissed her

soundly. She stiffened at first, surprised. But then slowly, her body relaxed and she slid her hands up behind his neck, pulling him even closer. A satisfied hum came to his ears, encouraging him further. He deepened the kiss.

A long moment later, she pulled back. "You kiss me like that and I can't think straight."

"Good, because it may take that to get you to listen to reason," he said, pressing his lips to her cheek, her forehead, her neck.

She moaned. Then her eyes flew open and she pushed against his chest. "It wasn't a dream!"

"What?"

"When you carried me back from the river! I thought it was a dream that you kissed me. It felt just like this."

He grinned.

He bent down and kissed her there again. "Like this?"

She shivered. "That makes me warm all over."

He chuckled. Her eyes were half-closed. Her black lashes swept down over perfect skin. Her swollen lips begged to be kissed again. Desire rushed through him. He had to have her. Had to make her his. Somehow.

He set her from him and took both of her hands in his. "I've told you before that I care for you, Sylvia. You kidnapped my doctoring skills that night. But since then, you have kidnapped my heart. I don't want to lose you. I want you to stay here with me. I want you to marry me."

Her eyes widened, and if he didn't know better, he'd say she wasn't breathing.

"Oh, Doc..."

"Nelson..." he corrected.

"Oh, Nelson—" She took a deep breath. "I never expected..." Her eyes filled with tears. "I didn't ever think... Wait—I got to gather my thoughts. I'm all scattered. I figured we were friends, but this is more..."

He smiled. "Definitely more. I love you."

"But why? How? I'm all wrong for you! And I'm afraid!"

"Afraid?" He almost laughed at the preposterous notion and then realized that she was serious. "You? The woman with the rifle? The woman strong enough and brave enough to live out on her own? What could you be afraid of?"

"That you'll grow tired of me. That I'm not your equal. Like your mother said, I can't hope to be the woman you wrote about on that list."

She might as well have thrown cold water on him. So that was what had happened with his mother. "I don't care about that list. Not anymore. I care about you."

"I—I do care for you too. So much." Her brow furrowed. "If you think there's a chance I could make you happy, and you're willing to take Tommy along with me—"

"Of course I want Tommy. And you do make me happy. We can make it work. I know we can."

"But *I* don't know."

He sighed. "Then we'll take it slow. We don't even have to tell anybody until you're ready. It will be our secret for now."

The furrow between her brows eased.

"Just say you're willing to consider it. You're willing to try."

She looked up at him, her brown eyes luminous. "I do love you. If you're willing to go slow, then…all right. Yes. I'll try."

He pulled her to him and kissed her proper to seal it. Yet she had planted a seed of worry in him. What would really happen in the next few days? Once the ferry was back in operation, would she leave and not look back?

Tommy met them back at Nelson's office, announcing that all his new friends were in school and that he wanted to go too.

Nelson couldn't have been happier to hear it. Sylvia, however…

"You look shocked," he said, grinning.

"I am and then some," she said, wonder in her voice. "Into the kitchen with you for now, Tommy. I heard that growl from your stomach." She straightened, looking from Nelson to his mother. "I'll make enough for everybody and call you when it is ready."

When they had disappeared down the hallway, he turned to his mother. "Come with me. It's time we had our talk."

She arched a brow and followed him. He ushered her into his office and offered her a seat—which she didn't accept.

He hoped for a way to connect with the woman, foolish though it might be at this late time of his life. "I don't know why you have set yourself up against Sylvia. You don't know anything about her."

"But I do. And I worry for your practice and your reputation."

"I don't know what you've heard, or where you've received your information, but may I suggest you ask her straight out rather than listen to gossip? You may find that she is an amazing woman."

"An amazing woman. Yes..." She looked down at her folded hands. "I have hopes that you will find such a woman someday, although I am certain it is not Sylvia."

"Why not?"

"From things that Mrs. Gallagher said at the mercantile. And a Mr. Caulder stopped by also and gave me quite an earful."

The two worst informants. "Mother—"

"Sylvia had the choice to marry when she found out she was carrying Tommy, the same as you. Only, she chose differently. Her path has been the harder."

She raised her chin. "I very much doubt that."

He wasn't about to feel sorry for her and her poor relationship with Ellison. "You had a roof over your head that didn't leak or have to be repaired constantly. You had enough to eat all the time— food that you didn't have to grow and harvest and preserve. You had friends and family nearby. You had dresses made of silk rather than dresses made from whatever was available."

"It sounds like I made the better choice, then, didn't it?"

He'd had enough of her high-and-mighty Boston ways. "No, Mother. You made the easy choice. With the options that Sylvia had at the time, she made a far scarier and, in my view, more noble choice."

She jerked up her chin. "You would see it that way. You are besotted with her. I agree that she is lovely to look at, but really, Nelson—"

"Enough, Mother!" He pounded his fist on the desk. Would nothing break the hard shell of her? "I've asked her to marry me."

"You what?"

"You heard me. I've asked Sylvia to marry me."

She stared at him. Obviously shocked. Then

her knees buckled and she started to drop to the floor.

"Mother!" He ran forward and caught her. He needed to invest in smelling salts with how often women fainted around here. He lowered her to the hardwood floor. "Sylvia! Bring me a pillow or a blanket!"

Sylvia came running in with the folded blanket from the exam-room cupboard. "What happened?"

He tucked the blanket under his mother's head and pressed the back of his hand to her cheek, then sat back on his heels. "I told her how I felt about you."

He glanced up at Sylvia. "She took it well."

His mother moaned.

"Just lie still, Mother. You are very pale."

Her eyes fluttered open. She focused on him first and then her gaze wandered to Sylvia. "I'll be all right in a moment."

He forced her to wait five minutes and then he escorted her up to her room. He removed her shoes and tucked her under the covers. As he was turning to leave, she grasped his hand.

"Nelson. Are you serious? What will our neighbors say when you return to Boston?"

"Boston?" He couldn't have been more surprised. "Is that what you hoped for by coming here? That you could talk me into going back with you?"

"I want you there with me. We've been apart for so much of our lives."

"There is nothing for me there. You made sure of that. I don't intend to go back."

Tears filled her eyes, surprising him further. He didn't know what to make of them. Were they for him? Or, more likely, were they because he would not agree to her plans?

"This Miss Marks has changed you."

"Yes. She has. She is a good woman, a good person, and she makes me very happy. I plan to marry her if she will have me."

His mother turned her head away from him and closed her eyes.

Chapter Twenty-Two

"I saw Wyatt and Rhett walk by, Ma. Can I go ask them if they can play now?"

Tommy was tired of sitting at the table. He'd been fidgety for the past twenty minutes while Sylvia cleaned up the kitchen from the meal.

"Go ahead. But make sure if they have chores to do that you either help them or you come back here so they can get them done."

Tommy jumped from his chair, grabbed his crutches and swung himself down the hall and out the door. He left the door wide-open. That boy! Guess she should be grateful that he'd found friends. She strode down the hall and closed it softly so as not to bother the men in the meeting with Nelson.

Mayor Melbourne, Teddy White and a few other townspeople had arrived to discuss the families that had been displaced by the flooding. She wished she could hear what they were saying, but she was confident that Nelson would tell her all about it later.

She still felt butterflies dancing inside from his kisses in the livery stable. The things he'd said had caused a glow, making her happy and nervous at the same time. She thought she might walk right off into the air. She wanted so much to believe them. She just wasn't sure that she could live up to his expectations.

A bowl of chicken and dumplings remained heating on the stove. Nelson had a regular order with Rollie and Sadie at the restaurant for lunch to be brought to him three days a week. Sadie had increased the portions to allow for his extra company. That last bowlful belonged to his mother who remained upstairs.

Mrs. Graham could have come down to get it for herself, but then, the woman was used to having someone wait on her. Sylvia had planned to spend the afternoon in her room, sewing on her new material. If she worked hard on it, she should have her dress made by tomorrow, and then she could clean and take Miss Simcock's dress back to her.

It would be rude to ignore the woman when she was ailing. Sylvia had a strong feeling that the reason she was ailing was *her*.

"Oh, bother!" She fixed up a tray with the

food and a glass of water and carried it up the stairs.

"Mrs. Graham?" She knocked softly on the door. "I've brought your noon meal."

The woman didn't answer. Was she asleep?

"I'm coming in." She hated to barge in, but someone should check on the woman.

The room was darkened with the shades drawn. Mrs. Graham was awake, sitting in bed and watching as Sylvia stepped into the room and put the tray on the bedside table.

"Are you feeling better, ma'am?"

She didn't answer.

"Your son is in a meeting downstairs with a few of the town founders. They're trying to figure a way to help get the families, like me, back to their land. I thought you'd like to know that."

Still no answer.

"Well. Let me know if I can get you anything. I'll leave you alone now."

"Close the door and come back here, Miss Marks. Sit down."

Sylvia hesitated with her hand on the glass doorknob. A conversation with this woman did not sound pleasant. Not after the things she'd said yesterday.

"I promise not to bite."

Sylvia turned to face her, her hands behind her on the knob.

"My son believes that I should speak with

you. That my information is somehow skewed due to my sources."

Sylvia stepped toward the bed—one step. "Doc Graham is a smart man."

Mrs. Graham pointed to the one chair in her room—a straight-backed chair with fancy scroll-work and a cane seat. "Please."

Sylvia wouldn't be cowed so easily as she was yesterday. Nelson had pledged his love to her. She was strong to begin with, had raised Tommy on her own and carved out a life for the two of them. The love of a good man only strengthened her further. She walked over to the chair and sat down.

"What do you want to know?"

"Tell me about yourself. Where you come from. Whatever you wish me to know."

She was a stranger, and Sylvia wasn't used to just blurting things out to strangers, but the woman was also Nelson's mother. "Only if you do the same with me."

That startled the woman. "What exactly do you mean?"

"For every question I answer about myself, you have to do the same. Answer one of mine."

The first hint of softening played about Mrs. Graham's eyes. "I suppose that is appropriate."

"Then we understand each other."

"I believe we do." She smoothed the covers over her lap. "I'll go first. I would like to know the circumstances of your son's birth. I've been led to believe, by Nelson, that the version I received from Carl Caulder is incorrect."

"We'll get to that eventually."

For the next two hours, they talked. Sylvia was cautious with her answers at first and likewise Mrs. Graham was the same. Sylvia talked about her home in Virginia in the hills, about the small coal-mining town and her mother and father and the things she did for fun. Mrs. Graham talked about her upbringing on Cape Cod and the clambakes and parties she attended. Then Sylvia told her about the Caulder family and particularly Thomas and Carl, the wedding that wasn't really a wedding in some people's eyes and the journey to Kansas.

"I was sixteen and full of a love so big that it couldn't be contained. Back then, I never doubted that things worked out in the end, that a ring given in a meadow on bended knee and words in front of my family were as binding as vows said before a preacher and that nothing would keep Thomas from marrying me proper-like as soon as we got more settled. But then he left for Texas and that cattle drive and he never came back."

Mrs. Graham listened. When Sylvia got to the part about learning of Thomas's death on the cattle trail and then Tommy's birth, Mrs. Graham grew very silent.

"How did you survive?" she finally asked. "Why didn't you move into town where people could help you?"

"Nelson asked the same thing. I was fearful of being alone, but I had to stand on my own two feet. Thomas paid good money for us to homestead that land. I couldn't just leave it."

"But you weren't married. Was it even yours?"

She nodded. "Carl tried to tell me it wasn't, but that was because he wanted to move in there himself. He had helped build the soddy and figured his sweat and labor made it part his. Julian DuBois, my neighbor, said the land was surely mine. As long as I stayed there for five years it would belong to me free and clear and Tommy too."

"My son said you were stubborn."

"It's a fact."

"You could have married Carl. It would have made things easier. Why didn't you?"

Sylvia blew out a breath. "Easier. If you ever met him, you'd see right off that he's nothing like Thomas. Carl has a mean streak. He doesn't let it out much, so we probably could have made a life together. He can turn on the charm the same as Thomas, but it's different. He's got no patience. He wasn't good with Tommy. I couldn't see him raising my son. And more than any of that—I didn't love Carl the way a body should that's gonna say vows to last a lifetime."

Something subtle changed in the woman's expression. She coughed lightly. "At the mercantile, he did say some rather unflattering things."

"Then you have met him. That's his way. He got mad when I wouldn't agree to marry him. Then he told all the folks in town that my real name was Marks and that his brother had never married me. Folks looked at me different after that. Some wouldn't barter with me for my goods anymore. It made it real hard for me and Tommy. Adele's husband would sometimes bring my things to trade so that folks wouldn't know they were mine. Otherwise, I probably would have starved."

She gazed out the window. "Ever since then, I knew the truth about myself. I wasn't a proper lady. It didn't matter how much I wanted to be or how careful I was around men or how I held myself apart, I couldn't go back and change the way things had been. All I could do was make a good home for Tommy and see that he was raised the best way I knew how."

Mrs. Graham fumbled with her handkerchief, worrying it in her lap. "Has Nelson— Has he told you about his father?"

Sylvia shook her head. "Just that he recently passed away. He said he was sick."

"For a short while. Not long."

Sylvia waited. It seemed Mrs. Graham was trying to gather her words. "He was a lawyer," Sylvia said. "I know that much. And he and the doc didn't get along all that well."

Mrs. Graham smiled sadly. "No. They weren't close at all."

"I'm sorry for that. A boy should be close to his father."

"Ellison did try at first." She hesitated. "You love my son, don't you?"

Sylvia met her gaze. "Completely."

The woman took a deep breath. "I thought so. And he loves you. It is obvious in the way he looks at you, in the way he was frantic with worry when we found Tommy on the steps after the rain." She looked down at her handkerchief again. "It has nothing to do with him being a doctor?"

"I can't say that I can separate the man from the doc. That's how we met."

"I heard about that. Have you agreed to marry him?"

The question took Sylvia by surprise. She thought that remained a secret with Nelson. He'd said they wouldn't tell anyone until she was ready.

"Don't look so surprised. I'm not blind. Nelson acts quickly once he makes up his mind. I can see that he has made up his mind about you."

"We talked some. I'm—" She didn't want to

tell this woman that she was afraid to marry her son. "There's a lot to do before I can think about something like that. I need to check on my land. I need to find out how my animals are doing."

"But you love him."

"Yes. I don't see how it can work out. I'm too different from him. I know that. And when a body loves someone, they want what's best for that person."

"A dilemma for you."

There was a lot going on behind what Mrs. Graham was saying. Sylvia could see it in her eyes and the careful way she spoke.

"You can take the tray down now. I'm not hungry. I'll be down soon."

Sylvia stood.

"You've given me a lot to think about, Miss Marks. Thank you for being so candid."

She gathered the tray and untouched food and took it back to the kitchen.

The meeting must be over—she no longer heard the booming voice of the mayor—yet the door remained shut. Nelson must have someone in the exam room who needed his doctoring skills.

The sun was shining and the breeze light. She gathered her sewing things and took them outside to the swing. Her thoughts had eased some with talking to Mrs. Graham. It was interesting how going over something like that could make it clearer just by talking about it. She still didn't see answers. It was too big. Too much to think about all at once.

She could hear Tommy playing with the Blackwell boys, whooping and hollering. It did her heart good to hear him so happy.

She started to hem the sleeve on her dress.

"Heard you was here." Carl sauntered up the walkway.

Immediately, her senses were on alert. Where was Tommy? Oh, yes—out playing with the Blackwells. She had been so engrossed in her sewing that she lost track of her surroundings. "Carl. What are you doing here?"

"Came to town for supplies." He sat down on the swing beside her. He had let his beard grow since she last saw him. It was coming in with all kinds of corkscrew gray hairs. His shirt and overalls reeked of sweat and cattle from the stockyards.

She scooted over and tugged her material closer, hoping to keep his odor and dirt from it.

"Oh, don't be like that, Sylvia." He shoved off with his foot and gave the seat a big swing.

"Stop that, Carl. I'm trying to get this done."

He let the swing come to a stop and then watched her sew for a minute. "I got a leak in my roof. Had to get some things to fix it at the hardware store."

She came to the end of the hem, tied a knot and bit the thread with her teeth to separate it.

"You look real nice in that new dress. Doc get that for you?" He fingered the gingham material at her collar.

She scooted over again. "No. One of the women at the hotel lent it to me. My dress got ruined. This is my new one." She concentrated on the next sleeve.

"Should have let me know. I could buy you a new dress."

"Ha! With what? Anytime you get a couple coins, you drink it away at the Whistle Stop."

"That ain't true!" He watched her for a few minutes, then he looked up at the house. "What are you staying here for anyway?"

"I can't get back across the river until the ferry is fixed."

"You could have asked me. You know where I live."

"That's...kind of you. I felt poorly and the doc wanted to keep an eye on me."

He snorted. "I just bet he did. Is your boy staying here too?"

Her eyes narrowed on him. She hadn't forgotten his threat. "You keep away from Tommy. You hear?"

"That land, you, Tommy... You know I been looking out for you all these years. I was never real close 'cause you been touchy about it, but I've always been willing to help."

"I know." But there were always strings attached to his kind of help.

He gripped her arm and held it up so she would have to look at him. "You don't belong here, Sylvia. Don't let yourself forget that. You're not like them."

She squirmed, trying to wrench from his strong hold. "Carl, you're crowding me! I can't sew this if you don't give me some room."

"Hello, Mr. Caulder."

Carl stood up immediately at Nelson's voice. "Doc," he said, acknowledging him. He stepped away from the swing and her.

"Are you ill? In need of my services?"

"No. Just came to check on Sylvia. Had to know she was doing all right, what with the flooding and all." Carl rubbed his hands on his thighs.

"Last time I saw you two together I didn't realize you were friends."

"She's like my kid sister. I tease her a lot is all."

"I have seen the evidence of your teasing. Bruises you left as presents."

Carl narrowed his eyes. "I don't know what you saw, Doc, but I never hurt Sylvia."

"Hmph. I'm glad to hear that." Nelson walked over to her to offer his hand. "You'll have to excuse us now. Sylvia promised me a walk this afternoon and at the moment I am free."

Carl's brows shot up. He laughed once—a sarcastic-sounding laugh. "Well, that'll be a sight."

Nelson ignored him. "Ready?" he asked her.

Without hesitation, she took his hand and rose to her feet, then put down her sewing on the swing. She was relieved that he had suggested a walk. Her first thought on seeing Carl had been to check on Tommy.

Nelson tucked her hand into the crook of his arm.

"Sylvia." The dark warning in Carl's voice was unmistakable. He hooked one thumb in his overall strap. "When the ferry starts up again, I'll come for you. Don't you forget what I said before, 'cause I won't."

Footsteps sounded on the porch. Sylvia looked up to see Mrs. Graham standing there.

"We'll be back in a few minutes, Mother."

She nodded.

Carl glanced at Mrs. Graham, then at Sylvia and Nelson, and then turning away, he strode angrily toward the main street of town.

Nelson took her in the opposite direction. "What did Carl mean by that last remark?"

She blew out a breath. "He can't take no for an answer. I sure wish that woman in Fort Wallace hadn't up and married a soldier. As long as Carl was seeing her, he left me alone. Now he's right back at it like a dog worrying a stick."

Nelson stopped and lifted her chin with his finger. "You didn't answer my question."

"He thinks I'm putting on airs, being here—that it's not my place. He figures I should be with him. Tommy too."

"Then we better go check on Tommy first."

Peace like she hadn't known existed rolled through her as Nelson turned toward the sound of laughter and hollering that came from behind the blacksmith shop. Nelson understood. He would protect her if need be from Carl or anyone else. She had never had that assurance before, not even with Thomas. Thomas had left her to fend for herself and she had done all right. But the way Nelson looked after her, she felt precious and special. She laid her head against his strong arm for just a second as they continued their walk.

Chapter Twenty-Three

Nelson knew Sylvia would need to check on her son after Carl's visit. He wished the man hadn't shown up. Sylvia had enough on her mind without him causing more turmoil.

The large back door of the smithy was open, and a breeze swirled through Brett's shop. Wyatt, Rhett and Tommy were out back, practicing roping a wooden crate, with no sign of Carl's presence.

Nelson and Sylvia walked on and found Hannah White outside her house, trying to quiet her four-month-old, Dora, and at the same time take her dry clothes off the line.

"I don't know what the trouble is," Hannah said when she saw them. It was obvious she was frazzled as the baby kept fussing. "Could she have a tooth coming in this soon?"

Nelson examined the baby's gums. "It's early for teething. Have you eaten anything different in the past day or two?"

Hannah blushed. "Some canned beets."

"Dora probably isn't ready for them in your milk."

"Here," Sylvia said. "Let me take her a minute so you can rest your arms. I remember how mine ached from holding Tommy when he would get this way. He didn't want me to put him down or sit down myself. All he wanted was for me to walk with him."

While Hannah took the dry clothes off her line and folded them, Sylvia walked back and forth with the fussy baby. She smiled as she handed the baby back. "It seems babies this age just know when their mother has her thoughts on other things and they don't like it. They like to be the center of their mother's world at all times."

Dora wasn't any less fussy, but Sylvia's attention to Hannah and her frustration made a decided difference on Hannah. She was calmer and ready to try again with renewed patience.

It was such a little thing, but Nelson would remember it in the future in dealing with those who came to his office for help.

They strolled past the school, and the new schoolteacher stepped out the door.

"I'm Miss Burnett. Kade Austin told me about

Tommy being in town because of the flooding. Your boy is welcome to come to school while you are here. Some of the other children in your same situation have been coming."

Sylvia thanked her.

They walked on, and when they were out of hearing distance, she stopped him. "You were right about there being a lot of new folks in town."

"Oak Grove is growing, with an eye for the future. I want you to be part of it."

She squeezed his arm. "It sure would be something."

In his room now, and thinking of their walk, Nelson smiled to himself. Sylvia had managed to walk through town on his arm without incident and had even relaxed somewhat and enjoyed it. It had been a test, of sorts, and it had gone well. She didn't know it, but tonight was the second test. He was taking her and Tommy to supper at the restaurant. Surprisingly, it was his mother's suggestion. He wasn't sure what to make of that. His mother said she had talked with Sylvia and that was all he could get out of her.

He finished tying his shoestring tie and made sure his collar stood up straight. He straightened his vest. Hooking his coat off the end of his bed, he shrugged into it. Being black, the coat served well as a mourning frock, but it had always been his standard clothing ever since he became a doctor.

His initial shock at Ellison's death had worn off and he remained conflicted about the man. Learning the truth had freed him in one sense—he now knew why he'd been a thorn in the man's side—but it also gave rise to so many more questions about his real father. Questions that had no answers.

His mother could not be persuaded to join them. She still wore black in respect for Ellison's passing and would for some time yet. Any semblance of enjoying herself in public was out of the question for at least another year. If he were to marry Sylvia, there would be no reception or celebration. He hoped, however, that his mother would attend the small ceremony.

Tommy waited on the top stair for a piggyback ride down to the main floor. Nelson scooped him up, surprising him and carrying him down instead. Then he let him scramble onto his back and handed him his crutches. The boy wouldn't want to be seen being carried into the restaurant, but Nelson was certain a ride *to* the restaurant was another thing.

Sylvia stood at the door, looking resolute and nervous all at the same time. She wore the same purple-and-white checked dress. Seeing her so fresh and becoming, with her hair done up, it was hard to recall the woman he'd first met at the mercantile, when the man's hat she wore hid her lovely face and eyes. That seemed like a year ago, not just four weeks.

They arrived at Austin's Hotel and Eatery at the same time that Sadie was lighting the candles on each of the tables. Sylvia moved in closer to his side when they entered the large room. Tommy swung in on his crutches like he knew just what to do and showed Sylvia the way to Nelson's regular table. Although it was only the second time Tommy had been there, he acted as though he ate there every night.

Nelson held the chair out for Sylvia. After a brief hesitation, she slid into the seat.

"Hiya, Tommy!" Wiley ran in ahead of his brother, Kade. Kade brought in saucers and teacups. They wobbled precariously in his hands.

Sylvia quickly grabbed them. "This is kind of fancy, don't you think?"

"It's perfect. I'm glad you agreed to accompany me. I don't like to take my meals by myself. Before you or my mother came, I ate here nearly every night, often with the mayor or one of the other bachelors in town." He felt a twinge of guilt at playing to her sympathy, but if it kept her in town, he'd worry about his conscience another day.

"Never thought of that. I never had much time to get lonely. Not with Tommy around. There was always something to do and Tommy to talk to."

"I'll admit, sometimes I would take the meal back to the house so that I could study. There is a lot to know, a lot to keep up with in medicine. I want to provide Oak Grove with the best, most current medical care."

As he spoke, the restaurant filled up with other residents of the town. A few of the women from the train gathered at one table. Miss Weber and Miss O'Rourke smiled and waved cheerfully at him and Sylvia. Miss Pratt shot him a sour look and then slid her focus to Sylvia, obviously displeased that they were together. He hoped some man would come along and soften her up. In her present state, he had a hard time believing anyone would marry her.

Rollie came from the kitchen and approached the table with a puzzled look on his face. "Doc. Miss Marks, ain't it? This is a surprise."

"Hello, Rollie. Sylvia and Tommy are staying with Mother and me until she can get back to her land. Although I am trying to convince her to stay in town."

Rollie's expression cleared—a little. "Tommy is your boy?" he said, turning his attention to Sylvia.

"Yes. He's been playing with the Blackwell boys, and I think with Kade and Wiley a time or two while we have been here. You have real nice boys there, Mr. Austin."

"I like to think so. What are you having tonight, Doc? You know the choices. Steak or stew."

"Steak, I think. For all of us."

"All right. Three plates."

"I will take a fourth plate to take back to my mother."

Rollie scratched his head. "I'll let the cook know."

When he had gone, Sylvia leaned forward. "Are they busy like this every night?"

Nelson nodded, enjoying watching her take in the townsfolk in the room.

"Sure seems like those gals have a lot of bachelors eyeing them. When do they have to choose?"

"The weddings are set for Sunday at one o'clock. Would you like to go?"

"I don't know any of them but Miss Weber and Miss Vandersohn." Her eyes brightened. "Oh—I guess I do know Miss Simcock. It would sure be a sight to see. I guess the entire town will show up."

She shrank back in her chair.

He smiled and reached across the table to clasp her hand for a quick squeeze. "You're doing fine, Sylvia."

He almost suggested that they join the brides

and add one more couple to the celebration, but he knew Sylvia wasn't ready for that yet, and if he mentioned anything, it would probably scare her away. Besides, if she did agree to marry him, he didn't want to share the moment. He wanted her to have a wedding beyond anything she could dream up. She deserved it after all she'd been through.

Their plates came then, carried in by Rollie, and followed by Sadie with hot tea.

"Mrs. Austin," Sylvia said, straightening. "I want to thank you for the fine meals that you've been sending over to the doc's."

Sadie smiled warmly at Sylvia while she filled the teacups. "He saved little Wiley's life not too long ago. Did he tell you? The doc is a blessing to us. We've got to keep him happy here."

After she'd left them to their meals, Sylvia leaned forward. "Does Mrs. Austin's gushing make you uncomfortable, Doc? She's right. We do want to keep you happy here, don't we, Tommy?"

"Sure do!" Tommy said, starting right in on his steak, making the table shake as he cut a piece.

Sylvia grabbed the table but still wasn't quick enough to keep the tea from spilling out of their teacups. "Tommy! Put down that knife! Sorry,

Doc," she said with a mortified expression. "He isn't used to steak."

"Hold on there, Tommy!" Nelson said, chuckling. He reached over and helped him cut his meat into small pieces. "Take your time. No choking."

Although Sylvia kept very still and looked dignified, her gaze darted about constantly, watching him, watching Tommy and watching the other patrons in the room. He wished she would enjoy herself a little more. She was a bundle of nerves and looked uncomfortable. It was as if she expected something terrible to happen. That bothered him. Hopefully, with a few more visits here, she would learn to relax.

Charming him, Sylvia waited until he had taken the first bite and followed his motions. It made him wonder if she had ever been in a restaurant before in her life. He listened to the chatter going on around him. At first other men walking into the restaurant would stare at them both, but after a moment they went on about their business.

"Did you enjoy our walk today?" he asked her, hoping to get her mind on something else.

She nodded but didn't say anything.

"I thought Miss Burnett, the new schoolteacher, seemed nice." When that garnered no response from her, he focused on Tommy. "She asked about you, Tommy. She said you are welcome in class as long as you are staying here in town."

Sylvia stiffened. "Doc—"

Maybe he should have waited to speak with her about it more, but he was anxious to move ahead with his plans—and have her a part of them. She had to understand how important it was to him to have her and Tommy with him. He was tired of being alone. Tired of being lonely. His mother would soon return to Boston and that house would be too big for just him.

"Growing up, I lived at a boarding school. I only saw my mother on holidays like Christmas and Easter. Sometimes my father would be there, but not every year. The older I got, the less he made it a point to spend time with me. Tommy, you are very lucky to have your mother with you all the time."

Tommy looked over at Sylvia and a silly grin spread across his face. Nelson chuckled. Sylvia smiled.

When they were nearly done with their food, Jackson Miller walked over. His clothes were spattered with mud, so he was careful to stand back from the table. He swiped his flat cap from his head. "I just got back into town. Thought I'd let the folks staying here and Miss Marks know that we found the ferry. It's at the landing now. It held up. Won't take much work to get it back in shape for use. If everything goes well, it should be ready for use by noon tomorrow."

The man couldn't have brought more unwelcome news.

"Thank you, Jackson."

Jackson nodded a goodbye and headed over to speak to another family at a table by the far wall.

"I never would have believed it if I hadn't seen it with my own eyes!" Mrs. Gallagher stood in the large doorway to the restaurant. Her sharp voice cut through the light dinner conversations going on around the room.

Sylvia slowly lowered her teacup, the contentment on her face fading away.

Mable Gallagher marched over to their table with a haughty look on her face. The space by the table that Jackson had just vacated immediately filled with the loud woman.

Nelson rose from the table.

"I am surprised to see you here, Doctor. And with Miss Marks."

"Why is that?"

"I assumed you would be in mourning over the death of your father. To see you enjoying a meal with *her*—well—after speaking with your mother, I was led to believe Miss Marks had left town."

"I'm not sure why it should matter to you, but there are extenuating circumstances concerning the mourning that I'm afraid you are not privy to."

The woman's nostrils flared at the dress down.

"And with the river flooding—where do you propose Sylvia go? The hotel rooms are full."

"I thought—uh—to Mr. Caulder's place. He did offer to take her in."

"Mr. Caulder isn't the most upstanding citizen in Oak Grove."

"But he is the boy's uncle."

He pretended to consider her words. "That could create talk of a disagreeable nature, wouldn't you say? I would hate for that to happen to such a lovely woman as Miss Marks."

Mrs. Gallagher nearly gagged. "But her reputation is already questionab—"

"I believe you've said enough." Tommy listened, wide-eyed and impressionable, as did everyone else in the room. The woman should have better sense than to say such things in front of the boy. "Sylvia is comfortable at my house. With my mother there to chaperone, it seems the most sensible place for her and her son until she can go back to her own home. They are welcome there for as long as they wish to stay." He wanted Mrs. Gallagher and everyone else in the town to know he wasn't going to tolerate anyone smearing Sylvia's character ever again.

"Well," Mrs. Gallagher sputtered. "Well! You

surprise me. I thought, with the things your mother said— Enjoy your supper, Doctor."

She turned to her husband, Henry, who stood behind her. "I believe I'll fix something at home after all. The company here disagrees with me."

With that, she stormed out of the restaurant with her husband trailing her like a puppy.

Nelson relaxed and turned to take his seat. Hopefully, this made up for his silence last week when Mrs. Gallagher had hurt Sylvia at the mercantile. He couldn't completely remove the sting of that altercation, but at least now the woman would think twice before being rude to Sylvia.

Across the table from him, Sylvia looked pale and shaken.

"It's over now," he said. "She won't dare say a thing after this."

Sylvia shook her head and stared at her half-eaten steak. "How can I go into the mercantile ever again?"

"Don't let her get to you. You won't have any more trouble with her." Didn't she see that it was over?

She met his gaze, her own fierce, her jaw set. "I want to go back."

"Sylvia, you haven't done anything wrong." He didn't want the evening to end like this. "If we leave now—"

"I want to go back. Now, please."

"All right. All right," he said, disheartened.

"We'll go." He pulled his money holder from his vest pocket and withdrew two bills, dropping them on the table. "Come on, Tommy."

He said his thanks to Rollie, who handed him a covered plate of food for his mother. Rollie had witnessed the entire spectacle, as had every other person in the restaurant. Nelson took hold of Sylvia's elbow to help her down the two steps to the boardwalk. Once on the road, she moved from his reach.

"Sylvia, talk to me." He sensed a desperation rolling off her. Tommy too could tell something was very wrong and kept silent.

At his house, she climbed the stairs to her room, went inside and shut the door.

He stood there in the hallway, staring up the stairwell. What had just happened?

His mother called from the kitchen. "How did it go?"

The fact that she asked was odd. His mother had expressed little interest in Sylvia or Tommy.

He walked toward her. "She said she wants to go back. Whether that meant back here to this house or back to her own place—I don't know."

Then another thought, more suspicious this time, came to him. "Tell me, Mother, did you know Mrs. Gallagher would be at the restaurant? You saw her earlier today. Had you said something to her?"

She stared at him, her gaze cool, neither confirming nor denying her involvement. "Sylvia will come to her senses. Give her time."

A heaviness settled in his gut. Everything was spinning out of his control. He was losing her. He set the plate of food on the table. "I don't think time is going to help. As of noon tomorrow, the ferry is operational."

Chapter Twenty-Four

Sylvia sat in the chair by her bed, the same one Miss Weber had used to watch over her the first day that Nelson had rescued her from the river. Tommy had long since gone to sleep, sprawled sideways across the middle of the bed. She hadn't bothered to straighten him out. She couldn't sleep. She couldn't do anything but replay that horrid scene at the restaurant over and over in her mind.

Mrs. Gallagher had the ear of everyone in town and the woman knew it. Sylvia had witnessed it from the first time she'd entered the mercantile, back when she had come for supplies with Thomas. The store was barely more than a way station then, but the power Mrs. Gallagher wielded then was nothing compared to what she had now. The mayor, the bankers, they all wanted her opinion on things. Her opinion mattered.

Sylvia would never be able to trade there again. With all that Mrs. Gallagher had said the last time she was in the mercantile, and now at the restaurant, she was sure of it. The woman wouldn't let her through the store's front door again. It wouldn't matter whether she had real money or not.

Nelson had confronted Mrs. Gallagher in front of everyone. *Everyone!* How could he have done such a thing? If forced to pick sides, people would side with her. They had in the past. Nelson had been here only two years. He was the newcomer and towns like this rallied with their own. It had been the same in Virginia, in the town where she had grown up.

She had spent only a few days here and look at the mess that had become of it! Nelson was wrong to have pushed her. They had feelings for each other, but those feelings didn't mean anything in real life. They both had to live among other folks. They needed other folks to survive out here—Nelson more than her.

Opinions mattered. In a small town like Oak Grove, where his livelihood depended on his standing in the community, he couldn't be nose-to-nose with one of the most powerful people in town.

In the end, Carl was right. She wasn't any

good for Nelson. She would—she already had— drag him down. It was as simple and as sad as that. Her chest ached with the thought. She had to face reality. He'd come to hate her eventually for holding back his career, his position in Oak Grove. He deserved a woman like Miss Weber.

Perhaps she and Tommy could survive until a new crop could be harvested in the fall. That depended on rounding up her chickens and sheep. And she had to find Berta. She just had to. If she couldn't find her animals, guess the only option left was to sell her land and try to find a job in a town far, far from Oak Grove.

The next morning, she told Tommy they'd be going back home. Tommy's ankle wasn't strong enough to walk the entire distance, so she would have to depend on Nelson to take her. If he couldn't take her, well…then she guessed she would have to depend on Carl.

The thought wasn't a pleasant one.

"Can I play with my friends till we have to leave?" he asked plaintively.

"It's Friday. They're in school today."

"I won't see them at all? Not even to say goodbye?"

"You might. I guess it depends when I hear about the ferry."

"Well, what am I supposed to do till then?"

It wasn't like Tommy to talk with that whine

in his voice. She sighed. "Have breakfast, and then go check on Penny. We'll take her with us when we go. If you want, you can lead her back here and tie her up outside. That way, we'll be ready when the time comes to leave."

"What are you going to do?"

"I'll be down as soon as I'm dressed."

Once Tommy left the room, Sylvia removed her nightgown—the one Miss Weber had lent to her. She'd have to wash it that morning and take it back. She wondered who the woman would chose for her husband. Then wondered if it would be Nelson and what he would do if that happened. He had a right to marry Miss Weber—or any of the women from the train. When the time came that he made a choice to wed, Sylvia would just have to accept it. All she knew was that it wouldn't be her. She wasn't right for him.

She dressed in the mustard-yellow skirt and blouse that she'd made over the past few days. It was plain, but it suited her. The buttons down the front of the blouse were the only decoration at all, and with the stiffness of the new material, they were difficult to button. She gathered up Miss Simcock's gingham dress and the nightgown and carried them down the stairs. She would set a pot on to warm some water so that she could wash them.

When she walked into the kitchen, Tommy

had just finished his oatmeal. Nelson and Mrs. Graham sat at the table with him. Everyone was quiet.

Tommy grabbed his crutches and swung down the hall. He was already an expert with those crutches. She'd have to remember to leave them behind. They'd worked their magic. Having friends to keep up with and play with had done the rest. He still had pain with walking, but he could bear weight tolerably well on that leg now. The front door swished open and then closed with his leaving.

Nelson stood. "Tommy said that you are leaving today." He searched her face with that green gaze of his.

"Yes."

He whipped his cloth napkin onto the table.

"Don't go, Sylvia. If this is about last night with Mrs. Gallagher, we can work through it. Together."

She glanced at his mother. Was she aware that her name had come up last night too?

Mrs. Graham rose from her chair. "I'll leave you two to discuss this. However," she said, focusing on Sylvia, "there is one thing I want you to know. I'm sorry I didn't talk to you first rather than Mrs. Gallagher. After our conversation, I changed many preconceptions I held about you. I'm sorry it took me so long.

"You will find it difficult to build a life together if you go back to your land. Nelson is a strong man, Sylvia. He can handle the Mrs. Gallaghers of this world. You can trust that." She took her teacup and walked from the room.

Sylvia was overwhelmed. Mrs. Graham was on her side? She turned, in her confusion, to Nelson. "How can the few words I said to her make that big a difference? It doesn't make any sense to me."

"From what she told me, you did most of the talking. There is more to my mother's story than she told you."

"Well, I didn't want to pry, and you know how I can talk on and on once I get going."

"Mother learned long ago to keep her thoughts bound up inside. She's only just now opening up. She probably wasn't ready to share it all with you in one sitting."

"What made her change her mind about me?"

"She realized she has a lot in common with you. I'll tell you about it someday. After we are married."

She looked down at the bundle of clothes that she'd placed on a chair. "About that..."

"You said you'd try," he said with an urgency to his voice. "One day doesn't amount to a 'try.'"

"It's just no good."

"You said you loved me."

"I do. There's no question on that."

"Then I don't see a problem."

"I'm not right for you and I never will be. People here know my past and aren't about to accept me." She walked over to the water pump and worked the handle, filling his largest pot with water. It didn't matter what he said. She wasn't changing her mind.

He came up behind her and placed his hand on her shoulder. "You won't give them a chance to know you—not the you I have come to care for."

"Well, I can't face them." She turned from the pump to meet his gaze. "Last night I was so mad at myself for letting you do the talking. You shouldn't have had to do that. If it's about me, then I'm the one who should be standing up for myself. Only trouble is, some of the things she said are true. How can I argue with that?"

"Thomas had some part in it too. It shouldn't all be on your shoulders."

"Well, that's neither here nor there because Thomas is gone now."

"What you did happened a long time ago and you've paid for it. Whether anyone else agrees with that or not, you should believe it yourself. Don't let what happened eight years ago ruin the future we can have together."

She sighed. "Oh, Nelson. It just ain't going to be. You've got to leave it alone."

"Do you know what I see when I look at you?" Gently, he raised her chin with his fingertips. "I see a woman who loves her son and even the man who gave her her son, although he didn't treasure her enough and do right by her."

She tried to look away, but he held her with his gaze. Her heart was pumping fast. The words he spouted were so sweet. She wanted to see herself as the woman he saw. She wanted to be that woman.

"I see a woman who loves unconditionally." He huffed out a breath, a slight smile coming to his lips. "There aren't many of you around. Believe me, I know."

She tingled all over from the tenderness shining from his face. Her insides were mush with all that he'd said and still her heart pounded. How could he see all that in her? How? It would be easy to step closer, to touch her lips to his, to put her arms around his neck. So easy...

He waited.

Carl's words came back to her. *You're not like him. You'll only shame him.* She stepped back, away from his touch.

"I'm going home, Doc."

Nelson's jaw hardened.

Someone knocked at the door.

"Sylvia..."

They knocked again. More insistently this time.

"Probably someone in need of your doctorin' skills," she said, turning from him. "You should go see who it is. I need to get these clothes washed and back to their rightful owners."

His gaze turned to stone. She'd never seen him angry. Not like this. The only other time had been when he'd seen the bruises on her arm.

He left the room and answered the door. She watched from the kitchen as he spoke with Teddy White. Funny how he could act like the world was still spinning and everything was all right, when for her, her world was falling apart. She placed her hands over her abdomen, as a weight shifted and dropped inside. There was no turning back now.

The sun was straight overhead when Carl rode up on a horse. He had tethered a mule to his saddle. Sylvia figured that one was for her and Tommy. She wasn't surprised to see him at all. Growing up from childhood with Carl, she'd become accustomed to his ways. Angry at Nelson, he might be, but he had been clear enough yesterday that he'd be back for her.

He'd known about last evening before it even happened. He'd known, eventually, that she would face her situation in town and see that the small amount of pride she still possessed wouldn't allow her to stay.

Tommy was out on the swing, hanging on to his goat and waiting. She felt bad that he wouldn't get to say goodbye to his new friends.

She rose from a chair in the parlor, where she had been waiting.

Mrs. Graham came in from the kitchen with a basket of food. "You won't have time to prepare anything for tonight." She pushed the basket into Sylvia's hands and gave her an awkward hug. "I don't know that I shall see you again. I'll be going back to Boston in another week, so I'll say my goodbyes now."

The exam room door remained shut. Nelson was in there with a family from a nearby ranch. One of the boys had a spider bite that had festered.

She knocked on the closed door. "I'm leaving now," she called.

A moment later Nelson opened the door. "I can't take you just yet. You'll have to wait."

"That's all right. You've got work to do. Carl is here. He can take me back."

Nelson closed the door behind him, shutting out the curious stares of the boy and his parents. "You can't go with Carl! Wait for me to take you. I won't be long."

"You don't know that. Anyone could come, needing your skills. You've got to stay here. And I've got to go. I can't wait any longer. I need to get home."

He took her face in his hands, searching her eyes, her cheeks, her lips, as if he was trying to memorize everything about her. She didn't have to look far to see the pain in his eyes. Her own burned with unshed tears. "This is good-bye, then."

She couldn't trust her voice not to waver or betray the turmoil going on inside. She nodded.

He kissed her then—hard on the mouth. Then he spun around and returned to his patient.

She stared at the thick door. So much more separated them than a piece of wood.

Carl didn't get off his own horse to help her. She led the mule around so that she could mount it herself from the front steps. It was awkward in the new dress, but she managed. A saddle would have been easier, but with Carl she wasn't about to say a thing. She was lucky to have a mule. She picked up Tommy, sitting him down in front of her on the mule's warm, dusty back.

As he urged his horse over to her and took the lead rope, the smirk on Carl's face said plenty. He thought he'd won in some kind of crazy match between her and the doc.

Once they were out of town and over the train tracks, he started talking.

"Glad to see that you came to your senses, gal."

"Nothing has changed between you and me, Carl. Thank you kindly for helping me get home, but don't expect me to start setting a place at the table for you. I'm only going back because you were right about one thing—that's where I belong."

He smiled a big, toothy grin. "Glad to see you still got some sass in you."

"Ma?" Tommy said. "Think the doc will come visit us again soon?"

"No, son. He's where he belongs and we will soon be where we belong."

She knew he wouldn't come. It would be best if he didn't come.

Jackson Miller was still working on the ferry when they arrived at the landing.

"Is it safe to cross?" she asked.

Carl scowled at her for speaking first and not letting him do the talking. He always said that women should be quiet unless spoken to.

"Yes. Just be careful on the other side. The mud is still thick over there."

Carl dismounted and led the animals onto the raft. Sylvia used the railing to climb from the mule and left Tommy astride. If the mud was bad, it would be better for her to walk the rest of the way. She hated to think what it would do to her new dress and shoes.

The current flowed faster than she was used to, but they got across without mishap. Carl was a strong man from his work in the stockyards and he handled the raft with ease despite the push and pull of the water. On the opposite bank, she took the lead line and walked along beside him. Her shoes sank in the muck a few inches, but she managed to finally get away from the worst of the mud and onto higher ground.

"What if your place ain't fit to live in, Sylvia? Maybe you and Tommy should come stay with me for a time."

"I have to find my animals. They won't know to come home if I'm not there."

"Coyotes probably got those critters already."

She glanced back at Tommy. "Watch your words, Carl. You'll upset my boy."

He blew out a long-suffering breath. "We done talked about this. About mollycoddling him."

She didn't answer. Just kept walking.

The lake that had prevented her from going to the DuBois farm had dried and become a wide muddy ditch. There were no tracks through the mud except for a few rabbits and squirrels and birds. Guess Adele and Julian were still stuck at their place. She'd make sure to check on them in another day or two, once the mud dried further.

It was another half a mile to her place, but the trail was getting drier and easier to traverse. Another dip and they rounded the curve to her home.

She stared at the mess before her, her chest tightening at the sight. The place was in shambles. Water had shoved a wave of mud in through her front doorway, ripping the door off its hinges and breaking it completely away. The roof sagged dangerously in one corner, too unstable for them to sleep under it. She'd have to see about shoring it up somehow. Probably would have to put on a new roof altogether.

"Well, at least the roof didn't cave completely in," she said, mostly to herself.

She helped Tommy down from the mule and took the basket he held.

"Guess we better see what the house looks like on the inside."

"You are plum crazy, Sylvia," Carl said with a snort. "You can't stay here. It's ruined. The whole thing is falling in and I ain't helping fix this mess."

"I didn't ask you to, now did I? I'll figure it out on my own."

Gingerly, holding her skirt high, she stepped on the solidifying mass of mud that covered the threshold. Inside, her table and chairs had been shoved against the wall by the mud. It was still wet and mushy in places. It would eventually dry. She let out a long breath. "Looks like we have a new dirt floor."

Carl rolled his eyes.

Guess he was right, as much as she hated to admit it. They couldn't stay here. "Let's go see the shed, Tommy."

The scent of wet moldy straw stung her nostrils upon entering the shed. She stared in surprise at the center of the small building. There stood her mule!

"Tommy! Come quick! Look who is here!"

Tommy limped into the shed. "Berta!"

Sylvia giggled at seeing how happy he was at the sight of their mule. She smoothed her hand over the animal's mud-caked back. "We're back, Berta. We're back."

She looked through the dim shed and counted three chickens and the rooster. She'd had ten before the storm.

"I don't see the sheep, Ma."

"We'll go look for them soon."

Carl stood at the door. "You really are determined to stay here?"

"I am." She took hold of Berta and walked her outside into the sunshine, where she tied her up to the water pump.

"Tommy, you grab that rake and start raking all the wet straw out of the shed."

"Can't we go back to town, Ma?" Tommy whined.

"No, we can't," she said, but the idea tempted her more than she'd thought it would. It would pass, she told herself. "Get busy now. You too, Carl. Grab a shovel and help."

He stood there in the middle of her yard and laughed. "I ain't going to help you, you crazy woman. You've been hanging on to a dream for eight years, ever since my brother built you this place. It's time for you to wake up."

"I homesteaded it more'n five years. I own this place. Tommy does too. It's all I got in the world!"

"Look at it, Sylvia. It ain't worth all your hard effort. Let it go."

She gazed around at the mess of her house and property and the will to keep trying slowly seeped out of her. Carl was right. Maybe this was too much for any woman to take on by herself. Maybe she should give up.

"We've been friends since we was kids. You and Tommy need to come make your home with me now. I'll even say words in front of a parson if it's all that important to you."

She knew he meant what he said, but she also knew he was sober right now. Things always changed when he drank. There was no way she would soften toward him, no way she'd let him be more than an uncle to Tommy. She didn't love him in that way.

"Now that I know what is left here after the storms, I need to do some thinking, Carl. It was too hard to figure things out while I was in town and worrying about the animals. And it's too hard to figure things out all at once right now." She took a deep breath. "You are right about me holding on to dreams. Thomas and me had some powerful ones. Doc even said the same thing."

Carl scowled at that.

"I have to think what's best for Tommy." She had choices. There were always choices if a person looked hard enough.

He walked over to his horse and mounted. "You are so hardheaded! Always have been. Go ahead, then. Think on it. Nothing will change, Sylvia. Nothing. I'll be back in a week to see if you have come to your senses."

She and Tommy worked the rest of the afternoon, cleaning up what they could. Tommy talked a lot. He brought up things he'd done in town and things the Blackwell and Austin boys had said that made him laugh. He talked about the doc too. A lot of things he said squeezed her heart, things that made her realize he was growing up. He had been happy there in town and no one in that short amount of time had said anything hurtful to him.

It helped to work hard. It made the thinking easier somehow. Clearer.

That night she gathered her blankets and dragged the straw pallets from the house to the shed so that they'd have a soft place to sleep. It wasn't because she was so happy to have found Berta and a few chickens. It was because she was afraid of the roof falling down on Tommy and her if they stayed in the house.

Chapter Twenty-Five

The next morning, Tommy made a point of telling her his pallet wasn't nearly as soft as the bed they'd used at the doc's.

"I ain't whining, Ma. Doc says that a man don't whine. Says a man can feel a lot of things, but it ain't supposed to show on his face or come out his mouth."

"He did, did he?" If that was the truth, Nelson hadn't succeeded all that well when he told her not to leave. He hadn't whined—but the love he felt for her sure did show on his face. It took her breath away thinking of it even now. Had she been a fool to give up on that kind of love?

"Yep," Tommy said, continuing his train of thought. "Says he thinks about that and has to be careful when he is doctoring. If he sees something really ugly like a dog bite or a fishhook stuck in a thumb, he has to act all doctorly like it don't bother him."

She stood there while her son chattered on, her hands on her hips. She turned in a full circle, surveying all that needed doing—the house and all that was in it, the shed and the animals. She didn't know where to begin. Guess the first thing was to haul out the pots and pans and make a fire pit they could use for cooking outside. Then she and Tommy could gather some greens so they'd have something to eat for the day. It was a nice, warm morning, so she pulled the table and chairs from inside the house and set them in the middle of the yard.

Over the next two days they worked hard. Sylvia was proud of her son, but it bothered her that she had made him trade having moments of fun with his new friends in town for hours of hard work with her. A balance of the two would have been better.

"Ma! Look!"

The middle of the third morning that they were home, Tommy pointed down the lane. A horse and buggy came into view from around the bend. Sylvia walked over to stand with her son. Visitors? Here?

Tommy let out a whoop. "It's Rhett and Wyatt!"

Brett Blackwell reined the horse to a stop and climbed down. "We heard you came back to your place and my Fiona worried for you. She sent some things." He went to the back of the buggy and took out a large basket, carrying it over to the table.

Fiona had worried for her? Her vision blurred suddenly. She cupped her hand over her mouth and followed him to the table. What had he brought?

She pulled back the cover. Two loaves of bread sat atop jars full of fruit and others full of vegetables that filled the bottom of the large basket.

Behind her, Rhett and Wyatt jumped down from the buggy. Tommy called to them to come meet Berta and see his chickens. In a dash, they disappeared into the shed.

"This is so much, Mr. Blackwell."

"Fiona wants you to have it. She said you helped her with our baby and now she will help you."

That made her feel better. It was more like bartering and not really charity. "Th-thank you."

"Next time we visit, she will come." He grinned sheepishly. "I didn't want to travel with Cordelia over the river. She's so little."

She smiled back, remembering he was a new father. But *next time*? She liked the sound of that.

"What can I help with?" He stared at the house and frowned. "You need new roof."

She chuckled. "I think I need a new house."

"Ha!"

For the next half hour, the boys and Brett helped her drag everything from the house into the shed. Brett stood on a chair and used some of her oilcloth to cover the hole that Tommy had made with his foot. When that was done, he said he had to get back.

"I bring men from town in a few days and we cut new roof."

Now, that *was* too much! "Mr. Blackwell, I can't ask you to do that. You've got your work at the smithy."

"You are our friend." He said it as if that over-turned any of her objections.

Just like that she spouted tears. It was too much. His kindness, Fiona's kindness and Tommy laughing with his boys.

He stared at her, his expression troubled. "You should come back. Out here, alone. This is not good for you."

"I ain't alone. I have Tommy."

Brett shook his head. "It's not good. Doc needs your help."

With that, he called for the boys to get into the buggy and headed back down the lane.

The next day, Teddy and Hannah White came with their wagon. Hannah held her four-month-old in her lap.

What was going on?

Hannah waved from her seat. "Hi, Sylvia. Dora was fretful again, so we thought a ride in the country might be just the thing to calm her."

"This is a long way to come," Sylvia said, doubtful that they'd told her the entire truth, but happy to see them. They just happened to bring a picnic lunch with them to share.

"Doc said you liked to garden," Hannah said, handing Sylvia several seed packets.

Then Wednesday, another wagon came. This time it was Miss Weber and Miss Simcock and the two men they had married on Sunday. After the introductions, Miss Simcock handed down a bundle wrapped in brown paper. "You forgot some things at the doc's."

It was the dress and the nightgown.

"But they belong to you!"

"Mrs. Taylor made us both new dresses for the wedding," Miss Weber said.

"And nightgowns too," Miss Simcock said with a giggle and a glance toward her new husband. "We wished that you had been there. We looked for you."

"I bet it was really something," Sylvia said. "I've never been to a wedding with so many brides at one time." If she had lived in town, she would have made sure to go.

This was starting to be a pattern. So much so that when Thursday came, she was disappointed that no one came to visit and was lonely despite having Tommy with her. She and Tommy spent the day searching for their sheep for the second time. They were unsuccessful. She hoped the two had found their way to Adele and Julian's farm.

Then Friday rolled around and who should she see coming down the lane but Mrs. Graham and Abigail White.

Abigail, with her sharp reporter's eye, surveyed Sylvia's homestead from her seat on the buggy.

Sylvia could tell they were both shocked at the condition of things. "I know it's not much. But it's mine and Tommy's," Sylvia said, trying to keep the defensive tone from her voice.

"You have a lot of hard work ahead of you," Abigail said as she climbed from the buggy. "I don't know what happened between you and the doc, but he hasn't been the same since you left."

"He has been a grump," Mrs. Graham said. She peered down at the long way to the ground.

"I'll get a chair," Sylvia said, on realizing her dilemma. She dragged a chair over and assisted the woman down.

"Thank you, dear," Mrs. Graham said, giving her a quick hug.

Sylvia couldn't have been more shocked.

"I've been in the reporting business for many years," Abigail said, drawing her attention. "I have learned that everybody has secrets."

Sylvia stiffened.

"Now, don't be alarmed. Yours isn't really a secret. Not since Carl Caulder shot off his mouth years ago. That's done and over now."

She said it so easily, so directly. As if it didn't matter anymore at all. *Done and over.*

"Then whose secrets are you talking about?"

"Dr. Graham and the list he has of qualities he wants in a woman."

Sylvia stopped walking. That list was Nelson's business and no others'. She didn't like Abigail talking about it. "How did you find out about that?"

"I might have said something on our way here," Mrs. Graham said. "I also told Abigail that my son asked you to marry him, but that you declined."

Sylvia bristled. That wasn't anyone's business but hers and the doc's. "You got no call to do that! Nelson is a fine man and he deserves a fine wife. I can't meet any part of that list." She turned to Abigail. "Mrs. Graham even said so."

The two women looked at each other and then back at her.

"I regret those words I said in anger. They weren't true." Mrs. Graham took hold of her hands. "Why, Sylvia Marks. Don't you know? The reason you don't see yourself in that list is because you are *more* than that list. You exceed all the qualities he wants. Nelson understands that. He figured it out long ago, when he asked you to marry him."

Overcome with her feelings, Sylvia covered her mouth with her fingers and backed away. "That can't be—"

Mrs. Graham smiled sadly. "I wish you would reconsider, dear. I want so much for my son. I want him to be happy."

"I want that for him too."

"I know you do." She sighed. "I asked him to come with us today. He wouldn't. His pride won't let him."

When the two women headed back to Oak Grove, all Sylvia could do was sit down at the table in the middle of her yard and think on those words. Her past was *done and over*. And she was *more*.

Chapter Twenty-Six

"Ma? Are we done working?" Tommy whined.

Sylvia appraised Berta with a critical eye. The dust still floated in the air after her brushing, but her coat was cleaner than it had been in a long time. Sylvia tossed the grooming brush onto a sack of grain. "Done."

The physical work had been good for her. It gave her a chance to ponder things. All the people who had come by that week had said they missed her. She would have never thought they thought about her at all, but each of them recalled a time that she had done something for them that helped them in their time of need. They also said that the doc was grumpier than ever now, without her help.

She had thought about the doc all week and wondered a great deal how he was getting along.

They were both so different. Nelson came from a world of boarding schools and rides in the park and concerts. And she came from the hills of Virginia. Knowing that, it hadn't stopped them from becoming friends. He could charm the feathers off a bird if he had a mind to. Or milk from Penny—she started to smile—or love from a woman who had had too little of it.

Maybe it could work.

She was smart. And strong. And full of love for him.

Maybe, and she hated to admit this, but maybe she had been full of pride too. She'd held her past pulled around her like a shield against what others might say, when in truth, most had moved on and were concerned with their own lives. Not hers. The doc and Abigail had said that she let her past have too much power over her. They might be right.

"Ma! Look!"

She glanced over to see Tommy showing off, his hands on the ground, his feet in the air and braced up against the shed. He sure gave her joy. She wanted to do right by him. Could she give him a better life if she faced up to things in town?

She wondered if Nelson might have had something to do with all the folks who had come visiting. She surely did love that man. He had asked her to be a part of his life, and she had foolishly run back to what was safe for her—what she knew.

Maybe she had given up too soon. Mable Gallagher had been rude to her. Next time—she took a deep breath—next time she would stand up for herself. She was smart. And strong. She was *more*.

When she first spoke with Nelson, he had said the women from the train were brave because they'd realized their situation needed to change and they'd done something about it. Well—she could be every bit as brave.

It was worth another try. It was worth a much bigger try than the one she had given the doc and herself. He was a proud man. He wouldn't come after her. He'd respect her decision. That was his way.

She looked out across the land that she'd worked so hard for, that was now hers and Tommy's. When Carl brought her back, he had said that nothing had changed. He was wrong. The thing that had changed was her.

She wanted more—for herself and for her son. And she was ready to work for it.

"Tommy, come over here."

Chapter Twenty-Seven

An entire week had gone by since Sylvia left. The five women who'd arrived by train had married, their weddings taking place without a hitch. Nelson had attended the ceremony and congratulated each new groom, sincerely happy for each couple. He knew now that Sylvia was the only woman he wanted beside him in his life. No other would do.

His mother rose from the table and carried both of their empty plates to the counter. She could cook! That had come as a surprise after all these years. Something weighed on her thoughts this morning.

"I'll be returning to Boston in another week," she said. "I wish you would reconsider and come with me."

"I'm needed here, Mother."

"I see that. I...still won't give up the hope that someday you will return home."

"This is my home now. However, now that I know I am welcome, I will come to visit."

A small smile tilted her lips. "I'd like that."

She looked down at the handkerchief in her hands, picking at the lace edge.

"What is it?" he asked.

"I've been worried..." She met his gaze. "Did I do the right thing in telling you the truth about Ellison? About me?"

He mulled that over. Would it have been better to continue as he had, believing that Ellison was his father? Intrinsic to that was the belief that there was something wrong in himself because his father didn't want him.

He stood and walked over to her. "Knowing the truth is better. I can deal head-on with the truth. It's much harder to do that with secrets and lies." He slipped his arms around her. "It was the right thing for me." In a week, life would return to the way that it had been before his mother's arrival, with one big change. He would be at peace with the man who raised him.

"Thank you, son." She leaned into him, hugging him back.

It wasn't the least bit awkward. Nothing like the first hug they'd shared at the train station.

She pulled away, dabbing at her eyes with her

handkerchief. "Well. I must get ready for church. Give me ten minutes."

He walked into his study. All he wanted was to be a doctor and hone his skills so that he could help people. He had hoped to have Sylvia by his side on that journey. He stuffed his hands in his pockets and stared out the window, gazing out over the endless prairie behind his house. Maybe, after his mother left, he would head to Denver for a week or two. He could see the sights. Maybe attend a medical meeting.

He walked to the bottom of the stairs. "Mother? I'll wait outside for you."

Behind him, he heard the click of a rifle being cocked.

"I got me a gun here."

He froze. All his senses suddenly pulsing with energy. Sylvia.

"Don't turn around."

Hope expanded inside his chest. "I wouldn't think of it."

"Good. You got to come with me."

A smile twitched on his lips. "What is this about? Is someone hurt?"

"Hurtin' real bad, Doc."

"Sick?" Slowly, he turned around. Sylvia stood before him holding her rifle—this time pointed away from him. She wore the yellow blouse and skirt she had made and had her hair pulled back in a knot at the nape of her neck.

Tommy stood behind her, peeking around her hips. "Should I get my medical bag?"

Her brown eyes glistened. "Medical bag can't fix this kind of hurting. It goes bone deep." Her voice faltered as she said the word *hurting*. Her chin trembled. Her eyes filled with a tentative mix of hope and want and—

"I know just what you mean." He opened his arms.

She set down her rifle and came to him, slipping her arms around him and holding on as if she would never let go.

"Oh, Sylvia…" Her hair was warm against his jaw.

"I couldn't do it. I couldn't leave you," she said, her words muffled against his chest.

"Then don't. Don't ever leave. I want you by my side forever. You belong here. With me."

She looked up at him, her eyes shining with love. He leaned down and kissed her, slanting his mouth across hers, reveling in the feel of her in his arms. He kissed her forehead, her cheeks, and then came back to her mouth. When he pulled back, they were both breathless.

"Doc!" she said. "Tommy's right here!"

He glanced down. Her son watched them with round eyes so like his mother's. "Master Tom, do I have your permission to kiss your mother before I marry her?"

A big grin split Tommy's face.

"I think that is a yes on his face, Miss Marks."

"Well, I haven't said yes, yet."

"Hurry up, Ma!" Tommy said.

His mother came to the steps. Her hand splayed across her breast as she watched, a tearful, hopeful smile on her face.

Sylvia looked up at him, her eyes softening. "Yes!" she finally said. "Forever, yes!"

Chapter Twenty-Eight

It took Mrs. Taylor two weeks to make a wedding dress. Sylvia had never seen so many tiny beads and buttons on one piece of clothing in her life. During that time, Sylvia stayed at the hotel with Tommy. She and Nelson took a day to move her chickens and mule and goat to the Du-Bois farm and another day to gather up the items from her farm that she wanted in her new home.

Nelson invited everyone in town—even Mrs. Gallagher—for the ceremony. Adele and Julian DuBois came too. Even Mrs. Graham attended. Her son's happiness, she said, was more important than rules of etiquette.

Tommy, wearing his new knickers and shirt and suspenders, walked Sylvia down the aisle. He was proudest of his first shoestring tie, just like the one that Nelson wore, and kept fidgeting with it as they walked to the front of the church.

Sylvia thought her heart would burst with happiness. She couldn't take her gaze off the tall, handsome man who waited by the parson. Nelson watched her with a fullness in his gaze that said she was precious to him. In that moment, she felt completely and utterly cared for and content for the first time in her life.

Reverend Flaherty commenced with the ceremony, and as Nelson vowed to love her and cherish her, a warm glow rushed all the way through her. A glow of peace and happiness and a forever kind of love. Nelson's eyes shone as he listened to her repeat the vows to him. Then he kissed her, sealing their vows.

Afterward, at the celebration in the new town hall, pieces of wedding cake were passed out and Wally Brown walked up to the front of the room and announced he'd had the most important part in bringing the two together.

"If that old mule hadn't busted my arm, the doc here and Miss Sylvia might never have come together. They'd still be two wandering souls."

"That wasn't it," Brett Blackwell said. "It was when my Cordelia came. Miss Sylvia helped my wife."

"Naw," Tommy piped up. "It was Ma's molasses bread. The doc likes it more than anything."

Sylvia covered her mouth to catch the giggle

bubbling up. To think they all wanted to have a part in the matchmaking!

Nelson leaned into her, his green eyes twinkling. "Should we tell them?"

Sylvia smiled. Her heart was so full. She squeezed his hand. "Yes."

Nelson grinned and turned to their guests. "The truth is…it all started the night I was kidnapped…"

* * * * *

*If you enjoyed this story, you won't
want to miss these other great Western stories
from Kathryn Albright*

*"TAMING THE RUNAWAY BRIDE"
(in MAIL-ORDER BRIDES OF OAK GROVE)
CHRISTMAS KISS FROM THE SHERIFF
FAMILIAR STRANGER IN CLEAR SPRINGS
THE GUNSLINGER AND THE HEIRESS*

MILLS & BOON®
HISTORICAL

AWAKEN THE ROMANCE OF THE PAST

A sneak peek at next month's titles...

In stores from 25th January 2018:

MILLS & BOON®

Coming next month

THE MARQUESS TAMES HIS BRIDE
Annie Burrows

'Don't be ridiculous. I am not your fiancée. And I don't need your permission to do anything or go anywhere!' Clare said.

'That's better,' Rawcliffe said, leaning back in his chair, an infuriatingly satisfied smile playing about the lips that had so recently kissed her. 'You were beginning to droop. Now you are on fighting form again, we can have a proper discussion.'

'I don't want to have a discussion with you,' Clare said, barely managing to prevent herself from stamping her foot. 'Besides, oh, listen, can't you hear it?' It was the sound of a guard blowing on his horn to announce the arrival of the stage. The stage she needed to get on. 'I have a seat booked on that coach.'

'Nevertheless,' he said, striding over to the door and blocking her exit once again, 'you will not be getting on it.'

'Don't be absurd. Of course I am going to get on it.'

'You are mistaken. And if you don't acquiesce to your fate, quietly, then I am going to have to take desperate measures.'

'Oh, yes? And just what sort of measures,' she said, marching up to him and planting her hands on her hips, 'do you intend to take?'

He smiled. That wicked, knowing smile of his. Took her face in both hands. And kissed her.

And just as she was starting to forget exactly why she ought to be fighting him at all, he gentled the kiss. Gentled his hold. Changed the nature of his kiss from hard and masterful, to coaxing and…oh, his clever mouth. It knew just how to translate her fury into a sort of wild, pulsing ache. She ached all over. She began to tremble with what he was making her feel. Grew weaker by the second.

As if he knew her legs were on the verge of giving way, he scooped her up into his arms and carried her over to one of the upholstered chairs by the fire. Sat down without breaking his hold, so that she landed on his lap.

Continue reading
The Marquess Tames His Bride
Annie Burrows

Available next month
www.millsandboon.co.uk